To Seek a Master

'You are an old-fashioned girl. A girl who likes to wear stockings, who likes to feel feminine. You are a girl who enjoys novels in which the heroine spends a good deal of time tied up, or in chains, at the mercy of some powerful man, or having to go naked, or being spanked.'

He chuckled, and Laura realised that the sudden tightening of her muscles at the crucial word must have given her away. The blood rushed to her face, but there was not distaste in his expression, or even the crude, boyish lust Chris Drake had shown, only a calm appreciation and, more importantly, understanding. Instantly it was as if a great weight had been lifted from her shoulders, and her voice was full of gratitude as she answered.

'Yes. I like that, but I still don't understand?'

By the same author:

Noble Vices
Valentina's Rules
Wild in the Country
Wild By Nature
Office Perks
Pagan Heat
Bound in Blue
The Boss

To Seek a Master
Monica Belle

BL

This book is a work of fiction.
In real life, make sure you practise safe, sane
and consensual sex.

Published by Black Lace 2008

2 4 6 8 10 9 7 5 3 1

First published in Great Britain in 2008 by
Black Lace
Virgin Books
Random House, 20 Vauxhall Bridge Road
London SW1V 2SA

www.black-lace-books.com
www.virginbooks.com
www.rbooks.co.uk

Addresses for companies within The Random House Group Limited can be found at:
www.randomhouse.co.uk/offices.htm

The Random House Group Limited Reg. No. 954009

Distributed in the USA by Macmillan, 175 Fifth Avenue, New York, NY 10010, USA

A CIP catalogue record for this book is available from the British Library

ISBN 9780352345073

The Random House Group Limited supports The Forest Stewardship Council
[FSC], the leading international forest certification organisation. All our titles
that are printed on Greenpeace approved FSC certified paper carry the FSC logo.
Our paper procurement policy can be found at www.rbooks.co.uk/environment

Typeset by Palimpsest Book Production Ltd, Grangemouth, Stirlingshire FK3 8XG
Printed and bound in Great Britain by CPI Bookmarque

1

Laura slipped into the window seat just in time to prevent the Devil from getting it first. He was one of the regular commuters, nicknamed for his neatly trimmed beard and the dash of white in his hair which, with an aquiline face and a smart dark suit, gave him a distinctly Satanic look. Others included Darcy, Mr Brown, the Grey Man, Miss Scarlett, Hovis Boy and the Tramp. All seven took the same trains each day, into Cambridge on the 7:55 and back on the 17:40, providing fuel for her imagination to stave off the boredom of commuting.

She had no idea where any of them lived, or what they did, only at which stations they got on and off and a few personal habits that allowed her to invent fantasy lives for each. Darcy was the attractive one, tall, with an athletic build and an easy manner that suggested an appealing combination of humour and masculinity, perhaps appealing enough for her to have made an advance had the plain gold band on his ring finger not implied that somebody else had got him first.

In her imagination there was no ring and one day the two of them would be alone in carriage. There would be no need for any of the social niceties and careful testing of each other's defences so essential to real life. He would know she was willing and simply take her, calm and confident as he stripped her naked, had her kneel to take him in her mouth, lifted her onto his erection and had her, still cool and poised in his perfectly cut office suit as he brought her to heaven again and again.

None of the others had Darcy's allure. There was something stern about the Devil that she found intriguing but also disturbing in a way she didn't fully understand, yet he was at least twice her age, so she preferred to think of him as the villain from one of the old-fashioned crime thrillers she liked to read, the sort of man Darcy would rescue her from before taking her as his reward.

Mr Brown and the Grey Man made a pair, both middle-aged men of middle height, probably in middle management and middle everything else. Only in the way they dressed did they differ, the one in a scruffy brown suit that matched his thinning brown hair, the other plain and grey. Mr Brown, she liked to imagine, had a secret home life, perhaps attending wife-swapping parties where he would dress up in garishly colourful women's underwear and watch the other couples having sex. The Grey Man she thought of as an automaton, or perhaps an android, built at one of the research companies in Cambridge and being road tested to see if anybody spotted him.

Miss Scarlett was either a spy or the scheming mistress of some wealthy industrialist, depending on Laura's mood, while the Tramp was an eccentric millionaire who would one day drop dead and leave her his entire fortune for smiling at him twice a day for the last four years. Hovis Boy was simply Hovis Boy, a spotty youth whose sole distinguishing characteristic was the sandwiches he carried in a plastic bread wrapper.

Settling more comfortably into her seat, she spent a moment watching the lines of dark brick houses move past as the train gathered speed, before taking her book from her bag. It was one she'd found in a charity shop near work, a paperback published in the 1950s and full of the unashamedly red-blooded heroes and yielding heroines she enjoyed. It was called *Taken to Turkey*, and she had started it that morning, introducing herself to the beautiful Evangeline Tarrington, the superbly handsome Mark Frobisher and the wicked Lord Jasper Mauleverer. Just twenty pages in, and Evangeline had already been kidnapped by Lord Jasper, only for his car to be ambushed by Bulgarian bandits en route to Istanbul, a highly promising situation.

The Bulgarian bandits were everything Laura could have hoped for, and kept her occupied all the way to King's Lynn. As she walked from the station she was lost in a daydream, one in which she was Evangeline, but instead of being rescued in the nick of time by the gallant Mark Frobisher she was made the plaything of the bandit chief. Better still, the chief could have his wicked way with her, only for Frobisher to arrive a moment too late. The two men would fight it out as she lay naked and trembling in the furs beneath them, but when the Englishman finally triumphed he would be unable to resist, and instead of carrying her to safety would take his turn on top of her. Even better than that, Frobisher and the chief could turn out to be old friends from some earlier adventure, get thoroughly drunk on arrack and share her. She would kneel among the furs, naked, her bottom lifted to the chief's thrusts as she sucked on her supposed rescuer's erection, thoroughly used as they chatted casually of other girls they'd given the same undignified treatment.

Laura was smiling as she walked, oblivious to everything but the vivid fantasy in her head, so that it was only when she reached her flat did she realise that she'd left her smart leather bookmark on the train. It was only a company one, given out to all junior employees as a blanket Christmas present the year before, and she quickly put her irritation aside, along with her fantasy as she settled down to the mundane tasks of the evening. Smudge needed to be walked, and she had to eat something, if only beans on toast, while she'd also have to iron a fresh blouse for the morning.

The last detail turned her mind back to work, something she did her best to avoid when not actually in the office. Given what EAS paid her, it was hardly reasonable for them to expect her to devote her free time as well as the regular nine to five, yet that seemed to be what was expected of her, especially by Mr Henderson. 'Look smart,' was one of his many watchwords, repeated at every opportunity and underlined with numerous remarks on her appearance and a clothing allowance on top of her PA's salary. The clothing allowance at least was welcome, although she would have preferred to spend it on something other than designer suits and expensive blouses, at least occasionally.

Laura bit her lip as she considered her boss. His comments had never crossed the line into anything that could be considered harassment, and yet the implication that her looks were important to her job was clear. The little approving nods when she made a special effort with herself, the way he introduced her to clients as if showing off a trophy, even the way he'd positioned their desks so that she had to walk the full width of the office for every tiny thing, all of it suggested that a major part of her work was to look sexy.

The worst part of it was that in different circumstances she wouldn't have minded. He was tall, powerfully built and quite commanding, all features she liked in a man, so much so that when she had first joined EAS she had allowed herself to fantasise about being taken roughly over his desk. That was before she'd discovered he was married, while on closer acquaintance she had come to realise that there was something faintly sleazy about him, although she could never quite come to grips with what it was.

As she finished the blouse she remembered her resolve not to allow work to intrude on her private time. They were visiting clients in the morning, a Peterborough firm who wanted to upgrade their ancient oil insulated switchgear to SF6 gas.

Mr Henderson had stressed the importance of proper preparation, but then he always did and the situation with Evangeline Tarrington was far more interesting than any amount of switchgear.

Now a little tired but feeling pleasantly lazy, Laura turned on her bath, pouring a liberal portion of oil into the stream from the hot tap so that she could already smell the hot jasmine scent as she went to her bedroom to undress. The little ritual of dealing with her clothes was soon complete and she turned back to her book, eager to discover how Mark managed to rescue Evangeline from the clutches of the bandits, as he inevitably would.

He did, distracting the guards by exploding an old Mills Bomb he happened to have with him on the far side of their camp, rushing in to slit the chief's tent at the back, extracting Evangeline and make good his escape before anybody even noticed. As he fled he carried her over his shoulder, a thoroughly undignified position that brought a smile to Laura's face as she imagined herself as the heroine. It was much too early in the book for the couple to do more than share an uncertain kiss, but Laura read on, waiting for the subtle change in the sound of the running bathwater that would tell her it was full enough. To her surprise Mark Frobisher wasn't making gallant remarks but seemed to be rather cross.

'You little fool!' Frobisher blustered angrily. 'You might have got us both killed!'

Evangeline's pretty mouth fell open, too shocked by his unexpected wrath to respond. Frobisher shook his head, his expression setting in a determined scowl as he appeared to reach a decision. He sat down on the running board of the great Bentley.

'Come here,' he growled, commandingly.

Evangeline obeyed, unable to do otherwise. Frobisher reached out, taking her gently but firmly by the wrist to pull her in to his body. Her maiden modesty welling strong in her bosom, Evangeline struggled against him, although her true desire was to yield. He was too strong for her in any event, pulling her close with ease, but not for the intimacy of a kiss. Rather, Evangeline found herself drawn forcibly down across his lap and, as her clothing was adjusted behind, her mouth had come open in astonished outrage. She was to be spanked.

Laura's mouth had also come open in astonishment and outrage. It was not at all what she'd been expecting. Normally the hero and heroine didn't even kiss until the fourth or fifth chapter, while she had invariably had to fill in all the more juicy details for herself. Not this time.

She read the piece again, and a third time, enjoying the little thrill of indignation the words gave her. That wasn't how heroes behaved, not normally. They were supposed to be dashing and chivalrous, a little brusque perhaps, or strong and silent, but never the sort of raving pervert who'd get off on spanking a woman's bottom. Then again, there was no suggestion that he was doing it for his enjoyment. On the contrary, Evangeline had deliberately eluded her chaperone, allowing Lord Jasper to kidnap her. Then she'd failed to escape during a drive of several hundred miles during which there had been several opportunities to contact the authorities.

All this was pointed out to Evangeline while her bottom was smacked. There wasn't the slightest hint that Mark was doing anything other than providing some badly needed discipline to a spoilt brat. There was nothing remotely sexual in his actions, except in that it meant he saw Evangeline's bare bottom, certainly nothing perverse, but the same could not be said for the sharp thrill the scene gave Laura.

She was trying to push it from her mind as she hurried to the bath, which was now in danger of overflowing. Masculine confident men who knew what they wanted were one thing, but to be turned across a man's knee and have her bottom smacked was so far beyond the boundaries of acceptable behaviour that she felt as if she was a traitor to her sex just for reading about it, while to surrender to the warm need between her thighs was unthinkable.

It was also irresistible. From the moment she slid into the hot scented water she knew she was going to have to play with herself. The fantasies she'd deliberately allowed to build up in her head, her sense of gentle tiredness, the knowledge that nobody could catch her and nobody would ever know, all conspired to make her need too strong, and yet even as she allowed one hand to slip between her thighs and the other to one breast she was determined that whatever thoughts in her head at the moment of climax they would not involve having her bare bottom smacked as she was held down across a man's lap.

Evangeline had been bare bottomed too, of that Laura was certain. The words of *Taken to Turkey* were coy, but there could be no mistaking the implication of the expression 'adjusted behind'. Mark Frobisher had bared Evangeline Tarrington's bottom. Laura gave a shiver and her fingers began to work between the lips of her sex as she imagined how it would feel – the helplessness, the indignation, the shame – as her skirt was lifted up over her legs and around her hips, exposing the seat of her knickers to the man's view, to the utter bastard's view. No, that wasn't fair, because she'd have deserved it, just as Evangeline had.

In no way would that have lessened the awful feelings, and

they would have grown ten times worse when the time came to have her knickers taken down, a hundred times worse, unbearable, and yet she'd be trapped, held helpless across a strong man's knees, bare and wriggling and silly as her bottom was stripped for the final, intolerable outrage of being spanked.

Laura's back arched, her lips already parted in rising excitement, only for her to shake herself, forcing the disturbing thoughts from her head. It just wasn't right, not to imagine herself being handled that way. Fifty years had passed since the book was written, fifty years in which women had fought free from the sort of crass, macho bullshit represented by the scene in the book. Yet even as she struggled to think of something more acceptable to her personal values a sneaky little voice was whispering to her, and it was only a fantasy after all, that really being taken from behind across the seat of a commuter train wasn't so very much more dignified, and that nobody need know in any case.

Again she began to massage her sex, trying to imagine how Darcy might treat her if they were ever in a carriage alone, one of her favourite fantasies. It was always much the same, his voice as he told her she was to be stripped, allowing no room for refusal, his hands on her body as he peeled off her clothes, the feel and taste of his cock in her mouth, the curt order to kneel on a seat and lift her bottom, not for spanking, but so that he could enter her from behind, no, not for spanking ... not for spanking.

Laura gave in, a low moan escaping her lips as she surrendered to what she really needed to think about. It didn't even much matter who did it, just so long as he was big, and male, and took no nonsense as he levered her across his legs, stripped her bottom bare and spanked her. She cried out as she started to come, playing the same awful sequence over and over in her head, bent over, bared, and smacked. Her legs had come high and open, her hand was locked tight to her breast, squeezing so hard her nails had dug into her flesh, but she was unable to stop herself, her fingers working on the sensitive bud between her lips as peak after peak tore through her, stopping only when she could bear it no more.

With that she collapsed back into the bath, her breath coming out in a long sigh of absolute satisfaction even as the inevitable feelings of shame welled up inside her, made worse by the fact that she knew full well it wouldn't be the last time. Never before had she experienced an orgasm as intense.

2

Laura still felt guilty in the morning, but that did not dispel an underlying excitement for what she had discovered. For once she hurried, going through her morning ritual with considerably less care than Mr Henderson would have expected for such an important day, but his intrusion into her thoughts only bred resentment. She was his from nine in the morning until five in the evening, with an hour for lunch, and he had no right to expect her to waste what little precious time was left. That, or as much as was possible, she intended to devote to *Taken to Turkey*, largely in the hope that there would be another spanking scene, this time described in rather more detail.

She was disappointed, although not entirely. Mark Frobisher had no sooner dealt with Evangeline's bottom than he was neatly coshed from behind by Lord Jasper Mauleverer, who turned out to have watched the entire procedure. That was quite exciting for Laura, with the added humiliation of an audience, but Lord Jasper proved to be a pretty poor villain, enjoying the view and making a few intimate remarks to set Evangeline's upper cheeks aflame as well as her lower ones, but completely failing to take proper advantage of her dishevelled state.

He did force her to walk behind him on a string and with her hands tied behind her back as they returned to his car, but that was plainly necessary, as he'd already tied her up once when he first kidnapped her. Both scenes were good, but fell well short of the spanking, while the ensuing car chase through the Sredna Gora mountains provided no more than conventional thrills. Only when Mark Frobisher's Bentley overheated did things start to look up, with Lord Jasper declaring that it was about time Evangeline paid for all the trouble she'd caused before giving a single laugh of unspeakable malevolence.

The train had been filling up as she read, with a typical assortment of complete strangers, Darcy, Mr Brown and Hovis Boy at King's Lynn, the Grey Man and the Tramp at Downham Market, Miss Scarlett and the Devil at Ely. By then only a few free seats remained, and the Devil excused himself politely as his hip bumped against Laura's. She murmured something in reply and shut her book, embarrassed by the thought of him reading it out of the corner of his eye while she enjoyed the horrid thrill of discovering what Lord Jasper planned for Evangeline.

Instead, she let her thoughts drift, thinking of how much the Devil resembled Lord Jasper in her imagination, which presumably meant that she'd subconsciously connected the two. It was easy to go further with the idea. Darcy was the perfect model for Mark Frobisher, and Miss Scarlett perhaps not unlike the chaperone who might have been bribed to allow Evangeline to give her the slip. The only one remotely like the Bulgarian chief was Mr Brown, and he needed a darker complexion and rather more hair, including a large and bushy moustache, while he was really too dull to fit in with Laura's fantasies in any case.

She was still in a daydream when the train pulled in at Cambridge and as she walked to work, but was brought suddenly down to earth by the sight of Mr Henderson standing beside his company Mondeo in the car park at EAS. She ducked down to check her appearance in the wing mirror of a convenient 4x4, only to end up blushing as she realised it was occupied by an elderly woman with an expression of carefully cultivated disapproval. As she approached Mr Henderson she wished she'd spent a bit more time on her hair, gone for another suit, higher heels, a splash of colour somewhere and, most especially, the seamed stockings that always earned her one of his approving nods but cost the earth, were a pain to put on and seemed to ladder at a single glance. He clearly agreed.

'Not quite the style I'd have expected today, Laura. Look smart, look smart, that's my motto.'

'Yes, sir. Sorry, sir.'

'Well, we shall just have to do our best. This is an important contract, Laura, not just for the company, but for me personally. Land this one and there's every chance I'll be head of marketing this time next year. I need you to be one hundred and ten per cent behind me.'

'Yes, sir.'

Laura got into the Mondeo, wondering how it would be possible to be one hundred and ten per cent behind anybody, unless it involved having a bit sticking out to one side or at the top, which in Mr Henderson's case would have been impossible for her and most other people. She had at least got the relevant papers together, and began to go through them as he pulled out of the car park, heading east on the Newmarket Road.

Mr Henderson had begun on another of his pet peeves, other road users, who he assumed were all out merely to pass the time of day, while he alone had important business. Laura had heard it all before and made the appropriate comments at the appropriate junctures, meanwhile working through the order in which to present the virtues of their 24,000 volt SF6 switch-gear system. Mr Henderson knew it by heart, but would expect the papers handed to him at exactly the right moments and in the right sequence, thus demonstrating efficiency. Only when he'd got up to speed on the duel carriageway did he turn back to the task in hand.

'The meeting is at Setchal Manor.'

The name meant nothing to Laura, but she responded politely. Presently he turned north, into the flat fen country, and again, following the instructions of his satnav down a narrow straight lane raised above the level of the fields. After a mile the scenery changed to carefully landscaped ridges and hollows set with clumps of trees, small lakes, bunkers and carefully manicured greens. Mr Henderson gave a satisfied nod, stating the obvious.

'A golf club.'

'Yes.'

'An expensive one, too, unless I'm greatly mistaken. This Mr Drake has taste.'

'I hope he doesn't expect us to play.'

'Nothing was mentioned, but if he does, we'll have to. Be prepared for the unexpected, Laura.'

It was another of his pet maxims, and one she'd always felt was particularly silly. After all, if you had prepared for something then it wasn't really unexpected, while it was impossible to prepare for everything unless you were going to carry around an impossible amount of stuff, including, in this case, a full set of golf clubs. Not that it would have done her much good, as her sole experience of golf was being told off by a man who looked like a retired Colonel, while enjoying a hasty fumble with an ex-boyfriend on the links near Cromer.

Setchal Manor was a large house of red brick and flint, fronted by mature cedars and a weather-beaten stone colonnade, all of which gave it an air of prestige and made Laura feel small and nervous. An impressive set of double doors stood open, exposing a smaller, glass set within and the reception area beyond. Mr Henderson announced them and they were shown into the bar, a great panelled room hung with trophies and boards listing past luminaries of the club from a date well back in the nineteenth century.

Mr Drake was already there, a man even taller than Mr Henderson, also younger and with an open yet assertive manner Laura found simultaneously appealing and intimidating. His PA was worse, a Miss Manston-Jones, whose public school accent, tailored clothes and air of friendly condescension gave the impression that she was really only there because Daddy thought it would do her good to mix with the proles for a while.

Despite feeling well out of her depth, Laura did her best to remain businesslike and efficient, or at least to look businesslike and efficient. That meant following Mr Henderson's rules, which included never refusing a drink from a client. After two large gin and tonics she was feeling a little more confident and a lot less steady, neither of which helped when Mr Drake made the suggestion she'd been dreading all morning.

'I think that takes care of the business end of things. How about nine holes before lunch?'

Mr Henderson responded without batting an eyelid. 'An excellent idea.'

Laura knew better than to object, but clung to the hope that she and Miss Manston-Jones might not be expected to play. After all, they were hardly dressed for the part, in tight skirts and heels, with Miss Manston-Jones' skirt inevitably that little bit tighter and her heels that little bit higher. The hope was short lived. Mr Drake drained his Scotch before adding a fresh horror to the experience as well as dashing her hopes.

'How about fifty pounds a hole, just to make it interesting? No handicap, and that goes for the girls, too.'

Mr Henderson responded with another favourite line.

'I've never turned down a bet yet.'

'That's what I like to hear. We'll get changed then, and meet up at the first tee. I take it you brought something casual?'

'Never without it.'

Laura reached a decision. It was better to be ticked off by the boss immediately than make a complete fool of herself, lose him several hundred pounds and then get ticked off.

'I'm afraid I haven't. I didn't know we'd be playing.'

'Be prepared for the unexpected, Laura.'

Miss Manston-Jones had stood up.

'Don't worry, I expect I can find you something.'

As she spoke her eyes had flicked up and down Laura's body, a survey she seemed to find amusing, to judge by her faint smile. Laura soon found out why. She'd been telling herself that their figures were similar, but the white slacks she was given proved at least a size too small, making it difficult to wriggle her bottom into them and leaving her deeply conscious of her rear view as they walked out onto the links. Mr Henderson made one of his mildly ambiguous remarks.

'Glad to see you found something, Laura. You'll do very nicely like that, I'm sure.'

He had held out a club to her as he spoke, leaving it open as to whether he meant she'd do nicely at golf or for their visual entertainment in between strokes, and as usual Laura was left wondering if it wasn't just her imagination. Even if it was, she couldn't agree with him, as she was certain she wasn't going to do well no matter how she was dressed.

Both men had bags of clubs, and Laura felt her heart sink further as Miss Manston-Jones made a confident selection. She'd obviously played before, and when she hit her ball it flew arrow straight and over halfway down the fairway. Doing her best to feign confidence, Laura went through the same ritual, selecting a ball, noting the number on her score card, and balancing it on a tee, where it stayed after her third attempt. Standing back, she gave the club an experimental swing, which felt surprisingly good. Sure that she could hit the ball a reasonable distance and in more or less the right direction, she stepped forwards a little, braced herself and swung the club down as hard as she could, sending the ball backwards about three feet. Miss Manston-Jones was trying not to snigger as she spoke.

'Let me show you how to stand.'

Laura stood aside, feeling helpless as the other woman quickly teed the ball up a second time, then demonstrated the correct stance.

'You need to place your feet about shoulder width apart, with your knees bent slightly so that your weight is evenly distributed between your heels and the balls of your feet, and far enough back so that you're comfortable with the clubface positioned directly behind the ball. Try it.'

Laura nodded doubtfully and attempted the stance, immediately failing to meet Miss Manston-Jones' approval.

'No, no. The ball should be midway between your feet.'

Laura tried again, painfully conscious that both men were looking on with obvious amusement. Again Miss Manston-Jones was unsatisfied.

'No. Let me show you.'

Miss Manston-Jones stepped close behind Laura, pressed against her as she demonstrated how best to hold and swing the club. Laura did her best to concentrate on what she was being told and not on the fact that had either man been in the same position as Miss Manston-Jones it would have left what was between his legs pressed firmly against the over tight seat of her slacks. At last the other woman seemed satisfied and stepped back.

'Now try.'

Laura swung again, doing her best to follow instructions. This time her club hit the ball, sending it high in the air to fall at the edge of the fairway slightly less than half as far down as the others. Miss Manston-Jones gave a firm nod.

'Not bad at all, for a beginner.'

A grateful smile forced itself onto Laura's face in defiance of a deeper urge to plant one muddy shoe hard against the seat of Miss Manston-Jones' slacks.

The game began, for Laura, a long series of embarrassments. Not only did Miss Manston-Jones insist on correcting her at every opportunity, usually with physical assistance, but her ball seemed to be possessed by a particularly malicious gremlin with a taste for sand, water, trees and long grass. Despite Mr Henderson's best efforts they lost hole after hole, until Mr Drake finally inflicted the final humiliation by offering to scrap the bet.

Laura declined, adopting her stance for the seventh hole with a new determination, her muscles tense, her legs well braced, fired with aggression as she swung her club high and brought it down with a crack that sent the ball down the fairway on a perfect line, to bounce twice and land on the green no more than a yard from the hole. Thoroughly pleased with herself, she turned to receive the adulation she was due from the others, only to find all three of them looking at her, but not her face. Miss Manston-Jones' raised a finger.

'Laura, I think you ought to cover yourself behind. Your trousers have split.'

Laura spent the rest of the meeting flushing pink at every look from either Mr Henderson or Mr Drake. Both had thought her accident highly amusing, despite superficial attempts at sympathy. Miss Manston-Jones had been little better, helping Laura as best she could but with laughter in her voice even after they had changed once more. Most galling of all, when they gathered in the dining room she discovered that the incident had helped create camaraderie between the two men at her expense, which enabled Mr Henderson to leave with the coveted contract in his briefcase and his face set in what Laura considered a thoroughly fatuous grin.

As they drove back he spoke of his promotion, now considered in the bag, and hinted that as PA to the head of marketing she could expect an increment in her own salary. Laura gave an absent-minded thanks, wondering if she'd even have the nerve to stay on at all when the story of what had happened that morning was sure to have circulated around the entire company within days, if not hours. Mr Henderson was known for his fund of funny stories, often at the expense of his colleagues, and yet there had to be at least a chance of persuading him to keep quite. Asking couldn't make the situation any worse.

'Um ... Mr Henderson, I'd be very grateful if you don't tell anybody what happened this morning.'

He laughed.

'I bet you would! Don't worry, you can count on my discretion.'

He'd reached out as he spoke, and for one moment she thought he was going to place his hand on her knee, only for him to change gear instead. Laura let out her breath to dispel the sudden tension, wondering if the gesture had been innocent, or a hint that some little favour would be needed to ensure her silence. He said nothing more, instead starting to explain the work she would need to do in support of the order they'd secured. Laura relaxed, sure that she was being unfairly suspicious and that both his subtly ambiguous remarks and the implication of the gesture he'd just made were no more than the products of her over-active imagination.

Once back at EAS she was kept busy liaising with other departments to organise the work they had brought in and writing up Mr Henderson's report to his line manager. It was nearly five o'clock before she'd finished, and she opened Outlook Express in the hope that there would be no emails that needed attending to before she went home. There were only four in all, one from Brian, the company humorist, with a series of jokes about different farm animals changing light bulbs, two queries from colleagues she was able to answer immediately and without difficulty, and a fourth, from somebody called simply The Controller, which she nearly deleted as spam before curiosity got the better of her. Clicking on it, she brought the message window up to reveal a single line. WEAR STOCKINGS TOMORROW.

Laura stared at the message, possibilities flicking through her mind: first that it was merely spam after all, then that it was somebody playing a joke on her, which almost certainly meant that Mr Henderson had broken his promise, and finally that it might be from Mr Henderson himself, as the opening gambit in a game of blackmail and seduction. Immediately angry, she called up the message source, reading carefully though the data to see if she could shed any further light on the message.

It certainly wasn't from Mr Henderson's normal address, or anybody else's within EAS, but that meant very little. He, or anybody else, could have used an anonymous server, thus covering their trail in case she complained. That made it seem likely that it was Mr Henderson, and that her suspicions had been right all along, with him merely waiting his chance before making his move. She rose, determined to confront him, only to sit down again. He would simply deny it, and she had no proof. The accusation would annoy him, whether he had sent the message or not, and he would then undoubtedly tell everybody about her splitting her slacks, making her the laughing stock of the office. She could already imagine how much fun Brian would have, and they'd never got on.

After a moment's hesitation she deleted the message, then consigned it to oblivion, telling herself that whoever had sent it couldn't possibly know she'd read it first. She shut her computer down and began to tidy up, all the while with the incident preying on her mind. As she walked to the station she was trying to work out who could have sent it, why, and what she could do. There seemed to be three main options.

The message might simply be from a joker, a random pervert who didn't even know her, or some chancer, in which case it was best ignored and there would be no consequences.

It might be genuine, in which case she could ignore it and hope that whoever had sent it gave up, which was the sensible option but almost certainly meant she'd never catch him.

It might be genuine and she could do as she was told, pretending to go along with him so that she could catch the bastard. That would be highly satisfying, and there was no denying her curiosity, but the idea of putting on stockings at the command of some unknown man gave her an all-body hot flush compounded of indignation, shame and something else, to which she was very definitely not going to admit.

3

As she rode the train back towards King's Lynn, Laura found it impossible to concentrate on her book. It should have been a good part too, with Lord Jasper tying Evangeline to the branch of a tree with her hands above her head for some unspecified fate, only for her to be rescued in the nick of time once more. Normally her fertile imagination would have provided a dozen ways to specify the heroine's fate, leaving her in the state of arousal and anticipation in which she liked to keep herself for the evening. Now it was impossible, with reality intruding no matter how hard she tried to concentrate.

Nothing in the message had suggested any real threat, yet she found a new comfort in Smudge as she walked him along the river and she made doubly sure her door was locked. Simply ignoring the message was clearly not an option, and as she ate the Chinese meal she had treated herself to in order to compensate for a thoroughly bad day, she found herself thinking about it once again, but in terms of the sort of crime one of her favourite detectives might have been called on to solve.

Mr Henderson was definitely her prime suspect. He liked stockings, and seemed to fancy her, which supplied his motive, while he knew her work email and might feel he had a hold over her, which supplied his means. The only evidence against him was that in four years as her boss he had never actually made a move on her.

Everybody else at work, quite a few friends and numerous clients knew her work email, so that wasn't much help, but the message had at least implied that whoever had sent it knew she hadn't been wearing stockings that day. Mr Henderson had known, because it had been chilly enough on the golf course for her to want to keep her tights on under the now ruined slacks, so he'd seen. It was just as well she had too, because otherwise he and Mr Drake would have been treated to a view of her knickers, which showed a large pink teddy bear mooning and had 'A Bear Behind' written across the seat.

As far as she knew, the only other people who could possibly have known she had tights on were Mr Drake and Miss Manston-Jones, both of whom had seen, and both of whom had her work email on the information sheets she'd given them that morning. Miss Manston-Jones didn't seem a very likely suspect, even if she had seemed just a bit too keen to get to grips with Laura when trying to teach her golf. It wasn't hard to imagine her as a dyke, and quite a butch one at that, yet it was hard to imagine her, or any woman, using that approach.

Mr Drake was a more serious possibility, and one she found hard to resent. He was very much her type of man: tall, self-confident, just a little stern. The idea of being under his control appealed, so much so that she knew she would be prepared to forgive him what from any ordinary man would have been a disturbing, even creepy, approach. Unfortunately she would not be seeing him the following day, so he had nothing to gain from the knowledge that she was wearing stockings, nor have any way of finding out if she'd obeyed. The same was true for Miss Manston-Jones, which left the finger of suspicion pointed very firmly at Mr Henderson.

She could not be certain. Another man at EAS might have

seen far enough up her skirt to realise she was wearing tights, even Brian, who might well have sent her the message as a childish and kinky joke. There had been other women in the changing rooms at Setchal Manor, but they could be ruled out easily, as could any of her fellow passengers on the train into work. Neither group knew who she was.

Then again, if one of the commuters had picked up the bookmark she'd lost they would know her work email. She pondered the possibility, but she was sure she'd dropped it when she got out at King's Lynn, either in the train or on the platform and both Darcy and Mr Brown had got out before her. Hovis Boy had lingered, tangled up in the rucksack he'd been carrying, and it wasn't hard to imagine him as the sort of little pervert who'd look up her skirt. He had to be a possibility, which was a relief in that she would have no difficulty at all in confronting him.

In fact, it might even be possible to conduct an experiment.

As she rolled her stockings up her legs the following morning, Laura was telling herself firmly that she was not wearing them for the pleasure of a man, let alone the man who had sent the message. She was doing so in order to gauge Hovis Boy's reaction on the train. If he'd got her email address somehow and sent the message he'd be looking, but that wasn't enough. Only if she was actually wearing stockings would he be bold enough to make the move which would allow her to report the little pervert to the police. That meant flashing her stockings for him, and possibly others, perhaps even Darcy, a highly embarrassing prospect that was quite definitely not the cause of the arousal she'd been unable to shrug off ever since making her decision.

She walked to the station at her normal brisk pace, arriving a few minutes earlier than usual. Hovis Boy was generally among the later arrivals, often jumping aboard the first carriage moments before the doors shut and occasionally failing to make it. Laura reasoned that if he had sent the message he would be excited and so was likely to turn up early, but there was no sign of him. Her train pulled up to the platform shortly after she'd arrived and she got in, taking her preferred seat by the window.

It took a little courage to hitch up her skirt far enough to ensure that with her legs crossed a small section of the lacy top to her hold-ups was visible, leaving her feeling exposed and jittery. She took her book from her bag, feigning nonchalance as she pretended to read while repeatedly glancing from the side of her eyes to see who was coming along the platform. Darcy arrived first, treating her to his usual indifferent smile and taking a seat some way down the carriage, then Mr Brown, who ignored her completely. Others arrived, each one making it that little bit harder to maintain her pose. Not that she was showing much, but it was deliberate and so hard to shrug off the feeling that every woman who entered the carriage was thinking of her as a slut in the old-fashioned sense and every man as a slut in the modern sense.

Hovis Boy finally made his appearance, running along the platform with his sandwiches bobbing in his hand as the doors were about to close. He threw himself into the train just in time and collapsed panting into the seat opposite Laura, one of the few remaining. She immediately wondered if he'd arrived late on purpose, knowing where she liked to sit and taking a risk that one of the seats with a good view would be vacant.

He'd certainly got one, opposite her but at a slight angle, so that he'd be able to see as far up her skirt as was possible. Certainly he'd be able to see more stocking top than she'd intended to show, maybe even bare flesh. Not that he was looking, his expression one of fish-like vacancy as the train began to move, but that could simply be a ruse. In *Chilled Steel*, Rick Cane had tracked the villainous Magnus Abner from New York to Chicago by pretending to be a dullard. Perhaps Hovis Boy was doing the same.

Then again, perhaps Hovis Boy really was a dullard. He never seemed to be interested in anything, and now that he was actually there it was very hard to picture him as the scheming little pervert of her imagination. Feeling rather silly, she uncrossed her legs, and as she moved his eyes flickered towards her, for just an instant, but surely long enough to peep up her skirt and see what she was wearing.

Laura froze, her heart hammering as she struggled to keep her eyes on the open book in front of her. He had looked. He knew. It was him. Or maybe not. He was a teenage boy, and a skinny, spotty one at that, hardly the sort to be indifferent to a woman in a short skirt as she uncrossed her legs. Not only that, but if he thought she had obeyed his command he would surely have given her a knowing look, a dirty grin perhaps, rather than immediately returning to his imitation of a dead fish.

She shifted position a little, wondering if she should force the issue, perhaps tug her skirt up a little more to make absolutely certain he could see what she was wearing. If he'd sent the email he'd have to react, surely, and then she'd have him. She almost did it, only to lose heart at the last moment, aware that she'd be flashing her thighs and possibly her knickers to half-a-dozen other men as well as Hovis Boy.

Abandoning the idea, she readjusted her skirt, tugging it back down into a less revealing position. As she did so her wrist brushed against something sticking up from the crack at the back of the seat where her weight had pushed it down, something blue and embossed with the EAS logo in gold, her bookmark, complete with her name and email address.

She pulled it out, sighing with relief for not having made a complete fool of herself. Hovis Boy could be crossed off the list, along with the other commuters, which put Mr Henderson squarely back in the frame.

Her relief lasted only a moment before she remembered that she'd have been in a much stronger position had Hovis Boy been guilty. She'd now be coming into work in stockings, just as she'd been ordered to, and he'd be sure to react. The scene was already clear in her head. He'd know the moment he saw the seams at the back of her legs, only this time there would be no patronising little nod. There would be an order.

'Good girl. Now show me.'

Or maybe he'd be formal about it, exerting his authority as her boss.

'Very good, Laura. Now lock the door and hitch up your skirt.'

He might even use her surname, as he tended to if dissatisfied with her work.

'I'm pleased to see we understand each other, Miss Irving. Now take your skirt off.'

Or worse.

'Good. Now take your skirt off, Miss Irving. I am going to spank you.'

The loaded word sent a shock through her, powerfully erotic, immediately followed by guilt and shame for her reaction. That was not how it should be, not with her boss seeking to manipulate her, to take advantage of her. Besides, he might not be into spanking.

She shook her head, ashamed for her reactions, but unable to shake the thrill, or the memory of how good it had felt to come over the fantasy of being given a spanking as a punishment. Her boss was the right person to do it as well, only a fantasy boss, not Mr Henderson. He was a blackmailing bastard, and married as well, which gave her the answer to her problem.

No, she would not end up showing off her stockings, or with her bare bottom stuck up in the air to be smacked. If he so much as suggested a peep at her stocking tops she would threaten to tell his wife. Mrs Henderson occasionally attended office functions and was definitely not the sort of woman to put up with any nonsense from her husband. She was tall, quite heavily built, and a partner in a local law firm. The tactic would work, without question.

With the situation at least partially defused, Laura allowed herself to relax a little, but it was not easy. She'd had *Taken to Turkey* open in front of her all the way from King's Lynn, but she'd scarcely read a word. Real life had taken over, and not with some humdrum necessity. She felt resentful, a little scared, but also very more alive than she had done for years, since leaving university and giving up her carefree life for the endless routine of her work.

Her gaze shifted from the book to the landscape beyond the window, but she barely saw the flat black and green of the fields as they rushed past. She was thinking of friends, and of places she'd known, of playing in the woods near what she still thought of as home, of school and the elaborate webs of who liked who, of the thrill of male attention and being slowly teased out of her clothes by Tommy Fuller, of sitting up drinking tequila until the early hours and waking in the arms of a man she hardly knew.

She let her thoughts run, remembering how Tommy brought her an excitement she'd never imagined could exist. Before she met him boys had been cautious, respectful, timid, at best trying for a kiss and a cuddle at her door. Not Tommy. He'd got her drunk on beer and tricked her into playing strip poker. She'd ended up naked, and horny, and willing, while he sat there grinning in his red check shirt and underpants, with his cock a long hard bar beneath the cotton. He'd got it out. He'd made her suck it.

Laura gave a powerful shiver at the memory. She had been willing enough, more than willing in fact, or to be really honest, desperately eager. Yet it was important for her to pretend that he'd made her do it, not forced her, but left her with no option, no option but to get down on her knees, stark naked, and take his lovely big cock into her mouth. She could remember how it had felt with her mouth full of hot hard male flesh, the taste of him and way it had made her feel weak with need, and feminine in a way she had never experienced before.

She'd been quite bold then, and later at university, doing pretty much what she pleased with whom she pleased. If she'd got the email then she might have gone along with it for a laugh, at least until she discovered whom it was from. Then she'd have either told him to piss off in no uncertain terms, or let him indulge whatever wicked piece of kink he had in mind. She certainly wouldn't have gone running to the authorities.

Maybe she should play Mr Henderson's game, if only for a little while. Nothing serious, of course, but what was the harm in showing off her stockings to him? Nobody else needed to know, and it wasn't as if they were having a proper affair. He'd want to go further, yes, that was obvious, but she could control the situation, perhaps even steer him into playing out the fantasy sparked by *Taken to Turkey*. That would be wonderful, arriving at the office not to write up marketing reports and put together client presentations, but to be turned over a strong man's knee and given a bare bottom spanking, then to suck him off, which was only fair.

A sudden jolt from the train snapped her out of her erotic daydream. They were pulling into Cambridge, although she'd barely been aware of the passing stations. Reality came back with a rush, leaving her feeling nervous and fragile and she turned her steps towards the EAS building. She was wondering if she could really do it, but her arousal was mingled with resentment for being manipulated, caution for her job and her reputation at the firm and, she realised, fear of the redoubtable Mrs Henderson.

By the time she reached the building she had decided on a plan of action. When she came into the office she would go to the rank of filing cabinets opposite Mr Henderson's desk and, very deliberately, bend to take something from the lowest drawer. He'd see her seams, maybe even an inch of lace. He'd know she'd been a good, obedient girl. He'd say something, and she would take it from there.

Having made her decision, she went into automatic, no longer thinking but simply doing, something which had often helped her get through difficult moments, from her one and only job interview to her one and only public striptease. Pushing in through the big double doors, she greeted her colleagues with curt nods, speaking only to request her floor from a man in the lift. At the office door she went straight in, bidding Mr Henderson a brisk good morning. He looked up, returned the greeting, his eyes still on her as she put her things down on her desk, her heart now hammering as she took three quick steps to the filing cabinets, turned her back directly to him, bent low to show him what he wanted to see, the outline of her bottom and hips beneath her skirt, her smart black heels, her stocking-clad legs with the tell-tale seam running up to the where the lacy tops would just show beneath the hem of her skirt.

'Good. Now, Laura, we need to put together a quote. Rotary switches for a company in Birmingham.'

4

For the rest of the working day time dragged as never before. Mr Henderson's behaviour towards Laura had not changed in the slightest. He seemed to approve of the way she was dressed, but made no overt comment, let alone a sexual one. Instead he was consummately professional, immersed in work and expecting her to follow suit, to the point where she had begun to wonder if his concern for her appearance really was no more than a desire to present EAS in the best possible light.

If he had sent the email he had either lost his nerve and decided not to make a move, or was playing an extremely subtle game with her. Neither possibility seemed to fit in with what she'd learnt of his character, and she knew full well that if he'd meant the instruction without erotic overtones he'd simply have told her to her face.

Her thoughts turned to Brian and the possibility that the whole thing was a joke, although that didn't seem particularly likely. With his juvenile, smutty sense of humour he was more likely to have come up with something cruder, perhaps an instruction to go without bra and knickers, or to photocopy her bottom the way he'd made Tina do at the office party the year before last. At least he was fairly easy to test. Mr Henderson might just be able to play it so cool he'd give nothing away, but not Brian. Brian would snigger. Brian would make some dirty remark.

Unfortunately Brian was quite likely to snigger or make a dirty remark anyway. To him the mere existence of a woman seemed to be provocative, either sexually, if she was conventionally attractive, or as the butt of a joke if she dared to deviate from his ideal by more than a few years or a few pounds. Yet there had to be a good chance he'd give himself away.

By luck accounts queried the margins on the quote she and Mr Henderson had put together, giving her a perfect excuse to go over to Brian's department. Not that there would be any reason to talk to him, but she would have to pass his desk. Perhaps a smile would provoke a response, or a deliberately frosty detachment.

She decided on frosty detachment, marching towards him with her chin in the air and her eyes fixed firmly to the front. His eyes had been on her from the moment she'd come in, but that was usual, so was his remark to his sidekick, Dave.

'Is it getting hot in here, or is it just my imagination?'

Dave's reaction was equally predictable.

'It's getting hot, Brian. Hotter, even hotter.'

Brian's next remark was not.

'Hot enough for the girls to leave off their tights, Dave, don't you think?'

'Yeah!'

Laura stopped, reacting on the instant as she reached down and took Brian by his gaudy, pink silk tie. Pulling him up a little from his seat, she bent her face to his.

'Do not do it again. That's all.'

She walked on. A chorus of jeers and hoots followed her as both Brian and Dave did their best to reassert bruised masculinity. Laura ignored them, contenting herself with a smile for two of their female colleagues who'd begun to clap. Continuing into Mr Bannerjee's office, she quickly went through the quote, explaining the margins and why they needed to be so low. After a few questions and a few grumbles her reasoning was accepted and she left. Brian made a joke of her earlier reaction, pretending to shield himself from her, and as she reached the door making a remark about the Gestapo that set off Dave's high-pitched laughter.

Back in Mr Henderson's office she explained Mr Bannerjee's reservations and returned to her desk. Her emotions were complex, an almost savage satisfaction for what she'd done, mixed with the urge to burst into tears and undercut by a bitter disappointment. It had turned out to be just one more silly office prank, and from Brian, who had even less potential as a figure in her fantasies than Hovis Boy.

She hid a sigh as she tapped her computer off stand-by. Only now that the solution to the mystery had proved to be mundane did she realise how badly she'd wanted it to be something more. All the positive emotion she'd invested in the event was gone, leaving only the fear and resentment he'd managed to impose on her, but she found herself earnestly wishing the email had come from some attractive man.

As she checked her mail she was wondering if he'd sent something else, perhaps some smug little taunt or one of his stupid jokes. There was nothing from him directly, but there was something from the same address as before, and as before from the Controller. There was a sudden tightness in Laura's throat as she clicked open the message, expecting some predictable quip from Brian but praying it would be something else. It was. VERY PRETTY, BUT HOLD-UPS ARE SO UNFEMININE. TOMORROW YOU WILL WEAR SUSPENDERS.

Laura froze, her hand still on the mouse as she reread the message, and again, taking in the implications of each and every word. He'd seen. He knew, and whoever 'he' was, it could not possibly be Brian, because the message had been sent pretty much at the exact moment she'd been hauling him from his chair by his tie. She glanced at Mr Henderson, but if he was responsible then he was a superb actor, his brow furrowed as he tracked a pen down a column of figures.

A lump had risen in her throat, forcing her to swallow before she read the message yet again. There was something horribly compelling about the way it was worded, filling her with angry resentment, but also a sense of weakness and need. It was not 'you should wear suspenders', not even 'you must wear suspenders', but 'you will wear suspenders', a statement that went beyond mere confidence to an arrogant certainty that she would obey.

Her immediate instinct was to defy him, perhaps to send back a curt note telling him that he was a filthy pervert and that she would never obey his commands. It would have been a lie. She desperately wanted to obey, despite her resentment, despite knowing that it would be utterly inappropriate to submit herself to a man's will. In truth, none of that was important or, at least, not important enough to make her submerge her desire. What was important was to know who had sent the message. If it was Mr Drake, perhaps Darcy, Mr Henderson even, then she would wear suspenders, and anything else he thought right, but if Brian had somehow managed to trick her, or if it was Hovis Boy, then they were going to get their faces slapped.

Mr Henderson was still hard at work, and paying no attention to her whatsoever. Laura pretended to be busy, while desperately trying to decide on the identity of her lover, or tormentor. It had to be somebody who knew she'd worn stockings that day, and specifically stay-ups. How could he have known; from the tension in the material, because he'd expected the see the lines of her suspender straps under her skirt, because he'd seen far enough up to be sure?

In any case it couldn't have been Mr Drake, and was almost certainly somebody at the office, somebody she'd seen that day, or who had seen her. She thought of where she'd been, to accounts, to the canteen, to the loos, to production, which had meant taking the walkway above the factory floor. That had always made her feel uncomfortable. Some of the cruder men tended to ogle the girls, some openly, some not, some even wolf-whistling or making cheeky remarks. She had quickly realised that if she walked near the edge she'd be giving the men a view up all but the tightest skirts, and had always stayed close to the wall if possible. Nevertheless, somebody might have seen, most likely one of the machinists.

She had never had much to do with the men on the factory floor. A few were attractive, but it was very hard to imagine them as the sort of calm, arrogant alpha male she pictured as sending the emails. Some of them certainly qualified as alpha males, it was true, but in a much cruder way, all rough power and self-certainty, which had its appeal but came a very poor second to what she really liked.

Yet they couldn't be ruled out, making the situation more confusing than ever. Once again she felt a little frightened, adding to the muddle of her emotions as she finished up her work. Still Mr Henderson behaved as he always did, and she found herself starting for the station more puzzled and anxious than she had been that morning, only to reach a decision before she was halfway. She would reply to the email, promising to obey if the sender revealed himself.

She felt an immediate sense of disappointment, knowing that however sensible the idea seemed it was pointless. By trying to take control she would either drive him away or make him more determined to exert his authority, if he was the type of man she wanted. If he did as he was told then he wasn't the type of man she wanted and the thrill would be gone.

Still she told herself that she would not be going to work in suspenders the next day, even though there was no harm in taking a detour to look in the window of Pretty Things.

Nor was there any harm in going inside, as she needed some new stockings anyway if she was going to be wearing them regularly. They had some beautiful designs, and there was a sale on, so it was only sensible to buy a couple of packs of plain knickers, and some pretty ones just in case. Having spent so much, and while she was in there, it seemed silly not to buy one of the rather tempting suspender belts they had on display, or maybe two, although obviously she wouldn't wear them the next day, or if she did, it wouldn't be for him.

Back in King's Lynn, Laura went though her evening routine feeling even more nervous than she had the day before. It had been a long and trying day, and on the way back from walking Smudge she bought a bottle of red wine, telling herself that a single glass wouldn't hurt and that the rest would keep well enough for Friday night when she normally allowed herself some.

The wine was smooth and strong, very easy to drink and very soothing. After washing her dinner down with the first glass she decided that she needed a second, just to help her sleep and dispel the doubts crowding her mind. It didn't work, but the third did, leaving her feeling mellow and tired as she kicked off her shoes and put her feet up on the sofa.

As she poured the fourth glass she was wondering why men made such a fuss over women's underwear. It was pretty, yes, and then there was the thrill of seeing something secret or forbidden, but that didn't explain their obsession with detail. Tommy Fuller had liked her to wear knickers that tied up at either hip, but that at least made sense. He'd enjoyed tugging the bows open to make her knickers fall down so that he could get at her more easily. But then Tommy had always been very practical, and an unashamed pervert.

She'd read somewhere that men got fixated on the sexual

imagery of their youth, so that a young man who'd got used to girls in suspenders might come to associate them with sex for the rest of his life. That raised an uncomfortable possibility, because suspenders hadn't been normal wear since the 1960s, the 1950s even, which meant that her man might not only be older than her, which was good, but positively ancient, which was not.

None of her suspects were over fifty, and she dismissed the idea, concentrating on the idea of him being fixated with the way she dressed instead. The idea was both weird and exciting, to think of herself a doll, for him to dress as he pleased, and to undress. Maybe he would treat her the way she had once treated her dolls, none of which had ever kept any clothes for long, while her youthful attempts at fashion design and hair styling had quickly left them looking as if they'd just escaped a war zone.

He would be rather more gentle, hopefully, but he would also be fixated on sex. He would cut her skirts down, preferably while she was wearing them, so short that her knickers showed, also the stockings and suspenders he'd have put her in. It would be the same with her tops, the buttons snipped off her blouses so that she was unable to close them properly, and, with no bra, unable to prevent herself from showing off her breasts. He'd cut her T-shirts up too, so high that the underside of her breasts showed and that the slightest movement would risk baring them completely.

She imagined herself in her ruined clothes, walking around the house as his doll, her body displayed for his entertainment as he sat and watched, coolly sipping a drink she'd served to him. The thought made her shiver, and only the curious look in Smudge's large brown eyes prevented her from tugging up her skirt and slipping one hand down the front of her knickers. Instead she poured out the rest of the bottle into her glass, filling it almost to the brim, and went upstairs.

Her purchases were on the bed, thrown casually down when she first came in. Now too drunk and horny for reservations, she quickly pulled open one of the suspender belt packages. Her fingers were shaking as she tugged her skirt high, but the little shocked voice in her head only served to increase her excitement. The long mirror on her wardrobe showed her in reflection, the exposure of her stocking tops and knickers in striking contrast to her neat office suit, and deliciously naughty.

On sudden instinct she put her hands on her head and made a slow turn, imagining him ordering her to display herself. Who he was no longer mattered. In her head he was male, tall, attractive, commanding, sitting at his ease as she tugged up her skirt to show off her stockings tops and her knickers, front and back, tight against her flesh to leave her with only a minimum of modesty.

He would order her to put the suspender belt on, which she did, fastening it behind her back and clipping each of the four straps to her stockings. It felt snug around her hips and she could feel the tension in her straps, while in the mirror they seemed to make the V between her legs and her bottom look fuller, more prominent. Maybe that was what he wanted, to make her show off, to make her feel sexual, for him.

Already she wanted to throw herself down on the bed and bring herself to orgasm under her fingers, but she held back, deliberately teasing herself. Once he'd got her skirt up he would want more, she was sure of that. First she'd be made to go without her bra, to let the shape of her breasts show beneath the thin silk of her blouse and betray the stiffness of her nipples. Then he'd order her to undo her buttons, one by one, with her excitement and sense of exposure rising as her blouse came wide, to show the sides of her breasts, and then everything, bare in front of him as his cool, knowing gaze took in the contours of her body.

She had suited action to thought, slowly undressing herself with her eyes fixed to the mirror. With her breasts bare she had begun to look like the dishevelled doll of her imagination, and her need to masturbate was close to desperation. Still she held back, knowing that he would want to inflict one final, delicious indignity on her, and make her take her knickers down. That she knew how to do, the way Tommy Fuller had taught her, and which had always left her feeling exquisitely rude. First, to thumb down the front, far enough to let him see the crease of her sex, then the back, with her bottom pushed out to make her cheeks as full as round and she could.

Tommy had never been in the least bit reticent. He'd have had his cock out by then, pulling at the shaft while he mumbled obscenities, telling her that she had a 'pretty cunt' and that he could see her bottom hole. Her man, the Man, would be less crude, but he would be admiring the same view, stripping her of both her clothes and her modesty.

Now bare in all the places that mattered, Laura climbed onto the bed, crawling over the cover and twisting her head around to admire the view in the mirror as she finally put her hand back between her thighs. She looked impossibly rude, her smart office suit rearranged to show off every intimate detail of her body, while the busy fingers between her sex lips betrayed her excitement as no amount of exposure could ever have done.

In her imagination the Man was watching. He'd have made her strip, enjoying the view and enjoying her helpless arousal at being dirty, as if she were his doll, his rude little sex doll to be adjusted as he pleased, made to dress how he pleased, made to show herself for his pleasure and, lastly, used as he pleased. With that thought she came, imagining him climbing up behind her to thrust himself deep into her body and hold her in place until he'd satisfied himself inside her.

5

In the morning Laura found her enthusiasm dampened by a slight headache, which made the thought of dressing for sex less than appealing. Whereas the evening before arousal had been her dominant emotion, now it was resentment. Deliberately ignoring not just her new suspender belts but also her stockings, she put on a pair of tights under her most reserved skirt suit, with sensible shoes in place of her normal heels.

The wind had swung around to the north and east, bringing a cold drizzle in from the sea, which made her walk to the station distinctly unpleasant. She was still not entirely sure that the Man wasn't one of her fellow commuters, so broke the habit of four years by taking the front carriage instead of the first she came to, at the rear. The fresh air had begun to clear her head, and in the warm, dry interior of the carriage, looking out across rain swept fields her mood slowly softened.

She began to consider whether she should respond to the last message and, if not with a demand, then how? Possibly her answer could help work out who he was without challenging him directly, just as Dr Faulkner had eliminated the suspects in *Steel Trap*, by a series of carefully planned acts each designed to reduce the total. In fact she had already started, by disobeying and by avoiding her usual group of commuters, so that if she arrived at work dressed as she had been instructed the next message she received would very probably allow her to eliminate one group or the other.

Feeling rather pleased with herself, Laura made a quick detour to Pretty Things on her way to EAS, risking Mr Henderson's displeasure, to buy another suspender belt and a pair of seamed stockings, which she put on in the shop changing room. She was only a few minutes late, and he showed no great surprise when she blamed the train. Nor did he show any unusual interest in her, immediately launching into the day's work.

'Something rather tricky has come up, Laura. Drake over at Maxwell-Boyce is considering an additional five 36,000 volt units on their order. It should be straightforward, but he is one of those clients who appreciate the personal touch, while as you know I have to be here this afternoon. I'd like you to take Drake to lunch, if you wouldn't mind? On expenses, of course.'

'Yes, sir.'

'Good girl.'

His response carried just the note of condescension and affection she'd come to imagine from the Man, and instantly brought her the familiar prickle of resentment and arousal. Telling herself to be businesslike, she quickly gathered together the things she'd need as Mr Henderson explained what she was to do and that she was to meet Mr Drake at the Horseshoes in Abbots Ripton.

It was an unexpected treat, and not only because she would be out and about instead of stuck in the office all day. By the time she'd secured a car from the pool the weather had begun to break, with patches of blue showing among fast moving clouds and a wonderfully fresh feel to the air. It was also the first time Mr Henderson had ever trusted her to act on her own with a client, while there was no denying that the identity of that client made a lot of difference.

Even if Mr Drake wasn't the Man, he was very definitely a

man, and just the sort to make her melt. It was even possible that he'd leave Miss Manston-Jones in Peterborough, which opened up all sorts of possibilities. They'd be alone in a country pub on what was turning into a beautiful spring day. A little wine, and she might be able to suggest a walk to make sure they were safe to drive back to their offices, a walk on which he might very well try to take advantage of her.

She'd be made to squat down in some lonely copse, to take his cock in her mouth, all the while risking being seen by some walker or farmhand, very possibly with her blouse open and pulled back to show off her breasts as she sucked. Maybe he'd even take her all the way, kneeling in the grass, her suit dishevelled to show her off in the same rude way she'd been the night before, or stark naked, without a stitch to cover her modesty.

On the other hand it was still a bit chilly, while the grass was sure to be full of ants, spiders and other small creatures guaranteed to have much the same effect on her ardour as a bucket of cold water. It would be more practical to take a room at the pub, if less romantic. That way they could really indulge themselves, and with luck he would prove forceful and open-minded enough to want to tie her to the bed or, better still, to smack her bottom.

Only by jamming her foot on the brake did she prevent herself from running into the car ahead as it slowed for a red light. Telling herself that if he did spank her she would deserve it for not paying attention to the road, she forced herself to concentrate. The traffic was light, and she quickly realised she had made a mistake in setting off as soon as the car had been cleared, as she arrived only minutes after the pub opened, with over an hour to go before Mr Drake arrived.

She bought an orange juice and went outside, sipping her drink in the pale spring sunlight and letting her thoughts drift. The events of the last few days had opened up the possibility of exploring her sexuality in some exciting way, taking her back to the way Tommy Fuller had made her feel: rude, sometimes even dirty, occasionally a little scared, but every bit a woman. Mr Drake at least had the potential to do the same.

After a quick glance to make sure that nobody was looking, Laura quickly undid the second button of her blouse, then the third, only to do the third back up, open it again and close it again. She knew from bitter experience that a lot of men would be put off by too overt a display, while there was every chance that Miss Manston-Jones would be along as well. Miss Manston-Jones, Laura was sure, would never have to suggest that she was available.

A silver Mercedes was pulling into the car park, and Laura stopped fiddling with her blouse, watching as the driver eased himself into a parking space. He got out, a typical young businessman, alone and with no obvious reason for the guilty glance he cast in Laura's general direction before going inside. Moments later a second car arrived, small and red. This time it was a woman; petite, with dyed blonde hair cut in a bob and the sort of chest that made men talk down. Like the man, she went into the pub.

Laura could see in through the windows, to the bar, where the man and woman greeted each other with a kiss. They drank wine, chinking their glasses together and gulping the contents in an obvious hurry. Five minutes and they'd finished. The man came out, got into his car and reversed a little way, allowing the woman to nip quickly into the passenger seat as she emerged. Laura smiled.

Obviously the couple were having an affair, and presumably a clandestine one. It was hard to disapprove, when she didn't know who else might be involved, and easy to enjoy a vicarious thrill as she imaged the couple driving off for a bout of hurried, illicit sex. There would be no time for anything fancy, as both were presumably on their lunch hours. They'd kiss, clinging urgently to each other in a passion made hot by anticipation. He looked the type to take the lead and would unzip himself, pulling his cock and balls out from the fly of his suit and guiding her hand to them. As she began to stroke him erect he would fumble her breasts out of her clothes, enjoying their size and weight, running his thumbs over her nipples to make them pop out. As soon as he was stiff she'd get into his lap, her skirt pulled up, her tights and knickers pushed down, and the full length of his erection eased into her. They'd do it like that, with her bouncing on his cock and him with one big breast in either hand, to reach their satisfaction in just minutes.

She was smiling to herself as she pictured the scene, and now earnestly hoping that Mr Drake would turn up alone, and make a move on her. Another car was approaching, a black one, very similar to his. Her heart had begun to beat faster as she realised it was his and she quickly composed herself, pretending she hadn't noticed him until he was actually walking towards her, his hand extended. There was no sign of Miss Manston-Jones.

'Another early bird, I see.'

Laura stood up, sure that he would realise the state she was in as she took his hand and responded.

'Mr Drake. Good morning.'

'Chris, please. Is everybody at EAS so formal?'

'Mr Henderson feels that I should address senior people respectfully.'

He chuckled.

'My PA's the same, maybe we should swap? Shall we go inside? It's a bit windy out here.'

'Yes, of course.'

'What are you having.'

The words 'rough sex' rose unbidden to Laura's throat and she ended up coughing in her effort not to actually say them. He made her choice for her.

'G and T. Have you been here before?'

'No.'

'It's very good. Miles from anywhere of course.'

Laura smiled and nodded, wondering if any of his previous visits had been liaisons such as the one she'd just witnessed. He set up a tab and ordered the drinks, refusing to allow her to put anything on her own expenses. Taking a menu and the wine list, he led her to a table by the window. Laura sat down, completely abandoned to his easy assumption of control. He was absorbed in the menu and she took a moment to watch him, admiring the lean contours of his shoulders and chest, but particularly his face. There was something patrician about him, yet with a boyish cast, so that it was easy to imagine him not as a businessman, but perhaps as a wealthy young idler from between the wars, or a Spitfire pilot. Certainly it was easy to imagine him as the hero in a novel, and one with a dark side, one who would enjoy giving a girl a bit of necessary discipline across his knee.

'Do you like spatchcock?'

'I beg your pardon?'

'Spatchcock. You know, it's a chicken dish.'

'Oh ... yes, of course. Yes, very much.'

'Well I'm going to have it.'

'So will I.'

'And a bottle of Chablis, I think, or would you prefer Sancerre?'

'Um ... whichever you think best ... no, let's have the Chablis.'

Laura had forced herself to make a decision, sure that she was making an exhibition of herself. He took no notice, but went to the bar and quickly gave their order, speaking the moment he returned.

'To business. I'll be straightforward with you here. I've managed to persuade my bosses to upgrade our 36,000 volt system at the same time as the general one, hopefully saving money in the long run. This is my idea, and a lot rests on my being able to justify it, so I need a good price. Presumably old Henderson has given you some leeway?'

'Some, yes.'

'Good. Then name your bottom line to save a lot of tedious argument, I'll accept, sign up to the deal and we can enjoy our lunch, how's that?'

Laura hid a smile, having seen enough clients try to steam-roller Mr Henderson over the years to recognise the technique. Hoping that Mr Drake was so sure of himself that he'd assume she'd accept his offer without quibbling, she named a price ten per cent higher than the one Mr Henderson had suggested. Mr Drake gave her a sharp look.

'Merlin Gerin can do better.'

'Then you'd have two companies trying to install switchgear at the same time. Please Mr Drake, if I don't manage to reach an agreement I'll be in trouble.'

He laughed.

'OK, I'll take it, if only for that naughty schoolgirl impression.'

Laura found herself blushing, as if he'd read her mind, and quickly busied herself with the paperwork. Having reached a decision he signed up without further discussion, and Laura was soon left with a satisfying sense of a job well done, while it was clear he was keen to flirt, and perhaps more. He spoke easily, asking questions and making her laugh with his wry, slightly self-effacing style. By the time they'd finished lunch what little resistance she'd had left was gone. He made it easy to melt, and when the couple she had seen earlier came back she didn't hesitate before leaning across the table.

'Do you see the man in the green tie and the blonde woman?'

'Yes.'

'They arrived shortly before you did, in different cars, then went off together in his. That was nearly an hour ago.'

He chuckled.

'The Horseshoes is well known as a rendezvous. There's a piece of forestry land a couple of miles away, which is, shall we say, equally well known. I suspect that's where they've been.'

'I'm sure it is.'

Laura hesitated, spinning the stem of her empty glass between finger and thumb as she wondered if she dared suggest a visit. He smiled, once again seeming to read her thoughts, extending one hand to gently stroke her fingers as he spoke.

'Would you like to?'

Laura nodded, a sudden, urgent motion, making no effort to conceal her passion. His smile grew a trifle broader and he squeezed her hand, then rose to pay the bill. Alone for a moment, she was sure that everybody else in the pub knew exactly what was going on, despite nobody paying any obvious attention at all. Not that she really cared. She was ready, and it had been too long.

He came back and took her by the hand, Laura walking as if she was in a dream as she allowed herself to be led to his car. It was new, the inside still rich with the smell of leather, the air warm and still. She relaxed, feeling safe and confident now that she was sure she had his attention, also naughty. Turning to him with a smile as they set off, she began to undo the buttons of her blouse, making it very clear that she was fully available and needed no further cajoling. His response was a knowing, amused chuckle.

The plantation was just minutes away, a stand of mature poplars and pines cut through by broad gravel roads, arrow straight but with turning places every so often that might have been designed for lovers in cars. He chose one well in from the road, but instead of taking Laura into his arms as she had been hoping, he climbed out, beckoning her to follow. She obeyed, not wanting to spoil the experience, but gave a squeak of alarm as he immediately pressed her against the side of the car, his hands circling her waist beneath her open blouse.

'Won't somebody see?'

'Maybe, another couple.'

He'd undone her bra as he spoke and the next instant her breasts were bare to the cool forest air. She tried to speak, not at all sure if she wanted to put on a show for other people, but he had taken one nipple between his lips and her voice came as a gasp. He was going to have her, just the way he wanted, and in the open, something so in tune with her fantasies she had quickly abandoned all thought of resistance.

'OK, do it . . . do as you like.'

'I intend to.'

He'd spoken as his mouth left her chest, but he stayed down, adjusting her clothes and kissing her flesh as it came bare, confident in his right to do as he pleased. Laura shut her eyes, holding him gently as she was exposed, her blouse opened wide to leave her bare breasts thrust high, her skirt rolled up to show her stockings, her suspenders straps, her knickers. A single, firm kiss was planted on the mound of her sex and he spoke again.

'Stockings and suspenders, I see. I do like an old-fashioned girl.'

Laura tried to answer, but again her words came out as a

gasp. He'd tugged her knickers down, in one sudden motion, exposing her to his mouth. Her legs began to shake as she was licked, her breathing growing deeper and harder by the moment, until she was sure she was going to come.

'Don't stop, please.'

He pulled away.

'Greedy girl, Laura.'

The tone of gentle admonishment in his voice was exactly what she needed as he set to work again. A few more words with that same easy authority would have been perfect, but her imagination had no trouble in keeping up. He was doing wonderful things with his tongue as she imagined how it could have been, for him to call her a greedy girl, just as he had done, but to refuse her request, then to tell her what happened to greedy girls, how greedy girls needed their bottoms smacked before being made to suck cock.

She cried out when she started to come, her fingers locked in his hair as her orgasm swept through her, only for him to pull sharply back a moment later. For one awful moment she thought they'd been caught, only to find herself gripped hard in his arms, twisted around, bundled over the bonnet of the car, her knickers jerked low and his cock eased into her from behind. The next instant he was thrusting himself into her with all his force, to leave her panting and clutching at the paintwork in exactly the sort of helpless ecstasy she had always craved.

6

Laura was singing as she drove back towards Cambridge. The encounter had been everything she could have hoped for and, unlike so many men, Chris Drake had known how to treat her afterwards, with a cuddle and assurances that there would be a next time. Despite his enthusiasm she'd made a conscious effort not to push too hard and risk scaring him away. He had been the one to suggest meeting up on Sunday, and had been keen to come to King's Lynn.

She already felt that she was more than a little in love with him, and everything else now seemed completely trivial, including the mysterious messages. When she got back she was obliged to clear her agreement with Mr Henderson and log the new order in, along with the necessary changes to the original one. That proved more complicated than she'd anticipated, and by the time she got back from production it was after four o'clock. All the while she'd been thinking of Chris and what they'd done together, so she was on automatic as she logged on and brought her email messages up, only to come suddenly alert as she saw the now familiar address.

Nothing had been said, but now that she'd got to know Chris she was certain he could not be the Controller, despite his enjoyment of the way she'd been dressed. He was forthright, assertive, but too passionate. The Controller's calm, reserved authority was very different, and while it might have been equally appealing, it was now no more than a distraction, and potentially an annoying one.

The message was short, just two words. GOOD GIRL. Laura paused as she moved to delete the message, biting her lip. Whoever it was, her best bet might now be to let him down gently, telling him she was with somebody else and thus hopefully avoiding any repercussions. Her reply needed to be short and to the point, avoiding any possibility of misinterpretation or keeping his hopes alive, yet polite. Hopefully he was as controlled as he seemed and would accept her verdict.

She typed her message in reply – I AM SORRY, BUT I HAVE A PARTNER – and was about to click on the Send button when she realised that there was something peculiar about his message. She'd only been a good girl to one man, and that was Chris Drake. Admittedly she'd put her suspenders on before coming into the factory, but the only person who could possibly have known was Mr Henderson, and he was his normal, businesslike self. She tried to tell herself it no longer mattered, but her curiosity was too strong. Could it have been somebody in the car pool, even one of the staff at Pretty Things? Both suggestions were ridiculous. It had to be Mr Henderson.

Laura turned her chair to him, determined to have it out once and for all, but found herself unable to speak. His calm, serious face made the idea of effectively accusing him of making improper advances an impossibility, besides which he would undoubtedly deny it and she would just end up feeling silly. He had noticed her attention and looked up.

'If you have nothing particular to do, Laura, you can go home. An early start to the weekend is the least you deserve.'

'Thank you, Mr Henderson.'

She deleted the message she had been about to send, now sure that if she left the mystery unsolved it would nag at her mind for months, if not years.

Mr Henderson had only given her an extra half-hour or so, but she put it to good use, calling in at Pretty Things again, but this time to buy a set of black silk camiknickers and matching bra, a treat both for herself and for Chris, who had made it very clear that he preferred her clothing disarranged rather than right off. He'd also made it clear that he liked the idea of being seen, which she found both frightening and exciting. Not that anybody had caught them, but they'd been right out in the open and another couple might easily have driven past, or worse, a logging crew, which really would have been embarrassing, too much so for reality, if not fantasy.

She buried herself in her book on the way home, once more enjoying the story now that she was sure none of her fellow commuters were spying on her. There was even another spanking scene, this time with a buxom Turkish girl turned over the knee of Mustapha bin Yunus, the villainous white slaver who had agreed to buy Evangeline from Lord Jasper. It was quite detailed, describing the unfortunate girl's bottom as a magnificent amber peach, wriggling in her struggles of desperation, a phrase that made Laura chuckle, then smile. An idea had occurred to her.

Saturday was spent tidying her flat, messing it up again in case he thought she was too fussy, and an attempt at some impromptu Feng Shui designed to give the impression of a casual, Bohemian lifestyle she felt might seem appropriate for the sort of girl who liked to be thrown over the bonnet of a car and rogered from behind or, better still, spanked.

It was an alarming prospect, for several reasons. The worst case scenario would be if, when she had finally managed to get the hint across, he didn't dish out a spanking but a lecture on human dignity and inappropriate sexual behaviour. That didn't seem very likely, judging by the way he'd behaved on the plantation, which meant she might succeed and end up having to cope with the pain and indignity that turned her on so strongly in her fantasies but might be very different in real life.

By the Sunday morning she was finding excuses not to go through with her plan, even to cancel their date, while she was convinced he'd be put off by her flat, either because it was too neat and tidy or too messy. Smudge was also a problem, apt to want attention at inappropriate moments and too big to be easily ignored. In the end she put him out into the tiny yard behind the house, assuaging her guilt by promising him the bone from the rib of beef she'd bought at the farmer's market. That left the flat dog free, but either a mess or not a mess, depending on his perspective.

As it was, he took no notice whatsoever, arriving half-an-hour earlier than he'd said he would, plonking himself down on her sofa and asking if she had any wine in the fridge. Laura obliged, selecting one of the four bottles she'd put in just in case – along with three brands of beer, a local organic cider and various mixers – and serving it to him before pouring her own glass. He took a couple of reflective sips and then began to talk, as casually as if he'd known her for years, with no hint of the tension she'd been suffering from since the moment they parted.

Gradually Laura relaxed, grateful for his casual manner. To let him take her to bed would be easy, effortless in fact. She considered postponing her attempt to get something more, but the idea brought such a sharp pang of disappointment that she abandoned it immediately.

Lunch was carefully planned, set early to ensure there'd be plenty of time to digest before an afternoon hopefully spent half naked in the bedroom with a red bottom, but his early arrival meant that she had to put the joint in the oven before they'd finished their first glass of wine. As she busied herself rolling potatoes in the minimum possible quantity of fat his voice carried through from the living room.

'What are we having?'

'Roast beef.'

'Delicious. Will you be in and out of the kitchen all the time, or can you spare a little for me?'

It seemed a peculiar question, but Laura answered anyway.

'Just let me get the meat in.'

'That can be arranged.'

She found herself blushing as she realised what she'd said and didn't reply but quickly finished her task before going back into the living room. He sat as before, sprawled comfortably on the sofa with his long limbs spread out, except that he now had his jeans open and his cock and balls bulging from the fly. Laura stopped, at once thrilled and disgusted, amazed that he could be so rude but unable to deny her instinctive reaction. It was also just the sort of thing Tommy Fuller would have done to her, expecting sex without the slightest attempt at seduction first, pulling his cock out and demanding it attended to in a way that no weaker man would have dared.

Chris Drake was the same, grinning as he waited, completely sure of himself and rightly so. Laura swallowed, managed a weak nod and got down on her knees, still in her apron as she crawled across to him on all fours. He gave a knowing chuckle and slid himself a little further down the sofa, opening his long thighs to make himself available to her mouth. She reached him, her excitement rising fast as she took in the faint but heady scent of cock mingled with some masculine body product. He looked at her, amused, but also appreciative as he spoke.

'I'd like your breasts bare.'

'Of course.'

Laura's hands went behind her back to the bow of her apron, but he wagged a finger at her.

'No. Leave that on. In fact, yes, take everything else off except that, and you can stay that way.'

A shiver ran the length of Laura's spine as she pictured herself cooking for him with nothing on but her apron, her bare bottom showing as she worked, at the stove, and on his cock. She knelt up and began to strip, too urgent to think of making a show for him, but he didn't seem to care, watching with that same boyish grin and stroking his balls and cock in an absentminded fashion.

She quickly had her top and bra off, kicked off her shoes and stood to get out of her skirt. His smile grew broader as her black silk camiknickers came on show, and she hesitated, wondering if he'd like her to keep them on. Her enquiring glance was met with a shake of his head.

'No, no, off they come, but you can keep your stockings.'

Laura nodded, fumbling her knickers down and stepping free to leave herself to all intents and purposes naked; nothing concealed from his gaze, or his touch. There was still some embarrassment at being so exposed, and she was glad to get her apron back on, leaving her concealed at the front, if hardly decent, but bare behind. Chris chuckled.

'That is a beautiful sight. Now down you go.'

She obeyed without hesitation, falling quickly to her knees, then to all fours. As she got down she felt her breasts loll forward beneath her apron and she knew he could see them, her bottom too. She nuzzled her face against his cock and balls, revelling in the feel of warm male flesh, before taking him into her mouth. He sighed, his hand closing in her hair to dictate the rhythm of her sucking as she got to work.

His cock immediately began to swell in her mouth, a sensation she had always adored and made all the better by the fantasy developing in her head. To be kneeling at his feet in nothing but her stockings and a cooking apron was good, but it would have been better still if she'd been spanked first, not as a sexy game, but as a punishment for some minor fault.

She moved forwards a little, making herself comfortable between his thighs so that she could play with his balls while she sucked. He was getting hard, and starting to push up into her mouth in his rising excitement, while the grip in her hair had tightened, keeping her firmly in place. She let her imagination run, playing the scene over in her head, how she'd be told off, maybe for refusing to work stripped, put across his knee, her knickers taken down and her bottom smacked hard. Once he was finished with her she'd be made to strip anyway and set to work in the nude but for her apron and stockings, only to discover that punishing her had turned him on, and being held by her hair as she was made to suck him off.

He was getting there far too quickly, already groaning and pushing himself deep, while Laura had hoped to carry on to the point at which she could no longer resist slipping a hand back between her legs. She tried to slow down, lifting from his now solid shaft to tease his balls and the underside of his cock with her tongue, but he quickly lost patience.

'Come on, Laura, in it goes.'

Being obedient to him felt too good to allow her to resist and she took him back in her mouth, still trying to take it slowly. He wasn't having it, holding her firmly by the hair as he fucked her mouth. Laura let her hand go back, feeling more than a little used and not sure if that was a reason for resentment or the perfect thing to come over. After all, if he'd spanked her and forced her to suck him off he'd hardly worry about her pleasure.

A powerful shudder ran through her at the thought, but before she could focus on her fantasy his cock jerked in her mouth. She did her best to swallow, still rubbing at her sex as she imagined having him come in her mouth as the final indignity of her ordeal, but he'd quickly pulled her head up, gasping as he spoke.

'Stop, stop, that's too much, Laura ... too sensitive. Oh, but you are good.'

She nodded and rocked back on her heels, eager to show him just how excited he had made her, but his eyes were closed as he spoke again.

'So good. Now, how about another glass of wine, darling?'

Laura stopped, her feelings a mess. It felt good to be controlled, but she needed at least some attention. Yet she knew that the longer she held off the better it would be and so reluctantly complied, returning to the kitchen to tidy herself up and retrieve the bottle from the fridge.

An hour later she was glad for her choice. Being in nothing but apron and stockings had kept her arousal high all the while, especially once he'd come into the kitchen to talk to her while she cooked the vegetables, sitting at his ease while his eyes caressed her bare bottom. She ate naked but for her stockings, constantly aware of her exposed breasts as her need rose and the level in the second wine bottle fell. By the time they had finished she was drunk and her inhibitions had gone completely.

They snuggled up on the sofa, Chris fully dressed, Laura still next to nude. He began to play with her breasts, idly, stroking her skin to feel their shape and teasing her nipples until she'd begun to arch her back. She let her thighs come wide, hoping for a yet more intimate caress, only to realise that if she was going to put her scheme into operation this would be her last chance, and that if she didn't the coming week would be one of agonising frustration. Twisting around, she reached for her book, which she'd left carefully placed on the lower level of her coffee table.

'Do you like dirty stories?'

Chris gave a low purr, which Laura took for assent. Opening *Taken to Turkey* at the bookmark, she began to read.

A gasp of pure horror escaped Evangeline's perfect white throat as she took in the scene in the harem. It was a great square room, lavishly decorated with all the opulence of the orient, the ceiling a magnificent mosaic of turquoise, cinnabar and gold, the walls hung with thick velvet drapes of a dozen rich hues before which stood huge negro slaves, their muscular bodies naked but for loose white pantaloons, their ebony skin glistening with oil, each as still as any statue and leaning on a great scimitar of finest Arabian steel. Enormous pillows lay scattered about the floor, their colours every bit as rich as the hangings, and on these pillows lay girls, some dusky, some Grecian olive in complexion, a few as pale as her own exquisite skin, but all young and as beautiful as the dawn.

At the far side of the room lounged Mustapha bin Yunus himself, a veritable giant, his great round head half hidden beneath a great black beard oiled and curled to the latest fashion, and crowned by a turban of viridian silk from the centre of which a ruby the size of a blackbird's egg winked like the eye of some malevolent demon. His own eyes were only a little less fierce, while his massive hirsute chest and monstrous belly protruded from between the wings of a red velvet waistcoat in a fashion so grotesque it brought her near to swooning. But none of these details held her eye, as she gazed at the girl who lay across Mustapha's lap – a dusky, painted houri, naked but for a scrap of dishevelled silk at the level of her ankles. Bangles and bells at her wrists, her lifted bottom a magnificent amber peach, she wriggled in her struggles of desperation as he applied smack after purposeful smack to her wildly bouncing cheeks.

'Don't you think that's fun? I'd love a man to handle me like that. Would you like to, do you think, Chris? Would you like to spank me? Chris? Chris?'

Chris was asleep.

7

Laura spent most of her journey into work the next day trying to place the blame for what had happened on herself. Chris worked hard and was entitled to be tired at the weekend, especially after sex followed by Sunday lunch. If she'd had any sense she would have sat down beside him when she first discovered him with his cock out and played with it while she read the passage from *Taken to Turkey*, either that or simply abandoned the whole over elaborate scheme and crawled across his lap, sticking her bottom up in an invitation that she was sure he wouldn't have refused. It had also been a mistake to drink two bottles of wine, and to cook such an enormous lunch, yet despite all her efforts she found it impossible not to feel a little resentful. She, after all, had done everything he'd wanted, and however much she liked a man to take control sexually he had to be considerate to her as well.

Her frustration had reached a peak when he'd woken up after two hours, demanded coffee and left almost immediately, applying a single firm pat to her bottom as they embraced at her door, as if to tease her, even to taunt her. She'd been too agitated to want to play with herself, either that evening or the following morning, leaving her still on edge as she got off the train at Cambridge. All the usual suspects had been there, and Darcy had even stepped aside to let her through the doors first, triggering a fantasy of giving herself to him in order to get back at Chris.

For once there was nothing urgent to do at work, with the

factory likely to be working at capacity for several months. Mr Henderson set Laura to the task of seeking out potential new clients, a routine job that allowed plenty of time for daydreaming, doodling and even the occasional glance at her book when he was out of the room. She also found herself checking her emails at what she knew perfectly well to be unnecessarily frequent intervals. Telling herself that she was now with Chris made her feel guilty, but it didn't stop her.

The email came shortly before lunch, much earlier than before. She opened it immediately, telling herself that it wouldn't do any harm just to look. Her eyes grew wide as she took in the words on the screen. SO, LAURA, DO YOU WANT TO BE PUNISHED?

She knew the answer – yes – but she could no more type it in than she could pull her eyes away from the screen. Whoever it was seemed to be able to read her mind. He knew her name, too, which had to narrow the field considerably, but made the question all the more alarming. She tried to tell herself that it was Chris after all, and had been all along, that he'd only been pretending to be asleep and had heard what she'd said, but her instincts told her otherwise.

Chris was really no different to Tommy Fuller, handsome in his maturity and confidence, but underneath all that a dirty little boy who liked to get girls out of their clothes and onto his cock. The Man, the Controller, was very different, calmer by far, with more authority, what Mr Henderson might have been in a fantasy world where bosses spanked their secretaries and nobody thought it wrong or even unusual.

She glanced across the room, but Mr Henderson was bending to return his appointments book to its drawer, apparently oblivious to her. New determination fired her. Chris or no Chris, she would find out who the Controller really was. That meant responding, playing him at his own game, although even as she began to consider her reply she was doubting her ability to outwit him.

It seemed pointless to answer his question, especially as she was pretty sure he knew the answer, or at least had a strong suspicion what it would be. Nor would admitting to her need help to identify him, while denying it seemed pointless. She considered conducting the experiment she had intended to, making changes to the way she was dressed in accordance with his instructions and seeing how he responded in order to eliminate each possibility until only one remained, only to dismiss the idea. Not only did it seem likely that he would catch her out, but he hadn't given her a specific instruction.

What his question did suggest was that she had been disobedient, presumably because she was wearing tights that morning, implying that she'd done it on purpose in order to provoke him into punishing her. Yet he hadn't threatened, but asked, which suggested that he wanted affirmation. If she gave it, perhaps he'd come into the open, but the thought of turning up at some private rendezvous ready in anticipation of getting her bottom smacked and finding Hovis Boy or Brian and Dave waiting for her was too appalling to be countenanced. Not only that, but it was not at all sensible to go to a meeting with a strange man on her own and she could hardly bring a friend who might end up watching her getting it knickers down across the Man's lap.

For a long while she sat staring at the screen before remembering how Hugo de Montvilliers had flushed the Human Chameleon from his hiding place by setting fire to the house in *The Marquis of Montauch*. She would set the Controller on fire, although not literally. He was a man after all, and obviously fancied her, so it surely had to be possible to prick his imperturbability? She nodded to herself, clicked on the reply button and began to type. I'M VERY SORRY, SIR. TOMORROW I WILL BE IN

STOCKINGS AND SUSPENDERS, AND FOR MY PUNISHMENT I WILL GO WITHOUT KNICKERS.

Having completed the message she hesitated, then clicked the Send button before her doubts could get the better of her. It was a good scheme and, after all, she didn't actually have to leave her knickers off. What mattered was that he would think she was bare under her skirt, and surely the man who could resist the opportunity to peep if he knew a girl was knickerless had yet to be born?

Conscious that whoever he was now had every reason to assume she was interested, she found herself nervous, sure that he would make a move at any moment, and dreading the approach of a leering Brian. Nothing happened, not a single one of the people she saw behaved in any way out of the ordinary, but with just a few minutes to go before leaving time another message arrived. DO SO NOW.

The words gave her a jolt of emotion worthy of the most hypersensitive of her literary heroines. It was an order, and the instinct to obey was so strong that she found her hands wanting to go to her hips. She closed her eyes, telling herself that she was now in a relationship, and that even if she hadn't been it wasn't right to take her knickers off for strange men. Another voice came back, a wicked insidious voice, telling her that it would do no harm, that it would be fun, and that it would change the journey home from work from a boring routine to a thrilling ride.

His message also suggested that he'd know if she obeyed, which had to mean he was watching, or at least expected to see her. She could hardly take her knickers off in front of Mr Henderson, which meant a trip to the Ladies. Very possibly he'd want to see, allowing her a chance to catch him out, which in turn provided the excuse she needed to actually do it, unless of course he was already watching her, and no doubt enjoying the state she was in. She cast yet another enquiring glance at Mr Henderson, but as always he gave nothing away.

Laura stood up, trying as hard as she could not to show her nerves as she made for the door, only to be brought up short by her boss's voice, cool and easy, just a little wry.

'Going somewhere, Laura?'

She spun around, stammering unintelligibly as she answered, now certain it was him after all.

'I, um ... that is, you ... I mean, I have to ...'

'Are you all right, Laura?'

'I ... I have to go to the Ladies. Unless ...'

'Oh, I see. I'm sorry. I thought you were hoping to get off early. Run along then.'

'Yes, sir.'

Laura turned for the door to hide her burning embarrassment. The awful words had been about to spill from her mouth when he had interrupted her, an offer to take her knickers off in front of him. She hadn't been able to stop herself, too weak with shock for what she'd thought was an admission that he was the Man, only to hold back at the last instant when he'd spoken again.

Yet it still might be him. Maybe he was toying with her, determined to extract every last ounce of emotion, to leave her a helpless wreck before he finally revealed himself. Maybe it would be when she came back from the loos, a curt order to lift her skirt, to show him her bare sex. She knew she'd do it as well, her feelings too strong to be denied, and as she hurried down the corridor she was cursing him under her breath even as her body grew hot to the thought of her coming exposure.

Only in the calm of the Ladies did she manage to get a grip on herself, sitting in a locked cubicle as she gulped in air. She hadn't realised how badly he'd got to her, if it even was him. Looked at sensibly, there was nothing at all unusual in what he'd said, while she was so tense that almost anything might have seemed provocative.

There was only one way to find out, to force the issue, because if she didn't she felt she was going to go mad. With her face set in a stubborn frown, she kicked her shoes free and tugged her skirt up, levered her tights and knickers down, then off, stuffing both garments into her bag. Naked from the waist down, she felt more exposed than she ever had before, in front of any man, even on the one occasion she'd allowed herself to be talked into performing a striptease, and yet she knew it was nothing compared to the way she'd feel if Mr Henderson made her show herself.

It took her a full five minutes to pluck up the courage to leave the Ladies, all the while wavering between going through with it and backing out. To her horror Brian and Dave were in the corridor, leaning on the coffee machine. Both turned to watch as she went by, making her painfully conscious of her bare legs and that only a thin layer of wool separated her naked bottom from their lecherous, penetrating eyes. Dave whistled at her, but it was Brian who spoke up.

'Hot, or what? I bet those go up all the way.'

Dave sniggered and Laura found herself blushing again, sure that they'd realise she had no knickers on and that the whole of EAS would know by the morning. Unless, that was, the Controller was some grotesque cyber creation of theirs, his firm authoritative manner no more than a construct made in mockery of the sort of man she would want to obey, and which they could never be. They were there, after all, and if it was them then they knew she was bare, yet it was hard to imagine them resisting the chance to make some dirty comment.

She had soon turned a corner, moving out of their sight, although their sniggers at some comment she didn't catch followed her as she walked. If she'd been nervous before, now she was completely off balance, and so filled with embarrassment at the thought of allowing them to manipulate her that as she pushed open the door to Mr Henderson's office she was praying he'd reveal himself as the Man, whatever the consequences.

He wasn't even there, and she saw that the clock stood at seven minutes past five. For once he had left on time, and she swore aloud in frustration. Now convinced that she was being deliberately and carefully manipulated, she checked her email, half expecting some new and yet more aggravating message. There was nothing.

With no choice but to get on with her normal routine, Laura closed down her computer and made for the station. She was a little later than usual, and the 17:40 was already standing at the platform. There seemed to be some sort of student event going on, with young men and women from the university crowding the train and every seat in her usual carriage taken, adding to her irritation.

Some of the regulars were there, Miss Scarlett immediately in front of her, Darcy sat with his handsome face set in an expression of profound thought as he read *Finnegans Wake*, Hovis Boy scratching his left buttock, the Devil occupying Laura's favourite window seat. There was nothing for it but to move down the carriage and hope that some of the students would get out at Waterbeach or Ely. She glanced down at the Devil as she passed him, hoping that he might prove to be the gentleman he looked, although with at least half the other passengers also female it seemed highly unlikely.

To her immense surprise he immediately got up, favouring her with a polite inclination of his head as he indicated the now empty seat. Laura didn't hesitate, moving before anybody else could take advantage of his generosity. As she passed the Devil he brushed against her and she felt the lining of her skirt move against the bare skin beneath. She was blushing again on the instant, sure that he must have realised she had no knickers on and imagining his disapproval. Still she looked up gratefully as she lowered herself into the seat, to find him looking down at her, his mouth curved up at one side into a smile that seemed to her both sardonic and wicked.

She turned to the window, telling herself that next she would be imagining that the crowd of students gathered on the platform had ganged together into a cabal dedicated to tormenting her. They certainly looked the part, and she didn't like the way Miss Scarlett was looking at her either, although she knew it was probably just because Laura had got the seat. It was best not to be paranoid, although as she took her book from her bag and settled down to read she was careful to keep her knees firmly together.

Taken to Turkey was hotting up, making it possible to at least partially distract herself. Evangeline had been sold to Mustapha bin Yunus with her purity guaranteed, leaving Laura imagining an intimate and painfully humiliating inspection, although no details were given. Satisfied with his purchase, Mustapha had given Evangeline over to the care of a pair of huge and vindictive matrons, who'd stripped her, scrubbed her down and, when she'd protested at the rough treatment, spanked her bottom.

It was the third spanking in the book, and in many ways the best, despite being dished out by two women rather than a man. The matrons were described as sitting opposite each other on the crude benches of a steam room, with other women watching and giggling as the hapless Evangeline was stripped out of her combinations and turned squealing across their knees. Laura found the idea of having other women laughing at her plight while she was spanked in the nude disturbingly strong, and read the passage with the book only half open for fear of her fellow commuters looking, as if they might realise what was going on in her head.

By the time she got back to King's Lynn her mind was buzzing with conflicting thoughts, some erotic, some frightening, most a little of each. Walking back towards her flat, she was looking forward to giving Smudge his evening exercise, which was sure to help her to cope with her now desperate sense of arousal, at least enough to allow her to focus on something less shameful than the choice between having gone without knickers for some complete stranger or being laughed at while given a public spanking.

He jumped up to greet her as she opened the door, licking her face in boundless devotion despite her best efforts to push him away, so that her nose and most of one cheek were glistening with doggie drool as she turned to the sound of her name in a curt male voice.

'Miss Irving?'

Laura twisted around, her heel slipping from the edge of the doorstep to send her sprawling on the pavement with Smudge on top of her, delighted by the new game. She looked up, expecting to find the Man looking down on her, and knowing full well that she'd just proven her obedience to him beyond doubt as she went down on her back with her legs open. He was middle aged, balding, dressed in black with highlights of reflective orange and trying not to grin after what he'd just seen as he held out an enormous bunch of roses.

'Delivery for you, Miss Irving. Compliments of Flowers within Hours.'

8

Instead of the guilty pleasures she'd been anticipating, Laura spent the evening chiding herself for being silly and letting her mind dwell on the possibilities offered by the note Chris had included with his roses. It was brief and to the point, inviting her to meet him in the lounge bar of the Esplanade Hotel in Sheringham on the following Saturday, with a ps written in tiny neat letters: BRING A TOOTHBRUSH.

There was no doubt at all what he meant. She was being invited for a dirty weekend at a smart hotel, which confirmed his interest in her and left the Controller once more a very poor second. Not that her curiosity had diminished, and as she showered she was trying to decide if what she had planned counted as being unfaithful to Chris.

Knickers or no knickers, that was the question, whether she should leave them off and indulge herself in the powerful and undeniably erotic thrill of going bare in order to discover the Man's identity, or put some on but still keep an eye out for men trying to peep up her skirt. The second choice was plainly the right thing to do, but the first was more satisfying because it had the great advantage that once she did identify him he would think she was his. That would allow her the pleasure of politely but firmly turning him down, and so getting back at him for what he'd put her through, from the first slight shock when she'd read his initial message to the hideous embarrassment of flashing the man who'd delivered Chris's flowers.

She wouldn't even have to expose herself, or no more than

she was used to at the beach. All she'd need to do was hitch her skirt up at one side, high enough to show off the top of her stockings and her suspender belt and to make it plain that she had no knickers on. He would be left boiling with frustration, with any luck, just as she had been the evening before, which would be a fitting revenge.

Even as she dressed doubts began to assail her. What if it turned out to be Brian, with or without Dave, or Mr Henderson, who could make her life a misery, or even some psychopath? She went without anyway, but put a spare pair in her bag, telling herself that she'd enjoy the thrill of going bare and do whatever seemed best at the time.

By the time she was halfway to the station she knew that she had made the right choice. It was a beautiful day, clear and sunny, with just a faint breeze that kept her aware that she was naked under her skirt with every step, the skin of her bottom and mound deliciously cool and sensitive even to the gentle rubbing of her skirt. She was quickly wishing that Chris was there, and that he knew, sharing her naughty secret until he could get her alone, when she'd be given the same rude treatment he'd dished out over the bonnet of his car, and perhaps somewhere even more risky.

Even if she failed to catch the Controller she knew she'd be on edge all day, while the sense of risk had faded with familiarity. On the train it was better still, with the added excitement of watching her fellow passengers and trying to decide who might be the Man. All the King's Lynn regulars got on, first Darcy, who barely glanced at her and went to sit well down the carriage, triggering a touch of disappointment despite her devotion to Chris.

Mr Brown was if anything even more detached than Darcy, but Hovis Boy sat down diagonally opposite her, immediately glancing at her legs. Laura felt her heart sink and a flush of embarrassment start to creep up her neck at the thought of him being the man she'd allowed herself to get into a state over, but the moment two girls from one of the local sixth forms got in he turned his attention to them, his mouth dropping open into his normal dead fish expression as he let his gaze feed on their slender legs and tiny miniskirts.

Laura began to read as the train pulled out of the station, enjoying Evangeline's consternation as the heroine was given clothes to wear in the harem: a pair of gauzy emerald-green pantaloons and a hopelessly inadequate halter top in the same see-through material. Only at Downham Market did she lift her attention to the train, but the Grey Man showed no more interest in her than the first two and the Tramp didn't appear at all. Ely was different, with Miss Scarlett getting on first to sit in the last remaining group of empty seats, then the Devil, who greeted Laura with what she was sure was a knowing grin and sat next to another passenger, in the one remaining seat in which he had a chance of admiring her legs.

She had started to shake, wondering if it was him after all, all her tangled emotions flooding back at the possibility that the cool, immaculately groomed man just a few feet away knew that she was naked beneath her skirt, and in stockings and suspenders as he had instructed. Rejecting him suddenly seemed an impossibility, an outrage even, her own behaviour teasing and flirtatious.

He'd be angry. He'd have every right to be angry. He'd have every right to put her across his knee and spank her in front of the entire carriage, on her bare bottom with the men grinning at her exposure and the women gloating over her humiliation, Miss Scarlett laughing at the sight of Laura's bouncing bottom cheeks, Hovis Boy leering at her naked sex and the tight little hole above.

Laura shook herself hard, desperately trying to dispel the rush of erotic thoughts and wishing she wasn't so helpless in the face of her own dirty and over-active imagination. The Devil had merely smiled at her, perfectly reasonably when they saw each other every day and he had given up his seat the evening before, while he'd simple taken the most convenient seat for the doors. Yet her heart was pounding and she felt hot and wet between her thighs, shamefully excited over nothing while a young, handsome and successful man had all but declared his love for her only the evening before.

Feeling ashamed of herself, she resolved to send the Controller an email as soon as she got into work, plainly stating that she was in a relationship and apologising if she had appeared to lead him on. With luck he'd accept her verdict, and if not he'd just have to be told more forcibly, whatever it took, even if it meant accepting a knickers down, bare bottom spanking for her atrocious behaviour.

Again Laura shook herself, fighting to keep her thoughts on track, but her need was simply too strong. She had to know who he was, to force a resolution, and it would be for the best if it did prove to be Brian, or Dave, or Hovis Boy, because then there would be only embarrassment, no regrets. With luck she would know by the end of the day, and the first thing to do when she got to work was to force the issue with Mr Henderson. Or rather, the second thing, because until she'd calmed herself down a little she wasn't sure that she could manage anything at all.

The moment she arrived at EAS she went to the Ladies, burning with shame for what she was about to do but telling herself she had no choice. It wasn't the sort of thing nice, properly behaved girls did, but maybe she wasn't a nice girl, maybe she was a dirty, badly behaved girl, the sort of girl who would benefit from a good spanking, preferably delivered in public.

She was early, having come from the station at something close to a run, and there was nobody about. Locking herself into a cubicle she closed her eyes, wondering why her head was in such a muddle. For one last time she tried to tell herself to stop being silly and dirty, but the thought of her bad behaviour forced her thoughts back to the spanking she felt she deserved, trapping her in a cycle of arousal from which there was only one way out.

Stifling sobs for her overpowering emotions, Laura surrendered, allowing her thoughts to drift. Still standing, her eyes still closed, she allowed her imagination to take its own path, back to the train and what might have happened. She imagined that all the regulars had been in league, planning to amuse themselves at her expense. They'd have know she was bare under her skirt, and that she would do as she was told.

In her mind's eye there was nobody else in the carriage, just the six regulars. The Devil would be in charge, his natural place. He'd tell Laura to get up, to go to the open space between the doors and stand still while the others assembled, some standing, some seated, but all with a good view of her body. She'd know what was coming, and so would they, but the Devil would make her wait, enjoying her apprehension until the moment was exactly right. Only then would he give his order.

'Lift your skirt.'

She would obey, unable to stop herself despite the agonising embarrassment of exposing herself, inching her skirt up to show off her stocking tops, the slices of bare white flesh above, her straining suspenders straps, the underside of her cheeks, her whole bottom, full and bare, and her sex. Miss Scartlett would laugh and make some unfair comment on the size of Laura's bottom. Hovis Boy would peer closely, determined not to miss a single detail as he enjoyed having a woman bare herself for the first time in her life.

As she played the awful scene through in her mind, Laura had tugged up her skirt, exposing her bottom and sex in the cubicle just as she was imagining herself doing so in the train. It felt good, far too good to stop, or to rush. Her fingers went to the top button of her blouse as she let the fantasy run on. It would be Hovis Boy who suggested the added and unnecessary humiliation, his voice a high demanding whine, full of dirty lust.

'I want to see her tits. Make her get her tits out.'

Darcy would agree.

'Yes, why not? She looks as if she has nice breasts.'

But it would be the Devil who gave the order.

'Bare your breasts, Laura.'

She began to undo her buttons, imagining the silent attention of all six people staring at her as she undid her blouse, pulled it wide and turned down the cups of her bra, leaving her breasts exposed, each plump pink handful of flesh nestled in the dishevelled silk of her clothing, her nipples stiff with involuntary excitement. To show them would be bad enough, but it would get worse, the Devil's voice cool and amused as he gave the next order.

'Play with them for a while.'

Laura's hands were already on her breasts, cupping them as she ran her thumbs over her nipples to bring her excitement rapidly higher. She was going to do it, all her inhibitions abandoned as she slipped a hand between her thighs, the other still stroking at her chest. As she began to masturbate she was already biting her lip to stop herself from crying out, and she had taken the scene in her head back to the beginning.

First she'd be made to stand, next to lift her skirt, showing that she'd gone without knickers at the Devil's command and that she was their's to amuse themselves with. The men would demand to see her breasts and she'd complete her exposure, standing bare in every way that mattered as the Devil spoke again.

'Get over my knee, Laura. I am going to spank you.'

She nearly came at the thought, rubbing hard between her sex lips and clutching at one breast as she imagined how it would be, bent over the Devil's lap, her bottom lifted, bare and pink and vulnerable, her cheeks a little open to show the tight little hole between, every rude fold of her sex on blatant display. Miss Scarlett would be laughing as it began, Laura squealing and wriggling across the Devil's knee as her cheeks bounced to the slaps and her legs kicked in the air, while her breasts would be squashed out on her tormentor's leg. Mr Brown and the Grey Man would take an ankle each, holding her down to leave her completely helpless as the spanking continued. Hovis Boy would start to take photos, hideously intimate ones that showed her face and her bare bottom at the same time, and her sex, and her anus. And Darcy, Darcy would wait until her poor naked bottom was bright red and glowing hot from spanking, and then fuck her.

Laura bit down hard on her lip as she started to come, the scene burning hot in her mind as she snatched and squeezed at herself: her hot spanked bottom raised and open as she was held helpless for penetration, Miss Scarlett's laughter shrill and cruel in her ears, Hovis Boy's camera clicking again and again as Darcy eased his erection deep into her wet, willing pussy, her shame complete as she begged him to fuck her as hard and as deep as he could.

Her legs had gone weak as she rode her orgasm, and as it faded she settled slowly against the cubicle wall, astonished at herself for what she'd done and how strong her need had been. Just a few days before the idea of being so powerfully aroused that she ended up playing with herself in the Ladies would have seemed as ridiculous as it did outrageous. Now she had done it, but while it was useless to pretend that her real motivation had been anything other than pleasure, it had certainly helped to calm her down.

She still felt nervous and more than a little ashamed of herself as she tidied up, but that only strengthened her resolve to sort out who the Controller was once and for all. Mr Henderson would come first, manoeuvred into an admission by means of a carefully crafted question that would allow her to back out unscathed if he wasn't the Man. He was already in the office, and glanced up from the papers he was studying as she entered, greeting her much as he usually did.

'Good morning, Laura. You're looking very smart today.'

It took all her courage to answer.

'Thank you, sir. I did as you asked. Would you like to see?'

His expression changed, but only to puzzlement. Laura switched to plan B, hastily letting go of the pinch she'd taken in the material of her skirt as she continued.

'About the Orwell B account. I have the figures ready.'

'Ah, yes. All in good time, Laura.'

Mr Henderson was innocent. No man, no matter how self-controlled, could possibly have looked so completely blank in response to a woman offering to lift her skirt for him. She relaxed a little, only for her tension to return as she remembered that her next option had to be Brian. Taking her seat at her computer, she pretended to start work while thinking of how best to catch him out. Unlike Mr Henderson, he couldn't possibly be expecting her to respond to him, and so presumably wanted her to think he was somebody else, another more attractive man. That made her task harder, as he wasn't going to admit to it whatever she did, while if she pretended to come on to him he would realise it was a trick. The idea also made her feel sick.

There were two things she could be sure of: that he would be splitting his sides with laughter at the thought of her going without knickers at his command and that if there was the slightest chance of getting a peep he would take it. She considered sending a message with some juicy content and then rushing over to accounts to watch his reaction, only to abandon the idea as impractical. The only way to get a view of his workstation without being noticed would be to stand on the table in the copier room and peer in through the glass partition, which was sure to cause comment.

Besides, there was a better way. Clicking up her email, she replied to the last message the Controller had sent. I WANT TO SHOW YOU. I'LL BE BEHIND THE VACUUM SHED AT TEN PAST ONE. COME TO ME OR WATCH ME.

He would watch, and from out of sight, which could only mean looking down from the window in the top floor fire door, that seemed almost certain. Just possibly he would try and catch her instead, but it didn't matter. She wouldn't be there, but she would be in the canteen, from where she'd be able to see him whether he went up the stairs to the top corridor or across the yard to the vacuum shed. He had no other reason to do either.

The answer came almost immediately. DO IT. I WILL WATCH YOU.

The rest of the morning passed at a crawl, until finally she was ready. Leaving her desk exactly at one, she made her way to the canteen, entering to find Brian and Dave in the queue, piling their plates high with curry and rice as they discussed the weekend's football matches. Puzzled, she stepped quickly back before they could see her and ran up the stairs.

As she had remembered from drill, the fire door looked down on the little triangle of overgrown land between the back of the vacuum shed, the factory wall and the perimeter fence. They would have had a good view, if perhaps from a slightly unsatisfactory angle, but both were down in the canteen, stuffing themselves with chicken tikka masala.

Hurrying back to the ground floor, she left the main building and made her way to the vacuum shed. Nobody was about and she had quickly pushed through the tangle of bushes to the area she'd been looking down on moments before. It was hard to see in at the fire door window, but she was pretty sure nobody was there, while the only other places anybody could possibly have watched from were the rooftops and, just possibly, the upper deck of one of the city car parks, but only if her watcher had a pair of powerful binoculars.

She hesitated, wanting to try and provoke a reaction but a little scared. Nobody had been crossing the yard behind her, and the silence was absolute but for distant traffic and the hiss and thud of equipment in the vacuum shed. In sudden decision she tugged up her skirt, enjoying the sharp thrill of exposure despite herself, and made a slow turn, ensuring that any hidden watcher had a full view of both her bottom and sex. Nothing happened.

Laura covered herself, more puzzled than ever. Now keen not to be caught, she started back for the canteen, where Brian and Dave sat with a group of their friends, just finishing their meals. She turned to Mrs Davies, who was stirring the scum back into a trough of curry.

'Excuse me, have Brian and Dave been here all the time since they arrived?'

'Those two? Almost first in they were, and been here since. Why's that?'

'Nothing, I just thought ... oh never mind. I'll have the fish please.'

As Mrs Davies began to serve her lunch Laura glanced around the canteen, now completely baffled.

9

The following day Laura came on her period, a relief both because she'd been careless with Chris and she was two days early, which meant she'd be clear for the weekend. It also went some way to explaining how fragile her emotions had been the day before, although she knew full well that she was only really trying to excuse her behaviour.

No more messages arrived from the Controller, also to her relief, or largely so. She also felt a little consternation, as his silence seemed to suggest that if he had watched her exhibit herself he'd been less than impressed, while she had no more idea of who he might be than before, only who he wasn't. It did seem at least possible that she'd been too bold for him and had scared him away, or that for some reason he was unable to use email.

By the Friday evening her anticipation for the coming weekend had all but pushed the Controller from her mind, and when she got home she was delighted to find another bunch of roses and a parcel containing a minuscule bikini with a designer tag that made it worth at least ten times as much per square inch as any other item of clothing in her wardrobe. It was brilliant scarlet, and very much the sort of thing only a man would have chosen, intended for the bedroom rather than the beach, as the back was little more than a thong and the cups barely covered her nipples.

She put it on as underwear the next morning, intending to give Chris a treat as soon as they arrived at the hotel, and perhaps even tease him into giving her the spanking she now craved almost as much as proper sex. *Taken to Turkey* hadn't helped, with Evangeline receiving a further three juicy punishments in the section she'd read over the week, including being made to line up with four of Mustapha's other girls and done in front of the entire harem. That had been near the end, and she only had a few pages to go, so she threw the book in with her luggage on the off-chance that she'd have time to finish it, or more probably that she'd be able to use it to guide Chris in the right direction as to how he ought to be handling her.

The day was clear and bright, and although the morning had been cold Laura was soon driving with the windows rolled down, in increasingly high spirits as she made her way around the coast towards Sheringham. Things seemed to be going well, and she allowed herself to daydream about a life in which she had Chris to fall back on as a partner, maybe even a husband, rather than having to take responsibility for every tiny thing.

She had been to Sheringham before, but could only remember the beach beneath yellowish cliffs, which as a child had seemed to go on for ever. The hotel was easy to find, a great red brick edifice with an air of faded grandeur. Chris was already there, and greeted her with a kiss that grew quickly passionate, leaving Laura more convinced than ever of his good intentions. He'd booked a suite looking out over the sea and with a huge old bed just the look of which sent a shiver down Laura's spine. It had been a long time since she'd been in bed with a man, too long, and although they'd only been together again for a few minutes she felt ready. Turning towards him, she put her hands to the hem of her top.

'Thank you for your present. Would you like to see?'

Chris's grin gave her the answer she wanted. She had already lifted her top a little, showing off the swell of her tummy, and pulled it higher as he sat down to watch from the comfort of a chair. That felt right, to have him as a relaxed and appreciative audience, fully dressed, while she stripped, tempting her to go naked once he'd enjoyed how she looked in her bikini. He was certainly doing that, the pleasure clear on his face as he admired the way the tiny cups struggled to hold in her breasts, which were in danger of spilling free if she wasn't careful how she moved.

Tossing her top aside, Laura put her hands to the buckle of her belt, opening it slowly and unfastening her jeans. His eyes had moved lower, glued to her as she exposed herself, showing off the tiny scarlet triangle that covered her sex but hardly hid it at all. She had shaved, leaving the material to follow every contour of her lips, an openly sexual display she was hoping he would be unable to resist. His nod of appreciation and the movement of a hand to his crotch suggested just that, but as she made to push her jeans lower he raised a finger to stop her.

'Turn around.'

Laura nodded, smiling nervously back over her shoulder as she turned to show him her rear view. He gave a pleased nod and spoke again.

'Stick out your bottom and push your jeans down, nice and slow.'

She obeyed, delighted by his rude instruction and imagining how she'd look as she eased her jeans down to show off the full, near naked ball of her bottom, barely covered. Chris gave a low chuckle as her flesh came on view and made a signal with his finger to indicate that she should carry on her strip. Again she complied, kicking off her shoes and peeling her jeans down and off, fully aware of what he could see from behind her.

'Very pretty. So pretty, in fact, that I think we should go down to the beach.'

'The beach?'

'Yes, why not? It's warm enough, don't you think?'

'Yes, but ... but this is for you, Chris. I mean, the way I am.'

'Oh, I don't know. I rather like the idea of other people seeing you like that. Think how jealous they'll be.'

'But ...'

'Come on. Beach.'

He had got up, and as he spoke he planted a single firm smack on Laura's bottom, leaving her skin tingling and warm. She immediately pushed her bottom out, hoping for more, but he had already walked past her, to look out from the window.

'Yes, why not? There are some old boys in deckchairs along the front. They'll certainly appreciate you, and I expect those men playing football will too.'

'Chris, I'm not sure ...'

'You'll enjoy it. Come on.'

Laura hesitated, hoping he'd threaten to spank her if she refused, which was sure to lead to sex, but quite wanting to do it. It felt daring, yet he would be with her to keep her safe, and to help her work out the arousal she knew full well her exposure would bring. She found herself nodding. Chris's grin grew wider.

'Good girl. I knew you'd see sense.'

He picked up the room keys and took her by the hand.

'Aren't you going to change?'

'No. I prefer to stay as I am. That way it will be more obvious that you're deliberately flaunting yourself.'

Laura shivered, intensely nervous but too aroused to back out.

'Can I at least have a towel? I mean, while we're in the hotel?'

'No.'

He kept a firm grip on her hand, pulling her towards the door. Laura went, half reluctant, her sense of exposure growing painfully strong as she was led out into the corridor. Nobody was about, but as they reached the stairs two elderly women passed, throwing Laura looks of disapproval and making tutting remarks as they continued up the stairs. Chris merely chuckled, leading Laura on down the stairs, her face now pink with blushes. She tried to turn back as she saw how crowded the foyer was, but he kept his grip, leading her across to the main doors with every pair of eyes in the room following her wiggling, near naked bottom.

It was worse on the street, where half the population of the town seemed to have gathered, and only the sure knowledge that her top would prove unequal to any more strain prevented her from making a run for the beach and the cover of the sea. A glance at Chris showed that he was enjoying himself immensely, and she managed a weak smile as they waited for the lights on a pelican crossing.

As they crossed a car hooted, maybe for Laura, maybe not, but the sound made her jump and set her blushes hotter still. Once across, they quickly reached the beach, reducing Laura's embarrassment, but only briefly. The large round pebbles made it hard to walk and hurt her feet, forcing her to support herself on Chris and making it impossible to walk with dignity. They had also passed the line of old men in deckchairs, who were now staring and making remarks among themselves. Laura couldn't make out their words, but she could imagine their mingled disapproval and amusement, scorn and lust. She tried to hurry on, slipped as a pebble moved beneath her foot, fought for balance, caught it, only for the motion to tug her bikini top up, exposing both shamefully stiff nipples to the gaze of the old men and several dozen others.

For one awful moment Laura was in a state of blind panic, clutching at her breasts in an effort to cover them but still not properly balanced, until a supporting arm from Chris and a quick adjustment of her bikini top saved her from at least the worst of her embarrassment. A few more careful paces and she had reached the sand, shaking badly, her body flushed hot, but at least able to walk without risking making a complete exhibition of herself.

Never has she been so conscious of her body, or of male attention to her bottom, breasts and the tiny triangle of scarlet cloth that alone shielded her sex. Not sure that she could cope for much longer, she turned away from the town and the long stretch of uncrowded beach beneath the cliffs. Chris made no effort to change her path, sparking her gratitude for all that he was the one who had pushed her into showing herself off, only for a sense of disappointment to well up as they drew clear of the busier areas.

'Do you think this is far enough?'

'Not for what I have in mind.'

Laura swallowed, sure that at the least she would be made to sunbathe nude, maybe to swim naked, thoughts that filled her with a delicious sense of arousal and naughtiness. Work and the routine of her life seemed distant and irrelevant, Chris the centre of her world and the perfect man, a man who would bring her out of herself, who could take her to heights beyond anything she'd known before.

She let him lead, far up the beach to where the crumbling yellow cliff had formed spurs and alcoves, each creating a private world of warm, golden sand, open to the sea, but hidden from curious stares. Some were occupied, some were not, but only when they'd moved well past the nearest group seated on the sand did he pull her in between two long spurs. His voice was a low growl as he spoke to her.

'Brace yourself against the cliff, as if I was going to give you a body search.'

Laura hastened to obey, setting her feet wide and leaning her hands against the surface of the cliff with her back pulled in to exhibit her bottom. Chris grinned and moved back to make a quick check to ensure nobody was approaching, then took out his mobile phone.

'One for the long cold evenings when I'm old. Say cheese, and stick that bum right out.'

She laughed and blew him a kiss, her bottom pushed well out as the phone camera clicked to record her rude position. Chris took several shots, with Laura happily showing off, even tugging her bikini open to show off her bare breasts before once more getting into position against the cliff as he put the phone away. Again he checked the beach, before tugging down his fly to free his cock and balls into his hand. He was already half stiff, and pulling at his cock as he stepped close to Laura. One quick motion and her breasts had been spilt from her tiny bikini cups, another and the pants were down. He came behind her, cupping a breast in each hand as his cock settled between the cheeks of her bottom. She stuck her hips out, accepting him as he guided his cock lower, to find the entrance to her sex and push in, deep and hard.

A sigh escaped her lips as she filled, and again each time he pushed into her. Never had she felt so feminine, so sexual, paraded for men's pleasure and then stripped and taken in the open air, her near naked body perfectly vulnerable to the man who seemed to understand her needs so perfectly. Better still, he was going to make her come, his hand snaking around her belly to find her sex and to rub at her as he continued to thrust himself deep from behind. She began to beg him to do it, lost in ecstasy too strong for her to care as the dirty words spilt from her lips. He chuckled to find her so abandoned, and with that Laura's reserve broke down completely.

'Do it, Chris, make me come ... make me come while you fuck me ... right in, deep in, and while you do it smack my bottom, please ... smack my bottom, Chris, rub my pussy and spank my bottom!'

He didn't answer, too busy with her sex and breasts, and the effort of thrusting into her and masturbating her at the same time. Again she cried out, begging to be spanked, but too late, her muscles locking in orgasm as he brought her off with a well-practised finger and a moment later he'd come himself, pulling free at the last instant to do it over her naked but unsmacked bottom.

Laura sank slowly to her knees, her muscles still twitching from the power of her orgasm, her ecstasy fading slowly to be replaced by embarrassment for what she'd said. Chris sank down beside her, to hug her and kiss her neck, then whisper into her ear.

'What was that you said? Does somebody like her botty smacked?'

At his words she seemed to melt, her muscles and her will-power giving way as one. Her bottom was still pushed out, ready, his hand moving slowly down the curve of her back towards his target, touching the swell of her cheeks, teasing between to make her sob and shiver, and stopping abruptly at the sound of voices.

'Bugger.'

Chris moved quickly away, leaving Laura to struggle back into her bikini before peering out from their hiding place. The group they'd seen playing football earlier were coming along the beach at a run, and it was only their coach's shouts of encouragement that had given them away. Laura shuddered as she imagined how they'd have seen her, kneeling all but naked with her bottom pushed out to be smacked, an image from her darkest fantasies and far beyond what she would have wanted in reality. Chris merely chuckled.

'Back at the hotel, perhaps?'

'Yes, please.'

Once more he took her by the hand, Laura now so far gone in her erotic haze that is was hard to imagine the other people around them as anything more than bit players in her fantasy. She was going to be spanked, and she was half wishing she already had been, so that they could all see her pink bottom and wonder, not knowing if she and Chris had being playing rude games, or better still, if she'd been naughty and he'd had to spank her for real.

As she was led through the foyer she was imagining that they all knew, every man and every woman, aroused or amused as she was taken upstairs to be punished, to be spanked like a wilful brat, perhaps for flaunting herself in her tiny bikini. Had Chris put her across his knee then and there, in one of the big overstuffed armchairs with everybody staring as her bikini pants were taken down, even then she wouldn't have resisted.

He had more control, but only just, kneading her bottom as they walked down the corridor and sending her into the room with a preliminary slap, the door still half-open behind them as he took her to the bed. Laura was in heaven as he went through the little ritual she had played over so often in her mind over the days before; seating himself comfortably and patting his lap.

'Bend over. I'm going to spank you.'

Laura obeyed, lost in bliss as she got into position, bent down across his knee, on tiptoe to make her legs as long as possible and bring her bottom up. Chris put an arm around her waist, holding her firmly in place as his other hand went to her bikini bottoms.

'Better have these down, don't you think?'

All Laura could manage was a sob, her eyes now shut as she concentrated on the overwhelming sensation of having her bottom exposed for a man to spank for the first time in her life. Chris tugged and it was happening, her tiny bikini bottoms drawn slowly down to lay her cheeks fully bare, and more importantly, what was between, exhibiting herself to him in absolute surrender.

He took them right down, easing them the full length of her legs to make sure that not a scrap of modesty was left to her, then completing her exposure by once again tugging the cups of her bikini top up to leave her breasts naked beneath her chest.

'Here goes. If it's too hard, just squeal.'

He'd laid his hand on her bottom, kneading her flesh, one finger tickling her anus to draw a weak gasp from her mouth. Her need was now desperate.

'Do it hard. Don't stop for anything.'

'OK. I'm going to enjoy this, Laura, and you do have a lovely bottom, just built for spanking. So ... shit!'

Laura twisted around at the sudden alarm in his voice, to find a woman stood directly behind her, tall, elegant, immaculately dressed, her patrician face twisted in fury – Miss Manston-Jones. For a moment the scene held, Laura bent down across Chris' lap with every rude detail of her rear view on show to the new arrival, all three of them wide-eyed in shock and surprise, before Chris finally found his voice.

'No, Hazel, this isn't the way it looks.'

Miss Manston-Jones' was a low growl as she answered.

'What? I suppose you're going to tell me you're punishing the little tart because she's been naughty? This is the last time you do this to me, Christopher Drake, you two-timing bastard!'

Her voice had risen to a scream on the last words and she launched herself forwards. Chris let go of Laura's waist, dropping her as he threw himself back to avoid his furious lover's talons. Laura squealed in shock as she landed on the carpet, rolled and tried to crawl away as the spitting, cursing Hazel Manston-Jones attempted to haul Chris back by one ankle. He kicked out, broke free and dashed for the door.

Hazel twisted around, eyes blazing as Laura struggled up, desperate to get away from the woman's fury, failing to remember that her bikini pants were around her ankles. Before she could even think about rising she was pinned, her arm twisting into the small of her back to hold her helpless as Hazel snarled out her words.

'So you like to be spanked, do you, you filthy little bitch! Right, I'll give you a spanking, you bitch, you little tart, you ...'

'No!'

Laura's plea went unheeded, as did her frantically wriggling bottom and kicking legs. Hazel laid in, applying smack after furious smack to the bouncing cheeks beneath her. It stung crazily, but the pain was nothing to Laura's furious indignation as she squirmed and bucked beneath the slaps, fighting to break free.

She failed miserably, Hazel only breaking off in pursuit of Chris, and Laura was left hot bottomed and gasping on the bed, as well spanked as she could possibly have wanted but feeling far from grateful.

10

Laura had pictured her virgin spanking somewhat differently, from a man for a start, and considerably less hard. She'd had no idea that it could hurt so much, or that she could feel so completely helpless in another woman's grip. Yet none of that mattered beside her feelings of anger and betrayal at what had happened, and which were made worse because it was quite clear that Chris and his Hazel had been together all along.

Nor did he come back, leaving Laura feeling numb as she dressed and made herself a cup of tea in the vain hope that it would help with her raging emotions. For over an hour she sat in the window seat, staring out over the sea as she struggled to come to terms with what had happened. Nothing she could say to herself helped, and yet she seemed oddly detached, as if the entire episode had happened to somebody else. She felt she ought to be in tears and yet they wouldn't come, while she kept wanting to laugh out loud.

Almost two hours had passed before simple hunger finally prompted Laura to leave the room. It felt strange to think that she had walked through the foyer semi-naked just hours before – so strange that only cold reason allowed her to accept that it had really been her. Quite a few people noticed her, some passing remarks, others smiling quietly to themselves, but their reaction no longer gave her the strangely thrilling embarrassment it had done before.

The beach was the same, physically no different to the way

it had been before, even to the line of pensioners in their deckchairs, but for Laura it was as if the colour had been washed out of the scene, while the tub of mixed seafood she had bought at a stall seemed without taste. She ate it seated on the lifeboat slipway, staring glumly at the waves and wishing that just for once she could pick a man who didn't seem to regard every single woman on the planet as fair game. Tommy Fuller had been the same, but he at least had made no secret of his behaviour.

Eventually she returned to the hotel, where she discovered that Chris had already paid for the room, dinner and breakfast as an inclusive package. His things were also in the room, but she resisted the temptation to purchase a pair of scissors and make some alterations to his clothes. He had kept his cards and money with him, which she decided was just as well, but went shopping anyway in an effort to cheer herself up. She failed miserably, as even scarlet high-heels and a poppy-red summer dress only served to bring back memories of the fun she'd had with Chris and his betrayal.

A large gin and tonic in the hotel bar helped a little, and a second rather more, if only to lift her sense of despair. After the third her choice in not ruining his clothes no longer seemed an act of mature restraint but rather pathetic, cowardly even. The shops were shut by then, but her nail scissors did well enough, allowing her to excise the crotches of two pairs of trousers and of three underpants, then indulge in some creative craftwork with a jacket and a couple of shirts.

By the time she'd finished the dining room was open, allowing her to enjoy a gourmet meal at his expense, including oysters and a half lobster washed down with Champagne, sticky toffee pudding and several cups of liqueur coffee. By then her tummy was a hard round ball beneath her dress and her head was spinning, while her emotions had finally come back, bringing her to the edge of tears.

Not wanting anybody to see her cry, she made her way back to the room, where she threw herself down on the bed. Her tears came immediately, hot and choking as she gave in to her hurt, but also soothing, until at last she began to feel that she was being silly. Another drink seemed to be in order, and there turned out to be a bottle of Champagne in the minibar. She opened it, sipping the sharp effervescent wine as she undressed and washed.

She had brought a baby-doll to wear to bed, but couldn't bear to get into it when it had been chosen for his pleasure, so pulled on a baggy top and a pair of knickers instead, before slipping into bed with the bottle at her side and *Taken to Turkey* to distract her from her thoughts. The story was almost at its climax, with Mark Frobisher threatening to drop Lord Jasper Mauleverer from the old city walls if he didn't reveal Evangeline's fate.

Laura had come to picture Chris as the hero, but now switched, thinking of him as Lord Jasper and earnestly wishing Mark Frobisher would drop him. Being a clean cut, English sort of hero, Frobisher hauled Lord Jasper in once he'd found out what he needed to know and made for the harem of Mustapha bin Yunus. The pace was picking up, and with it Laura's attention, although it was getting a little difficult to focus on the page, with the words splitting and reforming in the most annoying manner. She forced herself to concentrate, thrilling to the description of Mark Frobisher demolishing scimitar waving guards with his bare fists and tearing away the curtains across the harem entrance ...

... with a single, convulsive jerk of his muscles, to stand four-square beneath the high arch like some avenging angel of the Old Testament, his mighty fists bunched to strike down any opponent who dared to come against him, and yet the sight that met his ice-blue eyes came near to unmanning him.

Across the room sat Mustapha bin Yunus, naked but for a loin-cloth of turquoise silk, his great gelatinous bulk quivering with laughter, a goblet of beaten gold clasped in one hand and the rich red wine of sun-kissed Anatolia running down his blubbery chins. In his other hand he held a long whip of plaited leather, the tip an adder's tongue that whistled and snapped as he applied it to the voluptuous target made by the delectable dusky derrière of one of a line of unfortunate concubines. She was one of five such girls in a row along a wide bench, each as naked as the day she was born and kneeling in a pose so lewd, so redolent of the Turk's unbridled debauchery, that Mark's hand moved to shield his eyes for the sake of decency before he remembered where he was and the dangers that faced him.

The girl against whose succulent, rotund flesh the whip had just snapped was a dusky beauty born of India's jungle south, her neighbour an African wench as dark as ebony, the third an olive-skinned succubus of old Greece, the fourth a dainty yellow-hued daughter of the furthest east, and the fifth – the fifth was more beauteous still, her body a symphony in feminine delight, her luxurious tresses as golden as the midday sun, her skin as pale and smooth as Devon cream save only where three whip welts marred her perfection. The fifth girl – her pose no less lewd than the others – was Evangeline Tarrington.

Laura closed the book, blinking in a vain effort to make her eyes focus properly. She knew she was drunk, very drunk, and that seemed an excellent excuse for her being so horny despite everything that had happened. In fact it was good, because it meant she didn't need Chris Drake, who was a two timing bastard and didn't deserve her, or Hazel Manston-Jones, or anybody else. He was a rat, a pig, a snake, and it was just as well that they'd been interrupted before he could give her what had become such a special need: a good, firm spanking. Not that she'd gone without, because she had been spanked, spanked hard and by another woman, a taller, slimmer, stronger woman, just the sort of woman to dish out a well-deserved punishment. Maybe she'd even deserved it, in a sense.

'No. I'm not going to do that.'

She had spoken aloud, shocked by the path her thoughts had begun to take. Quickly she told herself that she hadn't deserved it at all, that in fact it had been unfair. After all, she hadn't known that Chris and Miss Manston-Vicious-Bitch were an item, and would never have allowed him to have her if she'd realised. It was unfair, grossly unfair, but she'd been spanked anyway and there was something horribly compelling about that very injustice. She knew what it was too, the added sense of indignation at being punished unfairly, which made the experience so much stronger. It had been bad enough to be helpless in another woman's grip with her bare bottom showing, let alone to be spanked, but the knowledge that it had been completely unfair was the final straw.

Tears of consternation and self-pity had begun to well up in Laura's eyes, but her hand was on her tummy, her fingertips beneath the waistband of her knickers. She tried to stop herself, imagining the scene from *Taken to Turkey* instead, and how Evangeline would have felt, kneeling naked at one end of a row of girls, her bottom lifted and open to the lecherous gaze of the grotesque Mustapha as she was whipped. It was good, an appalling humiliating situation fit only for her darkest, most private fantasies, and yet compared with what had happened just hours before, on that same bed, it was nothing.

She gave in, too drunk and too highly aroused to resist. Her knickers came down, but not off, pushed to her ankles in the same way her bikini pants had been earlier. Even the tension of the cotton between her legs felt exquisite, and she was arching her back in pleasure as her top came up to bare her breasts even as the tears began to trickle down her face. Her knees came wide, her fingers delved into the warm sensitive crease of her sex and she began to masturbate.

Her bottom still felt a little tender, a sensation she'd been doing her best to ignore ever since her spanking, but which she now needed badly. She needed it stuck up too, the way she'd been done, and quickly pushed the bedclothes down to expose her body. Turning onto her front, she spread herself out, her knickers taut between her ankles, her bottom slightly lifted, her face and breasts pushed into the now tangled sheets.

Again her fingers found her sex, teasing as she played the scene through in her head; trying to run, tripping over her own knickers, caught as she sprawled on the bed, and spanked. She nearly came on the crucial word, but still she wanted more. Reaching back, she began to caress her cheeks, feeling their shape and the texture of her flesh. Miss Manston-Jones had been fully dressed, but Laura had been to all intents and purposes naked, her bottom bare, her sex lips showing between her thighs, her anus exposed.

Thinking of herself nude and at the mercy of the cruel, imperious Miss Manston-Jones again brought Laura close to the edge, and again as she began to think of her spanking, how she must have looked, how her bottom must have felt to her tormentor's hand and the glorious sense of warmth once she'd been finished with. She began to smack her cheeks, determined to recapture the wonderful sensation that she knew would have had her playing with herself in any less emotionally fraught situation.

Miss Manston-Jones – Hazel – had done it hard, harder than Laura could manage with her own hand, but a quick rummage in the drawers by her bed solved that problem. Her hairbrush was far more effective, making her cheeks bounce and sting as she smacked at them, harder and harder, all the while running the details of her virgin spanking through her mind again and again, and thinking of how unfair it had been.

That was the key, the awful injustice of being given a bare bottom spanking by another woman, pinned naked on the bed, helpless and wriggling, smack after smack landing on her cheeks until she was red and hot, just as she now was, her bottom ablaze from the hairbrush, pushed up to meet the blows as her fingers worked between the lips of her sex. This time there was no holding back. Laura screamed as she came, smacking at her bottom with all her strength, tears of shame streaming down her face and her muscles contracting hard to climax after climax until at last she could bear it no more.

Laura collapsed onto the bed, sobbing and gasping, over-whelmed by what she'd done and yet unable to deny it or the heights of ecstasy she had achieved in response to what she knew any ordinary woman would have seen as an intol-erable outrage.

11

By the time she returned home to King's Lynn on the Sunday afternoon, Laura had come to realise that she was not an ordinary woman. She wanted the wrong things – punishment, exposure, humiliation, control – not at all what a modern young woman was supposed to want. Nor was it only a matter of being a little eccentric. To the world at large her choices were so obviously wrong that they were seldom even mentioned, or at best as problems to be got over with professional help, and yet they felt right or, at least, they felt good.

Three more times she had reached orgasm over what Hazel Manston-Jones had done to her, concentrating on different aspects: her physical helplessness and the way it had made her feel small and vulnerable, being nude while a fully clothed woman spanked her, and the knowledge that she'd been punished. The last was the best, bringing her to the edge of consciousness and leaving her sore and prickling with sweat.

As she drove back she had been asking herself if she was going mad, but aside from her strange sexual needs there was no evidence for it at all. She felt rational, and outside the sexual her emotions were completely normal: anger and contempt for Chris, regret for what might have been, and embarrassment for having allowed him to see so deep into her soul.

Her thoughts stayed on the same paths as she collected Smudge from her obliging neighbour, Mrs Phipps, and took him for a walk along her normal path by the river. It was a comfortably familiar thing to do, part of her old routine, soothing and yet bringing a touch of regret for the way she had felt at the beginning of the weekend, especially on the beach. She even thought of repeating the experience if the following weekend was warm and sunny, but she knew it wouldn't be the same alone. With that her thoughts turned back to the Controller, who seemed to have vanished as mysteriously as he'd come, possibly because he was dissatisfied with her display behind the vacuum shed.

On the Monday morning it proved depressingly easy to fall into her work routine, and there was really nothing else to be done. The train journey was uneventful, the day busy, her email box empty of strange and intriguing messages, save for an offer from a Nigerian widow to share in her late husband's multi-million pound fortune, which she treated with the contempt it deserved.

She had finished *Taken to Turkey,* which had ended predictably with Mark Frobisher rescuing Evangeline Tarrington and proposing to her after despatching three murderous Mameluks with an ornate fruit knife he'd picked up in the harem, and she was eager for more of the same, however poor a substitute it might be for what she'd lost. A lunchtime visit to the charity shop found another by the same author, *Brigands of Barbary,* which looked promising, although the thought of returning to exactly the same routine as before left her mood blacker than ever.

The journey home was particularly frustrating, with her usual train cancelled and the next so crowded that she ended up standing as far as Downham Market. By the time she got home she was on automatic, tossing the post onto the sofa, taking Smudge for his evening walk and eating a pre-made salad in front of the TV. Only when she'd finished did she open the letters she'd received, in her usual order of circulars, then bills, and anything that looked vaguely interesting last, in this case a plain brown envelope, handwritten. She guessed that this would contain something dull and impersonal anyway, until she opened it and a photo fell out, a photo of her standing behind the vacuum shed at EAS with her skirt lifted to show off her legs, her stockings and the suspenders that held them up, and her bare sex.

Her fingers were shaking as she burrowed into the envelope; thrilled, scared and embarrassed all at once. The only other thing in the envelope was a small piece of expensive grey notepaper, carefully folded and bearing a single line written in a neat, flowing hand – 'You are acceptable. If you wish to proceed, come on the train tomorrow without knickers or brassiere.' It was signed The Controller.

Laura read the note several times before putting both it and the picture back in the envelope. Excitement and fear vied for attention in her head, mixed with a dozen minor emotions. The picture had obviously been taken from the top of the municipal car park, and with a powerful lens, which, along with the mention of the train, left little doubt that the Man had nothing to do with EAS at all, but was one of her fellow commuters.

Whoever it was had her name, her email, her work address, her home address and very possibly more. She found herself reaching out to pet Smudge's head for reassurance, unsure if she was being stalked, or courted in the most delightful, arousing way, or whether the distinction was purely in her head. One thing alone calmed her fears, that she had been given a choice, to proceed, or not.

Something deep within her and immensely strong wanted to obey, and yet her reservations were equally powerful. What if the Man proved to be Hovis Boy or some other spotty teenager trying to get a rise out of her, or worse, hoping to start an affair, or he might prove unattractive for a dozen other reasons. She needed to know who she was dealing with before making any sort of commitment, and yet there would always be the chance to back out later, however embarrassing it might be.

Taking the photo and note from the envelope once more, Laura began to study them for clues. The picture gave very little away, save that he had access to the top of the municipal car park at lunch time and enough money to invest in an expensive camera and a long lens. The note was more telling, with the rather formal language and the use of 'brassiere' rather than 'bra', suggesting an older man, which fitted with everything else she knew about him.

The deduction was reassuring, calming both her doubts and fears although not eliminating them entirely, yet there was only one sure way to find out who he was, and that was to comply.

Laura's sleep was troubled by vivid dreams, in which the Controller turned out not to be a man at all, but Hazel Manston-Jones, who dished out a spanking on the train along with a lecture on the impropriety of surrendering to men in public places. Three times Laura awoke, only to sink back into the same dream, a cycle she only broke by masturbating over what had been done to her.

In the morning she felt off balance, her head crowded with the same conflicting emotions which had troubled her since she had first received a message from the Controller. Once she had showered and dried she went to her drawers, hesitant, only to reach a snap decision. She would do it, and cope with the consequences when they came, because not to was to give in to the dull routine of her working life.

To put on stockings with a suspender belt and to leave her knickers off was straightforward, but to go without a bra under her work blouse presented a problem. Her bust was a little too full to get away with it without somebody noticing, certainly Mr Henderson and very possibly others. If Brian and Dave noticed they would have a field day, so at work it would be impossibly embarrassing and very unpleasant, although on the train that same embarrassment would be crucial to her excitement.

The sensible choice was to bring a pair of knickers and a bra in her bag, which she could put on when she arrived at work, which she did, while wondering at the subtlety of the distinction between arousal and distaste. The wrong man, the wrong place, the wrong time and a delicious thrill could become a nightmare.

Fully dressed, she still felt as if she was naked. Nothing showed, save for the dark rings of her nipples beneath her cotton blouse and the curve of her right breast if she stood at a certain angle to the mirror. With the warmer weather other women on the train would probably be showing as much if not more, but her exposure was deliberate, a signal to a man she didn't even know that she was available, or at very least approachable.

Walking to the station gave Laura a thrill, with the sensation of the lining of her skirt moving on the bare skin of her bottom and the way her breasts moved with no bra to support them. Several of the men she passed seemed to notice, one even giving her a dirty grin, and she was sure that they not only realised she had no bra on but knew she was deliberately flaunting herself. Yet only one man had the right to respond, a man she knew would be on the train.

From the moment she got into the carriage she could feel her heartbeat picking up, while the skin of her neck felt warm and her nipples had grown obstinately erect, giving her the choice of keeping her jacket closed or letting them show. The decision to let them show put a lump in her throat, even though she was sat in her favourite window seat with nobody to see. She turned a little and took out her book, pretending to read although she knew that anybody coming in at the open doors would get the crucial angle that allowed them to see inside her blouse.

Her fingers were shaking, her face flushed hot with embarrassment, her arousal stronger than on many of the occasions she'd been naked with a man or even had somebody inside her. Hovis Boy got on and she quickly moved into a less revealing position, but he ignored her. A glance to the platform showed Darcy walking towards the train, tall and handsome and confident, bringing her pulse up until she could barely restrain herself and hold the position that would show him that she'd been a good girl and done as she was told.

He reached the doors, and stopped, turning aside to address a question to a member of staff. Laura stiffened, pushing her chest out a little and letting her jacket open fully, to leave a slice of her flesh on plain show and her nipples sticking up through her blouse in blatant betrayal of the state she was in. He stepped into the train, glanced from side to side, caught sight of her, his eyes flicking across the front of her straining blouse, and turning away even as her mouth had begun to curve up into a welcoming smile.

She cursed under her breath as she relaxed her body. He had turned the other way, taking a free double seat further down the carriage rather than any of the vacant singles near her. Only the thought of his wedding ring soothed her disappointment, and when the far less appealing Mr Brown got on a moment later and didn't even glance at her she felt only relief. Three of her regulars remained, and Miss Scarlett could be safely excluded. She hadn't seen the Tramp for a long while, which left the Grey Man and the Devil, unless the Controller was subtler still and had managed to completely avoid her attention.

With the train in motion she settled down to read her book, half-heartedly taking in the descriptions of the beautiful heroine, a fiery red-headed adventuress, and a hero who was Mark Frobisher in all but name. Yet the book helped her to relax, making the state of her nipples less embarrassing and helping the urge to play with herself to subside. Only when the train was pulling into Downham Market did she perk up again, wondering if the Grey Man's cold detachment might make it exciting to have him give her highly personal orders, but he came in through the other set of doors and took no notice of her whatsoever.

That left the Devil, who not only fitted her imagined description of the Controller better than any of the others, but who had the most authority. It was all too easy to imagine herself being put across his knee for a stern, no nonsense spanking, or kneeling naked at his feet as she attended to his cock and balls with her tongue, all of which increased her anticipation as the train drew nearer to Ely, until she was fidgeting uncontrollably and could no longer bring herself to concentrate on her book.

He wasn't going to be able to sit near her anyway, the only remaining seats being at the far end of the carriage, but her heart had begun to hammer once more as she adjusted her position to give him the best possible display of her breasts as he got on. That also meant showing off to Hovis Boy, who had begun to eye her cleavage with a sly, sideways look as the train slowed. Laura ignored him, doing her best to enjoy the humiliation and watching the doors as they slid slowly apart.

There was no sign of the Devil, until he came in at the other set of doors. He glanced around, ignored the two vacant seats nearby and began to walk down the aisle. Laura felt as if her heart was about to burst as he came nearer, and stopped, his hand closing around a support rail as the train shuddered into motion. She knew he was looking down at her, and turned to him, unable to look away, to find his bright pale-grey eyes looking into hers, then lower, to feast on the crescent of pale flesh showing within her blouse. He smiled, cool and certain and knowing. Laura felt her body tighten, a reaction like a small faint orgasm and a gasp had escaped her lips before she could stop herself. One edge of his mouth curled up, giving his smile the wry wicked edge she remembered from before. He spoke.

'Good morning, Laura. Stand up.'

She complied without hesitation and was rewarded with another smile for her obedience. The man next to her gave her a curious look, but it barely registered as she passed him to join the Devil in the open space between the doors. He looked her up and down, apparently in approval, then spoke again, softly enough to ensure that his voice was hidden from other passengers by the noise of the train.

'You have done as I said?'

'Yes.'

Laura had struggled to answer, wondering if she was about to be asked to exhibit herself to prove she had no knickers on, knowing she wanted to, but scared of the possible consequences. He glanced down to the front of her skirt.

'Good. You and I will get on very well indeed, I suspect, but naturally you will want to be sure of me first?'

'Yes.'

'Sensible girl. Perhaps you would care for dinner this evening? Shall we say seven-thirty at Brooke's?'

'That would be wonderful, but my dog ... no, never mind, he can cope, but I mustn't be back too late ...'

Laura stopped, aware that she'd begun to babble, but he merely returned his amused smile, then continued.

'Wear red, it suits you. Otherwise, come as you are.'

Laura nodded, despite an instinctive touch of rebellion at the order, unwilling and unable to argue the point. She could buy a dress at lunch time and change at work, while she was already naked beneath her clothes at his command. He spoke again.

'Excellent, I look forward to it. My name is Charles, by the way, Charles Latchley, although you may prefer Mr Latchley at times.'

'Yes, I think so.'

'Good. I had hoped we would understand on another.'

'Or ... I always think of you as the Devil.'

He laughed, openly this time, a deep, resonant sound, brief but without restraint.

'That might be very appropriate, on occasion.'

Laura shivered.

'How did you know?'

'How did I know who you are, or how did I know what you are?'

'Both, really, I mean ...'

'I have know what you are for quite some time, and so naturally I wanted to know who you are. My chance came when I found your bookmark the other day ...'

'My bookmark?'

'Yes, the one you've been using since Christmas. It was on the seat one evening when I chanced to come back into town late, an opportunity I was unable to resist, although I freely confess I had never expected you to respond so well.'

'Oh. You were watching me all along?'

'Yes. I do apologise if I caused you any alarm, but I am sure you will understand that I needed to test the water, and you do like stockings, don't you?'

'Yes ... I mean, my boss ... no, not really. I do. But how do you mean by what I am?'

'What you are? Surely you know what you are?'

'No. I don't understand.'

'You are an old-fashioned girl. A girl who likes to wear stockings, who likes to feel feminine. You are a girl who enjoys novels in which the heroine spends a good deal of time tied up, or in chains, at the mercy of some powerful man, or having to go naked, or being spanked.'

He chuckled, and Laura realised that the sudden tightening of her muscles at the crucial word must have given her away. The blood rushed to her face, but there was no distaste in his expression, or even the crude, boyish lust Chris Drake had shown, only a calm appreciation and, more importantly, understanding. Instantly it was as if a great weight had been lifted from her shoulders, and her voice was full of gratitude as she answered.

'Yes. I like that, but I still don't understand?'

His voice was rich with pleasure as he answered.

'No? How charming. What you are, Laura, is a natural slave.'

12

The day seemed to take forever to pass, with a hundred different thoughts crowding Laura's head as she struggled to concentrate on work. For all her excitement, she was not completely easy in her mind about what he had said, particularly about her being a natural slave. It seemed too extreme, far beyond her fantasies of capture and punishment, and suggested a permanent and deliberate inequality in their relationship rather than a purely sexual one. She had also become very much aware of the gap in age between them, and the inevitable social consequences. He was roughly the same age as her parents, which would make introductions difficult if it ever came to that, while she could already hear Brian and Dave sniggering and the catty remarks from the other girls at EAS if he accompanied her to company functions.

Despite her misgivings she was determined to go through with it, at the very least dinner and whatever came afterwards, almost certainly more. Not only did he seem to be the answer to many of her most compelling needs, but it would be immensely satisfying if Chris Drake was to discover that she had found herself a new partner just two days after Hazel had brought their liaison to an end.

At lunchtime she made a trip to Talitha Tabitha, a shop specialising in clothes for the richer female students at the university. After just a few minutes talking to a shop assistant who looked and behaved like an impoverished duchess, Laura chose a beautiful evening gown in heavy deep-red silk. The fit was perfect but the price came as a nasty shock, leaving her feigning nonchalance as she passed the Duchess her credit card.

When five o'clock eventually came around she went to change, agonising over the details of her make-up and hair but going without bra or knickers as she had been instructed. As she left the EAS building she felt more naked than ever, sure not only that everybody who passed knew that her pretty dress concealed her bare bottom and sex, but they also knew what was likely to happen to her later. None reacted, save to compliment her and ask about the date she was obviously going on. She replied cautiously, trying not to be so mysterious that rumours began to kick off, while also not giving too much away.

She was grateful for the anonymity of the university town, where she only looked slightly out of place, and in Brooke's not at all. Somewhat early, painfully nervous but determined to fit in, she ordered a glass of dry white wine and sat sipping it at the bar as she reflected on what the evening might bring. Charles, Mr Latchley, the Devil, had shown extraordinary confidence on the train, as if he already knew all about her, even her most private thoughts. It had been disconcerting, but also thrilling, especially to imagine that he would be able to fulfil her darkest fantasies without the embarrassment of having to explain them first. He knew.

At precisely seven-thirty he arrived, now wearing a perfectly cut dinner jacket and a black bow tie, giving him even more authority than before. Laura found herself smiling and rising at his approach, desperately eager to please, and yet her response felt entirely natural. He took command at once, announcing his name to the waiter, who escorted them to a table in the alcove formed by a bay window, ensuring perfect privacy.

Taking both menu and wine list, he spent a moment studying the selection with a critical eye, asked Laura a couple of questions about her personal preferences and ordered for both of them. The waiter bowed and withdrew, quickly returning with a bottle of Champagne in an ice bucket. Charles tasted the wine, approved it and watched as Laura's glass was filled.

'You're very generous, thank you.'

'Not at all. The wonderful thing about Champagne is that it can be drunk throughout a meal, unlike any other wine.'

'I didn't know that.'

'It's not something that's widely appreciated nowadays.'

'Are you in the business then?'

'Oh no, merely an amateur. I run an antiquarian bookshop in Sturton Street, although to all intents and purposes I'm retired. Originally I was in the City. And yourself?'

'I work for EAS, East Anglia Switchgear. We make sealed, middle and high-voltage units, but it's all very dull.'

'Not at all, although for a woman like yourself our modern world must seem stifling.'

'How do you mean?'

'Don't you find it so? The need to fit in with a society inimical to your personality, in which lip service is paid to individuality and yet you dare not openly express what is the very essence of your being.'

'My sexuality? You're right, and it's wonderful to be able to talk to somebody who understands. What's the right word, submissive?'

'No or, at least, only in a technical sense. Unfortunately the word has been hijacked by people who merely play games, whereas for you I suspect it goes much deeper. It's such a cold word as well, so scientific. I prefer to call you what you are in your heart, a slave.'

'I'm not sure I feel like a slave, although I do understand what you mean, I think.'

'Don't worry, full understanding will come with time. You have a long journey ahead of you, Laura, but at the end you will know yourself as few others do.'

'I hope so. It all seems a bit frightening.'

'If you'd rather not?'

'No, no, I want to, but it's so sudden, and I don't really understand my own feelings, and ...'

'That's what I'm here for, to be your mentor and, ultimately, your master.'

Laura responded with a nervous smile. What he was saying fitted with what she had known about herself for a long time but often tried to repress, while his calm, uninhibited confidence was immensely appealing. Yet a part of her wanted to get up and slap him across the face as hard as she could, for daring to assume that she was already his, and not simply her lover, but something more intimate by far. He was watching her face as she sipped her wine, and when he spoke it was once more as if he'd read her mind.

'It won't be easy. It never is. Society has conditioned you against your true nature, to the point at which it seems natural to rebel against your own instincts. Hence my little test, to see if you were capable of going against social pressure, and which you passed with flying colours.'

'Thank you.'

She had answered simply, ignoring the temptation to go into the emotional upheaval she had suffered. It was easy to go along with him, ignoring her misgivings and accepting the promise of what he was saying. Their starters arrived, thin slices of some dark rich meat accompanied by an apple mash, and he changed topic of conversation to fine food, Laura half-listening as her mind dwelt on how it would feel to be placed across his knee later that same evening. Once again he seemed to divine her thoughts.

'You are a trifle distracted, I see? I suppose that's hardly surprising, in the circumstances. You are ready, I trust?'

'I . . . I think so. What are you going to do with me?'

He gave a pleased smile.

'How perfectly you react, Laura. In the same situation, most girls would ask what I would like to do, or what I want to do. Not you. You ask what I am going to do. What indeed?'

He was teasing with her, his eyes twinkling with mischief. Laura could no longer hold back.

'Are you going to spank me?'

She'd spoken in a whisper, hot and urgent, but carefully modulated to ensure that the diners at nearby tables didn't hear her shameful demand. He didn't reply immediately, his full attention on his food. Laura waited, fidgeting, until he was ready.

'You crave discipline, that is your nature. You are also aroused by discipline, both the thought and the act itself as you will soon discover, but it is essential that you understand the purpose of discipline. If you misbehave, or fail at a task, or fail to meet my approval, you will be punished, always. You will not be punished without reason, ever, even though you may be smacked for other reasons, including simply to arouse you, or for my amusement. Is that clear?'

'Yes, I think I understand, but are you . . . are you going to do it?'

'If it needs to be done, yes.'

His answer made her feel weak with desire.

'You seem to know me better than I know myself. '

'That is hardly surprising, Laura. I have trained a number of girls across the years, and while each was individual in her own delightful way, there are certain basic verities, what I call the three Ps. One is the need for punishment.'

'And the others?'

'We'll come to those presently. For now I want to concentrate on the proper understanding of discipline as discipline rather than for erotic titillation.'

Laura could only nod, remembering how strong her reaction had been to her spanking from Hazel Manston-Jones. There had been nothing remotely erotic about the actual punishment, and she was no lesbian, yet she had not only wanted to come over it, but needed to, and repeatedly. What was being promised would be just as strong but he clearly understood how she would react. Less clear was whether he intended to take advantage of the state she would be in, something she could not do without. She was blushing as she struggled to find the words to express her need.

'You will enjoy it though?'

He laughed.

'I will enjoy you, Laura, very much. That will be an important element of your punishment.'

Laura managed a smile, unsure exactly what he meant but very sure indeed of what it was doing to her. Her whole body felt warm and sensitive, while she had begun to tremble. She wanted more.

'What else should I know?'

'Many things, but that will come with time. For now it is enough that you are willing to accept discipline from me.'

'I am.'

'Good. And one other thing. I advise against misbehaving in order to be punished. You will be, but perhaps not in the way you had anticipated.'

'How do you mean?'

'You will find out when the time comes, if it comes.'

Laura shivered, partly in fear, partly from a new surge of desire at the thought of having to give herself over to some unspecified punishment, something crueller still than the bare bottom spanking she needed so badly. He swallowed the last of his Champagne, then spoke again.

'What you can be sure of is that you are precious to me. I will discipline you, yes, but I will do nothing to hurt you deeply, nor to spoil your beauty, even temporarily.'

'Thank you.'

'You will, many times.'

Two hours later, drunk and aroused to the point of absolute surrender, Laura had given herself over completely to his control, knowing that whatever choice he made she would accept it with pleasure. She was his, and had said as much, so that even if he chose to simply put her on the train and leave her to travel home alone she knew she would accept his decision. That seemed to be what was going to happen as they made their way through the streets, only for him to turn aside, steering her into Sturton Street and to where shutters closed off the door of a shop painted black but for lettering in faded gold.

'My shop. Come inside.'

Laura waited as shutters were raised and the door opened, allowing him to usher her into a dim space rich with the scent of old leather and musty pages. He locked up behind her, turning on a single light to suffuse the room with a dull yellow glow. Bookcases stood against every wall and at the centre of the floor, creating a maze most of which was hidden in shadow, save for where the bulb he had brought to life created a puddle of light in front of where a single bulky armchair upholstered in green leather stood beside a plain desk. He sat down, gesturing to her.

'Come to me. Into the light.'

She obeyed, standing apprehensive before him, her fingers twining together behind her back. He put one hand to his chin, tugging at his small sharp beard, more demonic than ever as he spoke again.

'Remove your gown.'

Her hands seemed to move of their own accord, up to the zip of her gown, pulling gently downwards. She felt her bodice come loose, the heavy silk pulled down by its own weight to bare her breasts to him. He raised a finger and Laura paused, her gown at the level of her belly, allowing him to make a slow, unhurried inspection of her naked chest.

'Take hold of your breasts. Touch your nipples.'

Again Laura obeyed without hesitation, cupping her breasts in her hands to feel their weight as she stroked her fingers across the hard, urgent buds of her nipples. She wondered if she would be made to masturbate, her excitement rising steeply at the prospect, but he said nothing, simply watching until she could hardly resist touching lower. At last he gave another signal, motioning her to continue with the removal of her gown.

She pushed it down, shaking badly as she wriggled the silk down over her hips and legs, conscious of her naked sex as she went bare, and of her exposed bottom behind. He gave a brief, complacent nod at the proof of her obedience, waiting until she had stepped free of her gown to stand before him in nothing but her suspender belt, stockings and heels before once more addressing her.

'I had often imagined you naked, and I must say that I am not disappointed by the reality. Now turn around, and place your hands on your head.'

Laura shuffled quickly into position, glancing back over her shoulder as he began a leisurely inspection of her bottom. For a long while he was silent, until once again her sense of anticipation had risen close to breaking point.

'Bend forwards.'

A sob escaped Laura's lips, but she did as she was told, thinking of what he would now be able to see, the rear view of her sex, with every intimate little fold on show, also the tight pink star of her anus. She was hiding nothing, while he was showing nothing, and it felt perfect, exactly how they should be together, at least until he chose to fully enjoy her, which had to be soon or she would burst.

'Do you like what you see?'

'If you mean, do you have a pretty cunt, then the answer is yes, as I suspect you know.'

Laura let slip another sob at his crude words, her pleasure pushing higher still as he went on.

'A very pretty cunt. A very pretty bottom too, full, feminine, yet without surplus flesh. In fact, you are a very well formed young woman, but again, I suspect you know that. Now, as I recall, there was at least one day on which I instructed you to wear stockings but you disobeyed me. Is that correct?'

'Yes, I suppose . . .'

Laura never finished her sentence. His hand had closed on her upper arm and her words broke at the realisation that she was going to be put across his knee. A flood of emotions hit her, fear and desire and shame and a need so strong that she was already sobbing as she was manhandled gently but firmly into place, laid across his lap with her head hung low and her bottom lifted.

He began to spank, his hand smacking down on her bare flesh with hard, purposeful swats. It stung enough to make her kick her feet and wriggle her hips, but he had her held firmly around the waist, preventing escape. Not that she wanted to, because for all the hurt and indignity of her position she was filled with joy for what was being done to her, her bare bottom spanked across the knee of a strong dominant man, and not only for sex, but to punish her.

Laura burst into tears, not for the pain, but for wonderful sense of release as smack after smack descended on her cheeks. He never so much as paused, keeping up the same steady rhythm on her bottom and keeping his grip on her waist. She was now squirming freely across his lap, her legs wide and not caring what she was showing behind. It didn't matter, not for him. He could see anything, do anything, just as long as he kept her disciplined.

Her bottom was now hot, the pain dissolved to a blissful sensation that quickly had her sticking her hips up. He gave a knowing chuckle, sensing her reaction, and his hand had moved lower, smacking the tuck of her cheeks to send jolt after jolt to her sex. Laura realised she was going to come, spanked to orgasm, and that there was absolutely nothing she could do to stop it happening.

She cried out as the pleasure rose high, now on tiptoe, her bottom pushed as high as it would go. The smacks began to get faster, and harder, bringing her up and up until it happened, pushing her over the edge to a screaming, writhing peak. He never once reacted, holding her and spanking her as the orgasm tore through her body and stopping only when she was completely spent.

Laura slid from his lap to the floor, kneeling between his open knees. She was shaking uncontrollably, lost in a state of bliss she had never imagined could exist as she clung to the man who had spanked her. His arms came around her, holding her to his body as she let out her emotions against his chest, the hot, ecstatic tears streaming down her face, and only when her sobs had finally begun to subside did he ease her slowly down to feed his penis into her mouth.

13

They would meet again, properly, at the weekend. Until then, the Devil's instructions to Laura were simple. She was to do as she was told, without question and on the understanding only that he would take care of her and demand nothing that would risk her job or interfere with her work. He would monitor her.

What had been thrilling but also alarming was now a delightful game, or, as he had explained it, part of her training. Laura was singing to herself as she walked Smudge with a fresh spring in her step, while her mind seethed with memories of what had happened and thoughts of what might be to come. Simply knowing that she was now subject to his discipline would have been enough to keep her aroused, but there was so much more.

Just the memory of how he had handled her was enough to send a shiver through her body, while it was impossible to think of the actual spanking without wanting to touch herself. Then there had been the feeling afterwards, unlike anything she had ever experienced before, as she clung naked and trembling to his body. He had explained that it was normal for a well spanked girl to react that way, and it would now be a regular part of her life.

What was less normal was that she had reached a climax purely from the sensation of being smacked, something he knew about but had never encountered before, despite what seemed to be a great deal of experience. She felt proud and happy, while he had been openly impressed with her and hinted at the potential for yet greater pleasures. Twice more she had brought herself to orgasm over the memory as she lay in bed after catching the last train home.

He had also admitted to having been fascinated with her for a long time, simply for her looks at first, until her taste in books had hinted at her nature. Even then he had held back, knowing how few women suited his tastes and unwilling to compromise, until the day he had found her bookmark and decided to test her. He felt she had responded well, and had explained the mistake in her reasoning which had led her to assume that the man seeking to control her must have been one of her colleagues. He had sent the message telling her she was a good girl not because he'd known she was wearing suspenders at the office, but because he'd seen her with the bag from Pretty Things. The next morning she'd used a different carriage, so he hadn't known if she was actually wearing them or not.

Now she was obliged to go bare, or risk punishment, a subtle game that played to the ambiguity of her feelings, setting the pain of spanking against the pleasure it brought. The temptation to disobey on purpose for the thrill of knowing that she would have to face the consequences was strong, but her need to obey stronger still. She had dressed as instructed, and as before, bare under her skirt but for her suspender belt and stockings.

Her sense of anticipation as she sat on the train was stronger than ever, but she now felt protected, knowing he would be there. She also knew that he would not acknowledge her any more openly than before, and that this was an important part of her 'training', although she'd didn't know why. Feeling safe but aroused, she found the temptation to show off irresistible, deliberately adjusting her skirt as the train slowed for Ely station so that he would find her pretending to read *Brigands of Barbary* with a thin slice of stocking top on display when he got on.

Just to see him again made her heart jump, as did the slight rise of his eyebrows as he saw what she was showing, maybe suggesting amusement and approval, maybe the reverse, which raised the prospect of a spanking at the weekend. Nor was he the only one who noticed, Mr Brown taking a sly peek, and Hovis Boy positively goggle-eyed as he struggled to pretend he wasn't looking. Safe in the knowledge that she was the Devil's girl, both their reactions now amused her.

He followed her as they left Cambridge station, tempting her to walk with a deliberate wiggle that she hoped showed off the shape of her bare cheeks beneath her skirt. At one point he came so close he could have touched her, making her wonder if he would dare to smack her seat in public, which brought her feelings to a peak from which they subsided only gradually once they had parted and she made for the office.

It was hard to concentrate at work, her thoughts constantly drifting to him and all the possibilities life now offered. Fortunately she was given a simple task, updating Mr Henderson's filing system, which she could perform with mechanical detachment while her thoughts dwelt on other, more important, things and she waited for the instruction that she knew she would receive some time during the day. It came shortly before lunch, and was very different to what she had been expecting.

GO TO THE BASKET SHOP IN CLARE LANE. PURCHASE A ONE METRE LENGTH OF DARK CANE.

Laura's puzzlement lasted only a moment, to be replaced by a sick feeling of nervous excitement. It seemed very unlikely indeed that Charles wanted her to repair some wickerwork for him. Far more likely was that he intended to apply the cane to her bottom, something that had never been done to her but which she was sure would hurt a great deal. She was equally sure that if he felt it necessary, then she would accept it, although the prospect left her biting her lip as she made her way into the centre of town.

The Basket Shop was more or less as she had been imagining it, a small boutique specialising in old-fashioned wicker baskets, hampers, hanging baskets and just about anything else that could be made of bent cane. She had also been imagining the owner as female, middle-aged and kindly, so that the handsome young man behind the counter came as a surprise, and with no lengths of cane on display she was forced to ask.

'I'd like a one metre length of dark cane, please.'

He stood up as he replied.

'What's it for?'

Caught completely off guard, the blood rushed to Laura's face as she stammered out an answer, determined to say anything but the truth.

'Um ... what's it for? I, um ... does it matter?'

'Yes. We have several grades in stock, for different purposes.'

He was looking at her strangely, making her certain that he could picture her touching her toes with her skirt rolled up and her knickers pulled down, awaiting the cane like a disobedient schoolgirl. Her blush grew hotter still.

'I ... I don't know, um ... that is, it's not for me.'

The faint smug grin on his face suggested that he knew perfect well it was for her, in the sense that it was her bottom it would be used on. So did his reply.

'I see. Probably the medium grade then, which is about five millimetres thick?'

'Um ... I suppose so. Could you show me?'

His smile grew abruptly wider as she realised the implication of what she'd said, now picturing herself not only touching her toes to present her bare bottom, but doing so in the middle of the shop with curious passers-by watching as he tested the cane on her. At that she came close to losing her nerve and fleeing the shop, but he was already making for the back area, to return a moment later with a length of dark brown cane. He spoke again as he passed it to her.

'This will probably do the job, and they're only two ninety-nine each.'

Laura had taken the cane, which felt hard, cool and heavier than she had expected. Just to touch it made her fingers twitch and kept her face and chest hot as he waited for her decision.

'OK. I'll take it. Thank you.'

As she left the shop she was trying to tell herself that his knowing reaction had been purely in her head, but a nagging doubt remained. Maybe other people had been in to buy single canes and he had put two and two together? Possibly Charles had sent other girls to the shop before her, on the same errand, a thought that brought a touch of jealousy even though he has said he was single. Alternatively, the man in the shop might be into caning girls himself and kept a look out for possible candidates for punishment? Again she imagined being made to touch her toes in the middle of the shop, her bottom pushed well out, her skirt lifted to show that she was already without knickers, and given the cane in full view of the street or with other customers looking on.

The temptation to go back via Sturton Street was considerable, to call in on Charles and show him what she'd bought, perhaps to have it tested after all, or to admit to imagining herself being disciplined by another man, which she was fairly sure would earn her a well-deserved punishment. Only the certainty of being late back if she made a detour prevented her, and as it was she pushed open the door to Mr Henderson's office at three minutes past two. He glanced up.

'You're normally very punctual, Laura.'

'I'm sorry, Mr Henderson. I had to go into town.'

He glanced at the cane, which she hastily put down by her desk.

'For a garden cane?'

'And one or two other things.'

He gave a slight shake of his head, nothing more, but again Laura found herself wondering if he had guessed. Blushing once more, she hastily got back to work, wondering if Charles had been aware of how much of an ordeal buying the cane would be for her. The answer was almost certainly yes, and even if neither the man in the shop nor Mr Henderson had guessed its true purpose, there were undoubtedly other, more dirty minded individuals who would. Brian would guess, she was sure, which would mean lurid rumours circulating the office just as fast as the grapevine could carry them.

By the time she left she had managed to wrap the cane in brown paper, making her trip to the station a good deal less embarrassing, at least until she got into her carriage to find Charles already there. He glanced at the package in her hand and gave her one of his most wicked smiles. Digging into his coat, he produced an envelope, which Laura took as she spoke.

'You really know how to bring out my feelings, don't you? What's this?'

He immediately lifted a finger, wagging it gently before putting it to his lips. A lump came into Laura's throat instantly and the cheeks of her bottom tightened beneath her skirt as she realised that she had broken the rules. She had earned herself a spanking, maybe the cane, filling her with apprehension and excitement as she took her seat. He was close to her, but said nothing, merely enjoying the view of her legs until he got off at Ely station.

For the rest of the journey Laura was fiddling with the envelope, not daring to open it for fear of somebody else reading what might be extremely revealing contents, but tearing it open the moment she was safely home. Inside was a card, covered in neat handwriting on one side and with a picture on the other, a delicate watercolour showing a pretty blonde girl with her hair in a wavy 1950s style, dressed in red high-heeled shoes, stockings, suspenders and a full bra, also a pair of big white knickers. But they had been pulled down to the level of her thighs, baring her cheeky bottom to an older, fully dressed woman with similar features and hair. In the older woman's hand was a cane, not simply a straight length, but with a crook handle.

For a long moment she stood staring at the picture, doing her best to ignore Smudge's efforts to lick her face as she imagined the young girl's fear and humiliation, before curiosity got the better of her. Turning the card over, she read what he had written.

The cane is for your discipline. You will make it yourself, as a classic, English school cane as illustrated on the front of this card. You will keep it hung on the back of your bedroom door.

He had signed the card, but there were no further instructions. Laura read the words a second time and a third, then the first sentence yet again. To have guessed what the cane was for was one thing, but to see it written down quite another. She savoured the words – the cane is for your discipline – stated without emphasis or the least hint at the dark, sexual implications. Nor was there any ambiguity, no room for escape. She had confessed her need for discipline and now she would get it, with an implement she'd paid for and made herself, and which she would have to keep in plain view in her bedroom as a constant reminder that when, and if, it was necessary she would be beaten.

The thought made her weak with apprehension and need, but ordinary life had to be attended to. She went to fetch Smudge's lead, only to realise that it was important for her discipline to become a part of ordinary life. The cane would hang with her bathrobe. When she needed the bathrobe, she would put it on. When she needed the cane she would be made to bend over the bed and it would be put across her bottom, a thought very nearly too exciting to resist.

First she had to make it, and while he hadn't given her any instructions it seemed reasonable to assume that it would need to be soaked before the end could be bent to make the handle. Deliberately treating it as part of her normal evening routine, she ran a few inches of water in the bath and put the cane in, only then taking Smudge for his walk. Her head was still full of thoughts, in equal parts disturbing and delightful, of Charles and what he would expect of her, of the cane she was making and of the picture on the card.

It was impossible not to picture herself in the same vulnerable pose, perhaps even with another woman about to administer her punishment, so that it was not sexual at all, but done purely in order to discipline her. The thought was intriguing, and didn't even seem unfaithful, so she let her mind wander, trying to decide which of the women she knew would be the best. The obvious choice was Hazel Manston-Jones, who looked the part and would undoubtedly apply the strokes mercilessly hard. She had already spanked Laura, so might well want to dish out a few strokes of the cane.

As always when thinking of Hazel Manston-Jones, it took

Laura a moment to get over her pride before she could let her fantasy build up, but she was soon imagining a scenario in which she was caught with her brand new cane and made to take it as a punishment for going with Chris Drake. There would be nothing sexual about it at all, but Laura would still be made to go bare, purely in order to humiliate her and emphasise how low she was beside the tall beautiful Hazel. She would be put in a thoroughly lewd position as well, to make sure everything showed, kneeling on her bed, or bent over her kitchen table, perhaps even strapped in place to prevent her wriggling or trying to escape. She'd be lectured, told what a dirty cheating bitch she was, then caned, six hard strokes delivered one by one across her naked cheeks as she squirmed in her bonds before having her well-decorated bottom photographed so that Hazel could show Chris what had been done.

She had reached the marshes where a stream ran into the Ouse, the point at which she usually turned back to follow the field path into town. Tall brown and green reeds made a carpet in front of her, their stems temptingly like the length of cane now soaking in the bath. She stopped, scarcely able to accept that she could be so dirty, but the opportunity was too good to resist. A glance back the way she had come showed that nobody was about and her final chance of making an excuse was gone. Slipping Smudge from his lead she urged him to chase a flock of seagulls that she knew he had no chance whatsoever of actually catching. He went, bounding across the nearest field and she slipped in among the reeds, pushing through the tall stems until she was safely hidden from view.

Her fingers were shaking as she snapped off a length of reed. It was light and less flexible than the cane, but it would do. Closing her eyes, she began to inch her skirt up, imagining herself under orders from the cruel, vindictive Hazel Manston-Jones, who would laugh as Laura's bare bottom was revealed and make a joke about tarts going without knickers. The next command would be to touch her toes, and she would obey, bending down to leave her naked bottom stuck out and her sex peeping from between her thighs, much to Hazel's amusement.

She'd then be caned, six hard strokes, and as she pictured herself being punished, Laura began to switch her bottom with the length of reed. It stung, just enough, and after just three strokes the last of her caution was gone. Pushing her hand between her thighs, she began to play with herself, teasing her sex as she ran the punishment over and over in her mind: the sharp orders, the exposure of her body to another woman, the sting of the cane across her cheeks. Her knees nearly gave way as she started to come, threatening to pitch her forwards onto the soft black soil, into a kneeling position yet ruder than the one she was already in.

Laura gave in, deliberately going down on all fours, her bottom lifted and ready for entry from behind, enjoying the soft feel as her knees sank into the muddy soil, still thrashing at her bottom with the piece of reed and imagining Hazel stood over her, laughing.

14

The rest of the week followed a similar pattern for Laura, kept in a near constant state of arousal that could only be relieved, briefly, by playing with herself until she had worked out the memories and fantasies in her head. She finished the cane, with some difficulty and some time spent searching on the internet, first bending the handle into shape and tying it with string to make sure the crook stayed once it was dry, then sandpapering the ends and finally allowing it to stand in a pot of olive oil for a night in order to ensure that it stayed supple. By the time she was done and had hung it on the back of her bedroom door as instructed, the thing seemed to have taken on a life of its own, at once evil and sacred, an instrument of torture and ecstasy, both terrifying and compelling. Even to glimpse it hanging there ready to be put across her bottom if she was naughty was enough to make her want to touch herself, and she knew that once it had been used her feelings would be stronger by far.

He had made it plain that she would be beaten, but only when she needed it, which made her feelings more muddled still. That she deserved it, she had no doubt, not for any physical act, but because, try as she might, she was unable to keep her erotic fantasies focused solely on Charles Latchley. First it had been the young man in the cane shop, then Hazel Manston-Jones, and lastly Tommy Fuller during a nostalgic evening spent drinking wine, listening to old tracks from her teenage years and wishing that he'd taught her the delights of a well-smacked bottom. Each one had helped her to several exquisite orgasms under her own fingers. She was determined to confess, despite her very real fear of the consequences, and replied to Charles's Friday afternoon email with a question. SHALL I BRING THE CANE? There was no reply, but he was there on the train as always, greeting her with a smile and a quiet remark.

'Don't worry, I have several.'

Laura spent the rest of the journey and the night that followed in a sweat of anticipation, unable to keep still, unable to sleep properly for her fear and her longing, while every glimpse of the wicked looking implement on the back of her door brought a new surge of emotion. Nor was the cane her only source of excitement. She was to go to his house, presumably to spend the night, which would surely mean the full consummation of their relationship, presumably after she had been caned, a thought that had her hand back between her thighs twice before she finally got to sleep.

He had told her to surprise him, making her choice of what to wear difficult, but after an hour of laying things out and rejecting them she decided that it would be best to express their shared love of the styles of the 1950s. It took another hour to get her hair exactly right, and nearly as long again to make her final choice of a loose red summer dress over scarlet heels, seamed stockings and her favourite suspender belt, full French knickers that clung to the cheeks of her bottom and a bra that lifted her breasts into prominence. A black pork-pie hat with a feather at one side that she had found in a jumble sale but never had an excuse to wear added the final touch to her ensemble.

The combination made her feel gloriously sexual and drew glances from both men and women as she made her brisk walk to the station with her bag in hand. As always, it was easy to imagine that they knew, while the look Mrs Phipps had given her as she handed Smudge across had suggested both envy and disapproval. Laura didn't care, now proud of her choice and determined not to be coy about her relationship.

Being a Saturday, the train was almost empty, while getting off at Ely felt distinctly strange after passing through so many times over the years. He was waiting, as agreed, standing in the car park next to a bright red Morgan, smartly dressed as ever, and smiling his wicked grin as she approached.

'Laura, I'd hardly have recognised you. You look ...'

'Like a seaside tart from the 1950s? They seemed to think so in King's Lynn.'

'Well I dare say they'd know best, but seriously, you look delightful. Seams, I see, very right and proper. Do get in.'

He had opened the door of car for her, an old-fashioned courtesy that seem to fit perfectly with his assumption of the right to discipline her. She got in, trying to relax as he started the car and drew out of the car park but unable to suppress her nerves. He seemed as calm and in control as ever, driving fast but with patience as they skirted the town to head north and east across flat, open fields divided by rows of poplar and thorn. The top of the car was down, the fresh wind in her face making it hard to talk, but Laura didn't mind, content to soak up the atmosphere, so different from the life she had grown used to.

Laura had imagined him living in a town house, and was surprised when he turned down a short lane to stop outside what had once been a wind pump tower but was now missing its sails, while a two-storey cottage grew from one side in the same red brick and flint construction. A high, red-brick wall and a neatly tended garden surrounded the building, which was plainly quite old, with lichen covered red tiles on the roof and a wisteria trained above the windows and door, all in all creating the impression that she had stepped back in time at least half a century if not more. There was nothing remotely sinister about it, just the opposite, and yet it seemed entirely appropriate as the sort of place in which girls were not only spanked and caned, but expected to accept it as both normal and necessary. She thought back to the world of her favourite novels.

'You like old-fashioned things, don't you?'

'I do. Not that I make the mistake of imagining that there was a lost golden age. I was born just after the war and, frankly, things were pretty miserable, so it's more a case of rescuing what's good and doing my best to ignore what's bad. Come in.'

He opened the front door, which Laura noted had been securely locked. Inside was a living room, crossing the full width of the cottage to look out onto the garden and furnished in a comfortable yet distinctly male style. Doors led off either side, one to a kitchen and a small dining room, the other to what appeared to be a library or a study. A spiral staircase led up from one corner, which he indicated with a casual gesture.

'Go up.'

Laura obeyed, wondering if she was to be summarily spanked and fucked before they'd even had lunch, but he contented himself with a gentle but possessive pat to her bottom as they reached a landing looking out across the garden to the fields beyond. An open door to one side led into his bedroom, again simply furnished, with no evidence whatever of his unusual tastes. The door on the other side, the upper part of the tower, was closed and held shut with a heavy padlock, the sight of which gave Laura a twinge of apprehension. He noticed her expression and grinned.

'I'm not sure you're quite ready for what's in there.'

'I think I'm a big enough girl to see what I'm letting myself in for, aren't I?'

'Actually, I suspect you are. You made your cane for yourself, after all.'

'Yes, and hung it on the back of my door.'

'Ah yes, how do you feel about that?'

'It makes me dizzy just to look at it, scared and dizzy.'

'Which is exactly how it should be.'

'It's very clever, the way you always seem to be able to judge how I'll feel.'

'Oh it's an old trick, but a good one. There's nothing quite like having an implement she's been punished with on the wall to keep a girl on her toes. Then of course there's the matter of visitors. Anybody who comes into your bedroom will know what you get.'

'I wasn't planning on letting anybody else into my bedroom! Not men, anyway, and if any of my girlfriends are coming around I'm going to hide the cane. Sorry, but that I'm not ready for.'

He merely chuckled and she carried on, remembering her promised confession.

'Speaking of other men, and women too actually, there's something I really need to get off my chest. I love the idea of taking discipline from you, but when I think about it I can't help imagining other people doing it to me as well, mainly women … a woman, because that seems purer, if there's no sex involved, just punishment. That's wrong, isn't it? I want to be honest with you, Charles, right from the start, so I thought I'd better tell you, and … and …'

She realised she'd begun to babble, expecting to be whipped over the banister rail for spanking at any moment, or worse, real displeasure. He merely looked thoughtful for a moment before replying.

'You still have a great deal to learn, Laura, including what it means to give yourself fully to a man. I expect complete faith, of course, but it must be given freely, not forced. Do you want correction for your thoughts? Think carefully before you answer.'

Laura hesitated. Whoever she'd been with, however much in love, other people had always intruded into her darker fantasies, a habit she'd tried to put down to her vivid imagination rather than any real desire to be unfaithful. She doubted Charles could cure her of it, but felt she should be prepared to try.

'Yes. I think that would be right.'

'Very well. How many times did you imagine yourself being punished by somebody other than me?'

Laura decided she had to be fully honest.

'How many times did I think about it, or how many times did I come over it?'

His eyebrows rose a fraction and there was steel in his voice as he spoke again.

'You masturbated over other people spanking you?'

Laura looked at the floor.

'And caning me.'

'How many times?'

'Um ... about eight.'

'Eight?'

'Maybe ten, or twelve, but only other three different people.'

She raised her eyes, only to lower them abruptly, unable to meet his stern gaze as he continued.

'So let me get this straight. You have masturbated or orgasmed at least eight times over the thought of being punished by other people, and how many times thinking about me?'

'Oh, lots more. I can't stop it, ever since you spanked me. My head's just full of it, all the time. I have to do it before I can get to sleep, usually twice.'

She was blushing hot, wriggling her toes and fiddling with her fingers in her embarrassment. At last she managed to raise her eyes again, to find him looking down at her with a quizzical expression.

'I'm sorry. I suppose you think I'm a slut?'

'No. I like a woman to accept her sexual feelings, and I admire your honesty in telling me. I suspect these thoughts will die as you come to understand your true nature more fully, but for the time being, if you genuinely feel that you want correction, then perhaps we'd better go in after all.'

As he spoke he took a bunch of keys from a pocket, one of which he pushed into the padlock. Laura stepped close as he opened the door onto a bright, airy room, larger than she had expected and somewhat like a gym, with wooden bars against one wall of scrubbed brick and ropes hanging from the beams at the peak of the tower some twelve feet above her head. There were also pieces of padded furniture on the floor, but not vaulting horses or parallel bars. The nearest was a cage, constructed of thick wooden bars and just about large enough to hold a full grown woman if she stayed curled up or on all fours. Beyond that was a curiously designed bench, also of dark polished wood, but upholstered with black leather and plainly designed to be knelt on in such a way that her bottom would be the highest part of her body and completely vulnerable. Black leather straps on short chains hung from the legs of the device.

Laura swallowed and glanced at Charles, thinking for a moment of how little she really knew him and that nobody knew where she was, but he merely sat down on yet another piece of unusual furniture, a small stool topped with black leather. Behind him, to either side of the door, she noticed twin lines of hooks fastened to boards, and that from each hook hung an implement plainly intended for discipline, and therefore her own discipline.

To the left were ropes, chains, cuffs for her wrists and ankles, collars, an assortment of links and various things made of leather and metal the purpose of which was not immediately obvious. Nearest the door on the right, and most convenient to hand for somebody coming into the room, was a long dark cane not unlike the one she had made herself. More canes followed, of different designs, then leather straps, paddles of leather or wood, crops, various whips, and other things she had no name for but which were all too clearly designed for use on a human bottom, her bottom. He was looking at her, his face full of wicked amusement and she realised she had been staring open mouthed at the array of instruments. She managed to find her voice.

'Is this a dungeon?'

'Technically, I suppose it is, given that the term derives from an old French word for a Lord's tower. I prefer to call it my "necessary room", which suits my philosophy and makes it easier to mention in public.'

'I can imagine. Have you … have you had many girls in here?'

'No. As you can see, it's all very new. I've only just finished the conversion, although some of the equipment has seen some use, this whipping bench for instance.'

He had moved to the padded bench, smiling thoughtfully as if in memory of having some helpless girl strapped into place across it. Expecting a sharp order to get into some lewd position for her punishment, Laura hung her head and folded her hands in her lap, doing her best to seem contrite and accepting despite the frantic beating of her heart and the sick fear in her stomach. At last he spoke.

'But I'm being a dreadful host. I haven't even offered you a drink. Coffee, fruit juice perhaps, or a cold beer?'

Laura looked up.

'I thought you were going to punish me.'

'I am. In fact, I shall tell you exactly what will happen to you. I am going to introduce you to the cane, as you seem to find the idea of having it used on you so appealing. You will be given six of the best, the traditional punishment for unruly girls, on your bare bottom, of course, but not just yet. A little wait is always good for a girl's sense of apprehension.'

Laura was forced to swallow the word that rose unbidden into her throat and to substitute a response less likely to get her punishment increased.

'Yes, Mr Latchley.'

'Good girl, you learn fast. Now, pop off your knickers, just to keep you in mind of what is going to happen to you.'

'I don't think I'm likely to forget.'

'Nevertheless, knickers off.'

Laura had not intended to disobey, or even hesitate, and was already reaching up under her dress. He watched, cool and amused rather than lustful, as she levered her French knickers down and off, folding them neatly and placing them on the whipping bench. Only then did he speak.

'Now show me.'

Without hesitation Laura lifted her dress to her waist, displaying her bare bottom and sex for his inspection. She made a slow turn, and with her back to him pushed her hips out to fully show off her rear view before once more facing him, her dress still held up as she waited for the order to be allowed to cover herself. He gave an approving nod.

'Very good. One might even think you were already partially trained?'

It was clearly a question, but she hesitated before remembering her promise to be honest with him.

'There was a boy, once, Tommy Fuller. He taught me what men like to see. Some of my college friends used to strip too, to earn money for their courses. I did it once.'

'I see. Some argue that sexual display comes naturally to a woman, but I think it's important to distinguish between instinct, such as pushing out your bottom as if in invitation for entry, and what needs to be learnt, such as painting your lips red to mimic your cunt. With you I suspect there is more of the instinctive than the learnt, and that your friends really only helped you to express what you knew anyway. You may drop your dress.'

'But I thought ...'

'I said your punishment would come later. Now drop your dress, or I might be tempted to make you pin it up at the back and leave it that way until you are ready.'

Laura obeyed, covering herself in mixed relief and regret. Any other man she knew would have had her then and there, she was sure, first the cane and then his cock inside her, but not the Devil. With him she had to wait. He spoke again.

'How about that drink then? Don't worry, we'll come back later for your caning. I thought, perhaps, tea on the lawn, although it is a little breezy, so I'd better get you done first. Shall we say four-thirty?'

'That's four hours! I've already waited five days. Please, Charles, I need to get it over with!'

He merely chuckled.

15

They ate lunch in the dining room, Charles explaining the best way to make salad dressing and enlarging on the history of the building while Laura fiddled with her cutlery and thought of thin dark canes and sore bottom cheeks. He had also opened a bottle of white wine, which they finished in the study, a large book-lined room occupying the entire lower part of the old tower and which carried the same air of masculine well being as his living room and bedroom, but yet more pronounced. The big old-fashioned armchairs upholstered in studded green leather suited him to perfection, as did the dark wood of the other furniture and the ranks of books, as if it were all an extension of his personality.

With the wine and the overwhelming sense of his presence, Laura found it very easy to picture herself not just as his lover but as his plaything, even what he had implied she would become, his slave. She was also very aware of the time, with the constant tick of a grandfather clock between two high book-cases cutting down the time to her punishment. He seemed indifferent, a trifle sleepy even, talking casually and sipping his wine, but always watching her. It had been over an hour since he'd even mentioned what to her was the essence of their relationship before he suddenly changed the conversation.

'Going back to what I was saying about the word dungeon, it really is best not to use it. I fear that the popular press and the film industry link the word, and indeed any lifestyle that involves physical discipline for women, with the worst sort of people. You know the sort of things, maniacs in hockey masks with chainsaws, cannibals who dress in human skin, although I confess that I may be getting my references mixed up. Of course, nothing could be further from the truth, but I think it best to keep the fact that you are under my discipline private. A little exhibitionism is a different matter.'

'You did send me into Cambridge to buy a cane.'

'You didn't tell anybody what it was for, did you?'

'No, but I was sure they'd guess.'

'Unlikely, unless they themselves are corporal punishment enthusiasts, but what I was going to say was that it is important for you to be able to trust me. After all, we've only just met, and we will be alone a lot of the time.'

'I trust you, and I'm good at spotting creeps and nutters.'

'Your instincts are correct, although there are many who would classify me as a nutter simply because I like to give women physical punishment, and you as well, for enjoying being on the receiving end. The important thing is that your family, your friends, your work colleagues should know that you and I are in a relationship, but not the more intimate details.'

'That's fine. I didn't mean to keep it a secret.'

'Good. Then telephone somebody to let them know you're here; if you haven't done so already?'

Laura nodded, aware that she'd been foolish and once more grateful for his easy control. Taking her mobile from her bag, she began to punch out her parents' number, only to think better of it and ring Mrs Phipp's instead, to ask after Smudge and say where she was. Charles waited until Laura was finished.

'Smudge?'

'My dog. He's a mastiff, sort of. He came from a pedigree breeder but I think his mum must have escaped for a bit.'

'I would have guessed that you preferred cats.'

'That will be the first time you've been wrong about me, but why?'

'Dogs are loyal, devoted to a single master, characteristics you show rather than appreciate in others. Nobody ever really owns a cat, and so those who prefer to be owned themselves usually prefer cats.'

Laura shrugged, still unsure about the issue of being owned. To be faithful was one thing, to be punished something she craved, but to see herself as the property of a man still seemed a step too far. Charles didn't labour the point, leaving Laura to her still rising frustration. Any other man, she was sure, would already have tried to get her into bed, and after all, just because she had to wait for her beating didn't mean they couldn't enjoy themselves first. He didn't seem inclined to make a move, so after a few minutes more, with the last of the wine bottle finished, she took matters into her own hands.

'Aren't you going to take me upstairs?'

'It's only just gone two.'

'I mean, to the bedroom.'

He shrugged and put down his empty glass. Rising from his seat, he extended a hand to Laura. She took it, allowing herself to be led from the room and up the stairs. On the landing the view through the open door into the 'necessary room' gave her a sharp, sweet pang, but he took her the other way. His bed was a large solid affair, framed in plain polished wood much like the whipping bench and spread with a cream-coloured coverlet. There was a faint masculine scent.

Charles pulled her towards him, kissing her forehead, her cheek, her mouth, which came open to the pressure as he took her in his arms. He began to stroke her hair and the nape of her neck as they kissed, quickly bringing her desire to boiling point. Pushing a hand down, she tugged his zip low, burrowing within to free his cock and balls. Their kisses grew more urgent as she began to knead him and tug at his shaft, already desperate to get him erect and inside her.

He let her do as she pleased, yet stayed firmly in control, first easing her dress open and down then pushing her gently into a sitting position on the bed. Laura took the hint, pulling him in by his now half stiff cock to take it in her mouth, clumsy in her eagerness as she began to suck and squeeze at his balls. He took her by the hair, a gentle grip yet firm enough to let her know that she was being held in place while he stiffened in her mouth.

As she sucked she kicked her shoes off and unfastened her bra, freeing her breasts into her hands, to hold them and stroke her nipples hard, then to rub them against his now swollen cock as she lifted herself a little. Charles tightened his grip, pushing himself into her cleavage and rubbing harder until he was fully ready, his erection standing proud between her breasts, thick and long and pale.

Laura's thighs were open across his legs, her sex ready as she rubbed her breasts and face on his cock and balls, eager to get as much of him as she could until he chose the moment for her penetration. It soon came, as he pushed her shoulders down, laying her on the bed and lifting her legs to spread her open in front of him. She took his cock, rubbing it against her sex as his hands explored her thighs, stroking her flesh through her stockings and higher still, on the sensitive flesh at the tuck of her bottom cheeks and around her anus.

He touched, tickling the little hole and Laura felt herself tighten, giggling for just how open she was in front of him, with every intimate part of her body exposed to his eyes and to his erection. His cock was still in her hand as she rubbed it on her sex, knowing she could come if he let her be for a few moments more, but he took hold, guiding himself lower, and in, pushing himself deep with a single thrust. A moan of pleasure escaped Laura's throat as she filled and she surrendered, giving in completely to the glorious feeling of having his cock moving inside her.

Her hands moved to her breasts, kneading her own flesh and pulling at her nipples as her pleasure rose. He'd got her by her thighs, gripped hard to pull himself in, ever faster and more urgent. Her back began to arch and she was rubbing on him as he pushed inside her, completely abandoned to her pleasure and ready to come. The first contractions started and her hand went down, snatching at herself and gasping out her ecstasy as the thrusting motion inside her rose to a frenzied climax. She was coming, and so was he, a long moment of perfect bliss that she wished could last forever and faded only when he was spent and had pulled free.

They collapsed together on the bed, Laura quickly snuggling up to his chest, lost in a golden, happy daze. It had been brief, urgent, but a delightful culmination of her need for him, leaving her content just so long as she was cuddled into him. He held her, stroking her back and bottom, very gently, yet with a possessive intimacy that filled her with reassurance and a growing sense of love.

She had quickly lost all sense of time, while he seemed content simply to hold her, something none of the men she had been with before had done. After a while she went to the bathroom, returning to climb back onto his bed and once more snuggle close, relaxing in a state of bliss with the warm sunlight playing on her naked body, until at last a sudden, sharp slap to her bottom roused her from the edge of sleep. Laura purred as she snaked a hand to his cock, only to have another firm slap applied to her bottom.

'Oh no you don't, young lady. It's nearly half-past-four, time you were punished.'

Laura sat up, her stomach instantly full of butterflies and her throat tight. She had had no idea it was so late, but his bedside clock confirmed the truth. He spoke again as he put his cock away.

'Will this be your first time. Tell the truth.'

'Yes. I've been spanked, but never caned.'

'Then I'll warm you up, which I wouldn't normally do for a punishment.'

'Warm me up?'

'Like this.'

Laura squeaked in surprise and alarm as she was pulled face down on the bed. He leant over her, trapping her body, and began to spank, applying firm swats to her cheeks, which quickly had her kicking and wriggling in his grip, while the sudden transition from being held lovingly in his arms to being pinned down to have her bottom smacked was almost too much. It hurt too, setting her gasping and begging for mercy, but he took no notice, spanking her until at least her bottom had begun to warm enough to make her want to push it up in pleasure. He stopped immediately.

'That will do. Now, stockings off, please. I think I'll have you fully naked, as this is a formal punishment.'

She complied, snivelling a little as she rolled her stockings down and off, but keeping her feelings of fear and resentment to herself. It was what she had wanted, what she had agreed to, no more, no less, while she knew she should be grateful for having had her bottom warmed first, and that for her to be caned in the nude was entirely appropriate. He waited until she was ready, then once more took her by the hand, this time to lead her into the necessary room and across to the whipping bench. When he spoke his voice was calm, quiet and level.

'Do you accept my right to punish you, as I see fit?'

The catch in Laura's throat made her voice a hoarse whisper as she gave her answer.

'Yes.'

'I will give you six strokes of the cane, which will hurt. Do you want to be in straps?'

Laura hesitated, wondering if she had the courage to go through with her punishment if she wasn't restrained and deciding that she probably didn't. He waited, moving her folded knickers to the top of his cage before she made her choice.

'I think I'd better be, yes.'

'As you wish. Kneel on the bench.'

She obeyed, shaking badly as she climbed into position, with her knees on the lower of the padded surfaces and her body on the upper, which was short and sloped, leaving her bottom thrust high and open to his gaze, while her breasts hung down at the front. She braced herself, taking hold of the frame and looking back as he ducked down to put her in the black leather straps that hung from the device.

He worked methodically, calm and unhurried as he locked her ankle securely into place, the strap snug to her flesh and the chain allow her to kick only slightly. Just to have a single strap fastening her to the whipping bench brought her feelings of helpless exposure to a new height, and higher still as each of her limbs was fixed securely to the heavy wooden bench, leaving her completely unable to protect herself. Last came the belly strap, a wide, padded piece that held her midriff firmly against the upper part of the bench and kept her bottom up and spread. She could feel the cool air on her anus and sex, while her trembling had grown so bad she felt she was close to panic, but she was now held tight and knew that even if she struggled she would be unable to escape what she craved and dreaded. He spoke again, as matter-of-fact as ever.

'Do you want a gag? It is your choice.'

Laura nodded urgently, desperate to be given the full six strokes no matter how much they hurt, but sure that she'd be begging him to stop after just one, which would ruin the experience. He moved to the rack by the door, lifting a curious device, a red ball with a slim leather strap at each side, plainly designed to go in her mouth, only to put it back and select a short length of rope instead as he spoke.

'The ball gag would certainly shut you up, but as you are an old-fashioned girl I shall use an old-fashioned technique. Open wide.'

He had picked up her knickers as he came back, balling them in his fist. Laura realised what he was going to do too late, her protest coming as a muffled sob as her expensive French knickers were wadded firmly into her mouth. Her sense of humiliation, already almost as much as she could cope with, grew stronger still as he tied the piece of rope off behind her head to hold her knickers in place. She could taste herself, a sharp reminder of her own excitement, and she was sobbing as she hung her head in shame and contrition, ready for the cane.

Charles had walked back to the rack, and Laura watched in ever greater fear and consternation as he selected the dark crook handled cane, evidently a favourite. Her bottom tightened instinctively as he once more stepped close, and again as the thin cold rod was tapped to the meat of her cheeks. He lifted the cane, holding it high above his naked, vulnerable target, her stomach churning and her muscles twitching as she waited.

'One.'

The cane lashed down, landing full across Laura's bottom, a heavy blow immediately followed by a stinging pain, for too strong for her to control, her legs kicking in the straps and her hips wriggling in a frantic, futile effort at escape as she wondered how she could ever have been stupid enough to want to endure such agony. She tried to speak through her mouthful of silk and lace, desperate for him to stop or at least wait, but he already had the cane lifted a second time.

'Two.'

Laura's entire body jerked as the cane struck home for a second time, laying another line of fire across her bottom and sending her into a squirming, kicking frenzy.

'Three.'

Again the cane smacked down and she was sobbing through her gag and thrashing her ankles up and down in her straps.

'Four.'

Laura gave in completely, her body jerking without the slightest thought for anything save the pain of her punishment.

'Five.'

Another stroke, and even as her muscles locked in reaction she was thinking that there was only one more to go, and bracing herself.

'Six.'

The final stroke landed across Laura's bottom, leaving her treading her knees in a little dance of pain for several seconds before her reaction finally cut in: remorse for her behaviour, joy for her repentance and a vast sense of gratitude to the man who had beaten her. She was still shaking uncontrollably, and her bottom seemed to be on fire, but as he knelt down to pull the knot holding her knickers into her mouth free and tug the soggy bundle out she could only find three words.

'Please hold me.'

He kissed her and went to work on her straps, quickly freeing her into his arms. She clung on, shaking, overcome by a sense of catharsis stronger by far than what she had experienced after her spanking. He began to stroke her hair and whisper into her ear, telling her how brave she was and urging her to let her feelings out. Laura didn't need to be told, the tears streaming down her face, and as the pain of her welts began to fade to a dull heat her need began to flood back. She gave in immediately, sliding one hand back to touch the sensitive ridges of her welts and the other between her thighs to find her sex, without the slightest trace of shame for his presence or how open she was to him as she began to masturbate.

16

Laura's bottom was decorated with five perfectly parallel, evenly spaced red lines, with a sixth laid across them at a diagonal, a pattern Charles had described as a 'five-bar-gate' which was his personal trademark. As she inspected herself in the bathroom mirror while Charles made the tea, she was feeling happier than at any time she could remember, and also immensely proud of herself and of her striped bottom.

The caning itself had been an agonising ordeal, and she knew that she couldn't possibly have taken it without being both strapped down and gagged, but the after effects were a very different matter and the orgasm she had brought herself to while he held her had been among the very best, leaving her weak but deliriously happy. Being caned was horrible, but having been caned was wonderful.

She was walking with a deliberate sway to her hips as she made her way outside, still naked, and twirled to show off her bottom as she saw him. He had put out a pair of wrought iron chairs and a table covered with a white linen cloth and set for tea: china, silverware and a plate of biscuits and small yellow cakes. One of the chairs had a small cushion on it, which Charles indicated as she approached.

'You'll be needing that, I expect.'

Laura returned a grin and sat down, lowering her bottom carefully onto the cushion. Her bruises ached even when standing, and being seated made them more tender still, keeping her firmly in mind of what had been done to her as she reached for the pot.

'Shall I be mother?'

'Please do.'

'That was amazing, extraordinary. Thank you.'

'Do you feel better for it?'

'Yes, much better. I needed it, to punish me, but to get me off too if I'm honest. Now I feel as if I'm floating on air.'

'I warn you, it's addictive.'

'I don't care. I want more.'

'Once a week is the maximum recommended dose. We need to keep that pretty bottom in good condition, after all, and in-between times, you can be spanked.'

'Yes, please.'

Laura was smiling happily to herself as she completed the ritual of making the tea. Everything was perfect, sitting on her freshly caned bottom in the warm English sunlight in her lover's garden, casually naked but safe from prying eyes, sipping tea, the only sounds birdsong and the distant rumble of a tractor. Work was a distant annoyance, her life as she had imagined it in her fantasies, with Charles as Mark Frobisher or another of the strong masculine heroes she adored. She sighed as she settled back into her chair. Charles raised his cup in salute.

'I'm a lucky man. It's not easy to find a woman like you. Now, how about dinner at the Eel Net this evening. It's a little rustic, but the food's good.'

Laura walked swiftly through the twilight, guided by Charles' arm towards the lights of a thatched pub that looked as if it had grown into place rather than been built. She was naked under her dress, and still so pleased with herself that she kept wanting to show her bottom to passers-by, which in turn kept her smiling and trying to suppress her giggles. Charles was enjoying the state she was in, teasing her by threatening to make her lift her dress to display herself to the locals, but not really succeeding as the thought delighted her. Only as they reached the door did he place a warning finger to his lips.

'Not a word, remember. They all know me in here, but they do not know what I like to get up to, and I aim to keep it that way.'

'Ah, just a quick flash, please?'

'Behave.'

He patted her bottom to guide her through the door, into a low yellow lit space, warm and loud with conversation. She wrinkled her nose at the smell of beer, but it was mingled with frying onions and steak, making her suddenly hungry. Charles made for the bar, nodding right and left to other customers and twice introducing her to those he knew by name. Laura responded with shy smiles, a little unsure of herself and more aware than ever of the way her dress allowed the shape of her breasts to show. The male customers seem to appreciate her, casting glances to her chest, some frank, some furtive, but she felt none of the rancour she would have for uninvited attention at other times, secure in the knowledge of Charles' protection. He bought drinks and collected menus, taking both to a table in an alcove where they would be able to talk in reasonable privacy. Laura took a swallow of her wine.

'They would like to see me, wouldn't they?'

'I expect they would, and why not?'

'I'm yours, and yours alone now.'

'Are you?'

'Yes! I don't think I'll be ... be touching myself over other people again, not after the cane.'

'I'm sure you won't, but what if, let us say, they were holding a striptease competition here tonight and I wanted you to enter.'

'I'd do it, but it would be for you.'

'That's a good answer, Laura. As I mentioned earlier, while society frowns upon corporal punishment, the same is not true, or at least it is less true, for exhibitionism. If I were to spank you now, for instance, I'm sure that several of these lads would come to your defence, and Jack, our host, might even threaten to call the police. On the other hand, if I were to make you eat your dinner with your breasts bare he would take it as a joke, although he would no doubt ask you to cover up.'

'Do you want me to do it?'

'No, not at present, although I might ask you to do similar things at times. That is the second of the three Ps, the desire to prove your devotion to me. I take it you have that?'

'Absolutely. I'll do anything you ask ... within reason.'

'No, Laura. You must do anything I ask, abdicating your responsibility completely. You must trust me to decide what is reasonable.'

'What if you asked me to jump off a building?'

'That would not be reasonable.'

'OK, I think I understand, but I probably have a bit of a way to go yet. That's the third P?'

'Your desire to be my property.'

'Oh.'

'It is within you, Laura, although you may not fully realise it yet, and it may be a while before you are able to accept your own need. When you do, I shall have you sign an agreement binding you to me and put you in a collar.'

Doubtful, Laura quickly changed the subject.

'So, what sort of thing will you want me to do to prove myself?'

'We shall see. As I told you before, I won't ask anything that would put your livelihood at risk, which is part of being responsible. I'll email something to you on Monday, just to keep you on your toes, or maybe Tuesday.'

'And it's allowed to be exciting?'

'It's supposed to be exciting, but as with your discipline the pleasure may come later.'

Laura purred to the sudden thrill of fear and longing triggered by his words. If the experience was even a fraction as intense as being given the cane it would be enough to keep her warm all week. He treated her to his devilish grin for her reaction and turned to the menu.

'For now, let's eat. The steak is good, local and properly hung, which is so rare nowadays.'

'I'm worried that I'm going to put on weight, being with you.'

'I have ways of controlling a girl's weight, should it prove necessary.'

'I bet you do.'

'Jumping on the spot with a dog whip to encourage you if you slow down, for example.'

'Ouch! I think I'll have a salad.'

'No, no. Have the steak, and that's an order.'

By the end of the meal Laura was sat back in her chair, one hand resting gently on her swollen tummy, the other holding her still half-full glass of the delicious sweet wine he had ordered to go with her sticky toffee pudding. It looked as if she might well end up on the gymnastics and dog whip diet, but for the time being she could barely move. Charles seemed unaffected, dabbing a serviette to his lips before speaking.

'That was delicious. A coffee, perhaps, and then home.'

Laura didn't answer, content to follow his lead. He also paid without consulting her, something he seemed to take for granted, and once they had finished their coffee he offered his hand. She took it, allowing him to help her to her feet and guide her from the pub, with the landlord and several of the customers wishing them goodnight in tones Laura was sure held traces of both envy and smutty amusement.

Outside the night was cool and still, the road a ribbon of dark gunmetal between high, black hedges and trees silhouetted against a starry sky. Charles put his arm around her waist, steering her back the way they had come, to where a stile led to a field now silvered by moonlight.

'We'll take the field path. The moon's bright enough, and it's a much more pleasant walk.'

Laura bunched up her dress to cross the stile, her eyes still adapting to the dim light as she started cautiously along the footpath. Charles joined her, walking a little way before stopping to kiss her, then to speak.

'A little modification, maybe.'

He took hold of the front of her dress, tugging it down to spill out her bare breasts before adjusting each so that they sat, high and proud in a nest of cloth. The light was too dim to show the colour of her dress, but her breasts showed clearly, pale and bare, blatantly exposed if anybody happened to come the other way.

'What if somebody sees?'

'That's not likely, but it is part of the fun.'

'Shall I go naked? I'd like that, if you want me to.'

'Best not. A bare bottom is one thing, a caned bottom quite another.'

He took her hand once more, leading her back towards the cottage, very conscious of her naked chest and the playful thrill of being exposed. It was better even than in the train, because now she had nothing to cover herself at all, her bare breasts on show to anybody who happened to pass, while she had no say in who saw or what they thought of her. She imagined the landlord, Jack, coming after them, perhaps because one of them had left something behind, and catching her, maybe demanding a feel, only to stop herself as she remembered why she had been caned that afternoon.

At the far side of the field a second stile led them to a grove of poplar where a narrow wooden bridge crossed a dyke. The trees hid the moon, creating a confusing pattern of shadows, so that Laura never realised that somebody was coming the other way until the wet sound of a footstep alerted her, immediately followed by a greeting and a muffled snigger as the stranger was given a full view of her bare white breasts. She paused in shock, meaning to cover herself, but Charles' hand tightened on hers.

'Oh no you don't. You stay that way until we're home.'

'OK ... I mean, yes Mr Latchley.'

'That's better. Now come to me, and put your hands on your head.'

Laura cast a nervous glance in the direction they had just come, but the stranger was no more than a black mark some way across the field and she knew she was hidden by the trees. Putting her back to the hand rail of the bridge, she placed her hands on her head as Charles came close, to kiss her cheek, her mouth, and her breasts as he took one in each hand. Laura closed her eyes, shivering as her nipples were brought to erection between his lips and teeth, her feelings rising quickly until she was half hoping he'd bend her over the rail and take her from behind.

'Make love to me.'

'No.'

He had pulled away, his hands still cupping her breasts, one thumb rubbing over each nipple.

'Please.'

'No. Now turn around.'

Laura obeyed, unsure what was about to be done to her as she turned to face the railing, which pressed to her hips as she was pushed forwards. Her skirt was quickly turned up and her upper body bent over the rail, her breasts lolling forwards under her chest and her bare bottom thrust out towards him.

'Stay still.'

He moved away. Laura stayed as she was, wondering for a brief, awful moment if he might not have left her exposed for the next passer-by, only for him to return within seconds.

'All clear. Right, stay as you are.'

She heard the faint rasp of his zip and something warm pressed into the crease of her bottom, his cock. He began to explore her, tugging at himself as he stroked and slapped her bottom.

'I thought you said you weren't going to make love to me?'

'I'm not. You must understand the distinction between making love, which we do together, and a fucking, which I do to you. I'm going to fuck you.'

Laura gave a powerful shudder. What he had said might have been drawn straight from one of her favourite fantasies. She pushed her bottom out, her hands still on her head as he began to rub himself between her cheeks and fondle her breasts, amusing himself with her body as he pleased. Her cane welts ached where he was pressed to them, bringing her punishment back to mind as his cock grew slowly stiffer, her fear and the terrible pain, then the bliss that had followed.

'In we go.'

He had moved his cock lower, still holding one breast as he guided himself deep into her until she felt his balls press to her sex. Taking her by the hips, he began to thrust deep, making her gasp and moan as she thought of what he'd done and what he'd said. She'd been beaten and now she was being fucked, punished and then used, as if she were his property, to do with as he pleased. That was what he wanted, to make her his completely, not in the way most people meant it, as a promise of faith, but completely, his plaything, his slave.

Laura cried out at the thought, now fighting to keep her hands on her head as he pushed into her ever faster and harder. She needed to touch her breasts, her sex if she could, but he had told her to put her hands on her head and there they would stay until he gave his permission to move. Not that he would. He was having far too much fun with her, which made her frustration and denial all the more satisfying as she was brought right up to the edge of orgasm before he came deep inside her. Even then she stayed still, holding herself in place until he was fully finished with her, and after, in the same lewd, available pose as he tidied himself up. At last she could bear it no more.

'Can I ... please can I play with myself?'

He gave a soft chuckle.

'You want to masturbate?'

'Please, yes.'

'Say it.'

Despite her arousal, Laura felt herself colour at his demand, but said it anyway.

'I want to masturbate.'

He slapped her bottom.

'Properly, Laura.'

'Please, Mr Latchley. I want to masturbate.'

'Hmm ... I'm not sure. You're very sensitive to words, aren't you?'

'Yes ... yes, Mr Latchley.'

'OK. Ask permission to rub your cunt.'

'Oh God. OK ... OK ... Please, Mr Latchley. I'd like to rub my cunt.'

Her words broke to a sob as she said it and he chuckled, a sound so wicked that she found it easy to imagine herself really being tormented by the devil.

'Again.'

'Please, Mr Latchley. I'd like to rub my cunt.'

'No. I'll do it for you.'

As he spoke he had taken hold of her, his hand between her legs. Laura gasped as two fingers slid inside her, and his thumb had begun to rub on her anus as he spoke again.

'Tell me what I'm doing, Laura.'

'Oh God ... Charles, please ... you ... you're fingering me. You've got your fingers in me. You've got your fingers in my cunt.'

'And?'

'And ... and ... I don't know. Yes I do. You're touching up my bottom hole, and ... and now you're rubbing me properly, rubbing my cunt, right on my clit, oh God, Charles, your thumb's up my bottom you dirty pig. You're rubbing me off ... rubbing my cunt off with your thumb up my bottom, you dirty pig, and I'm going to come!'

Laura screamed as her orgasm hit her, scaring the birds from the trees. Charles laughed once more.

17

Laura awoke with her head cradled into the crook of Charles' arm and her mind flooding with bittersweet memories of the night before. They had stayed up late, talking and sharing a bottle of wine before retiring to bed, where he had made love to her with the same affection of their first time the afternoon before and a great deal less haste.

He was still asleep, and Laura made no effort to rise, instead thinking of all the things she had experienced and learnt during their short time together. She had realised so many of her fantasies, and more importantly come to understand them and accept them as part of herself, while it was wonderful to be able to discuss things that had previously been shameful secrets with a man who understood. Never before had she felt so free and yet at the same time so much under a man's wing.

When she finally got up she didn't bother to put on the pyjamas she'd brought with her, but went naked to the bathroom. Her welts had faded a little, but some bruising had come up around the lines, slightly spoiling the elegance of the striping that marked her as his. She was still tender as well, something she'd found had made a pleasant addition to sex and served to keep her constantly in mind of her position as a woman subject to discipline from her lover.

Having washed, she went downstairs, intending to make coffee and bring it up to him in bed, only to find his kitchen so meticulous neat that she didn't dare disturb anything, while she was sure that any attempt she made to use the new and complicated looking coffee machine would only end in disaster. There was orange juice in the fridge and she poured herself a glass, which she took out onto the lawn, enjoying the warm morning sunshine on her bare skin. It was gone eleven, bringing her a trace of regret for the first time that weekend, for the knowledge that in a few hours she would have to go home.

She began to explore the garden, admiring the way Charles had designed it to ensure that the lawn was invisible from all sides and sheltered from the wind, yet able to catch enough sun to be warm and pleasant. He had obviously thought it out in advance, while the bushes were only just tall enough to serve their purpose, presumably having been planted soon after he first moved in. One puzzling feature was a dense shrubbery at the end, where two fields came together to create a sharp angle.

A path led in beneath an archway covered in climbing rose, to a cool, dim passage flecked with sunlight. Intrigued, Laura followed the path, to find a hidden space in which a tall wrought iron structure stood on a concrete plinth, something like an aviary although the size of the door and the heavy padlock holding it shut suggested that it was not intended for birds. She reached out a hand to touch the cool hard metal, sure that it was built as a cage and wondering how it would feel to be locked within.

His voice called from the house and she started back quickly, unsure whether she was supposed to be exploring the deeper recesses of his garden. He was in the kitchen, putting breakfast together, and his eyebrows rose a fraction as he saw her. Laura laughed.

'Sorry, I almost forgot I was naked. It seems so natural.'

'Go as you please. The garden is designed for seclusion.'

'So I see.'

'Did you find my oubliette?'

'The cage? Yes. What was that word?'

'Oubliette, literally a "little forgotten place", although in this case a little place of forgetting would be more accurate. It's a French word, meaning a cell, usually underground and with only a hatch in the ceiling through which a prisoner would be lowered and then put out of mind. All very unpleasant, but it amuses me to borrow the names of real horrors, while my purposes are very different.'

'Would you lock me in there as a punishment?'

'No. I would lock you in to allow you to forget yourself.'

'I don't understand.'

'You would, after a few hours, although it's not easy to explain unless you try it. It's also the perfect place for a girl to meditate on her behaviour, or to keep you if I need you convenient to hand. Not today though. I want you with me.'

'I would like to try, but you're right. Time seems rather precious.'

'So it is, but I hope we'll have plenty together.'

'As much as I can spare. I need to be back by eight, or nine at the latest.'

'Then I suggest breakfast and a walk along the cut. We'll see what the afternoon brings. How do you like your eggs?'

'Why do I love what I ought to hate?'

Laura had asked the question as they reached the top of the long straight bank. Ahead of them the placid water of the New Cut stretched into the distance, a set of parallel lines vanishing to haze and with not another living soul to be seen. They had walked for miles, talking of this and that, occasionally stopping to kiss or for him to lift Laura's dress to her neck, exposing her, or for her to briefly take his cock in her hand or mouth, as if they were teenagers and exploring each other for the first time. Twice they had come close to being caught, helping Laura's mood of mischievous abandon, but as they approached the Cut their conversation had grown more serious. Charles didn't answer, but began to walk along the arrow straight path as Laura carried on.

'Because it shouldn't make sense, should it? I don't like pain, but I like to be spanked, and as for the cane, I couldn't believe how much it hurt, but afterwards, that was lovely ... a really beautiful experience.'

He treated her to a smile before replying.

'The scientific answer is that the pain makes your body produce chemicals called endorphins, which cause feelings of well being, even exhilaration. The exhilaration is sexual because it's your bottom being smacked, which brings the blood to your genitals and stimulates the nerves that supply the area. I suppose the smacking sensation may also be like the way a man's hips push against your buttocks when you are entered from behind, which would of course have been the normal position for sex for millions of years before we started to do it lying down.'

'Yes, but why me? Spank most girls and you'll end up with a knee in your groin, or in court.'

'Very possibly both. You're right, of course, it's mostly in the head, but the way I see it is that you are more in touch with your primitive sexuality than most women. They have allowed social constraints to overcome their natural desires. You haven't.'

'True enough. So you're saying all women should like a good spanking?'

'I'm saying all women are physically capable of enjoying a spanking. Whether they would be able to accept it mentally is a very different matter.'

'And the cane?'

'The cane is far more painful, as you found out yesterday. The principle is the same, but very few women could get past the initial pain.'

'I couldn't have done, not without being in the straps, and gagged.'

'There we are then. Most women, if not all, enjoy their bottoms patted as part of foreplay. Spanking takes that a little further, and the cane further still, but you each have your limits.'

'Fair enough, I suppose, but what about my sense of embarrassment? I mean, I ought to hate having my knickers pulled down to expose me for punishment, shouldn't I, and it is deeply embarrassing, but I love it?'

'That's rather trickier to answer. Exposure is all to do with social conditioning. It's natural for women to enjoy sexual display, which is all part of the urge to reproduce, but as we normally wear clothes nudity itself becomes sexual display. Then we're taught it's wrong by various idiotic institutions, and so it becomes embarrassing, even humiliating. Why you find that embarrassment exciting I can only guess. Perhaps if being naked is embarrassing then growing aroused when embarrassed gives you a better chance of reproducing?'

'Why?'

'Well, not to put too fine a point on it, the girls who get embarrassed and turned on get fucked, the ones who get embarrassed but don't get turned on don't get fucked. No fucking, no babies. But that is just a guess.'

'It makes sense, I suppose. So how about being helpless?'

'Perhaps a man who can hold you down is likely to be a better protector and provider than one who can't?'

'So it's all in my genes?'

'I suspect so, although no doubt your environment has some

effect. You were saying that you didn't want to be spanked before reading about it in a novel?'

'Pretty much so. It still seems unacceptable, but now I realise it was what I needed all along, or at least, part of what I needed. I always liked my men to be in control.'

'You've come a long way, and much faster than most.'

'I'm like that, impulsive. But what about you, have you always liked to be in charge, and when did you find out that you got off on spanking girls?'

'I've liked to be in control for as long as I can remember, and I suppose my desire to keep my partners disciplined is part of that. As to getting off on it, show me the man who doesn't get turned on by having a wriggling, bare-bottomed girl over his lap.'

'Most men wouldn't dream of spanking their girlfriends!'

'More fool them, but I didn't say anything about spanking, just enjoying a girl's bare bottom. But the power is intensely erotic as well. Just as you enjoy feeling helpless, so I enjoy having you helpless, whether I'm holding you down, if you're tied up, or simply because you're too excited to resist, like last night.'

'That was nice.'

'Yes it was. I thought you might appreciate being made to use crude language.'

'I never do, but it really got to me.'

'Exactly. Just as with exposure, so with crude language. You find it exciting to break your social conditioning. There are other ways of doing that too.'

'Such as?'

'You'll learn.'

'You seem to know so much. I like that, but it makes me feel a bit small.'

'I'm experienced, it's true, but if I'm to be your mentor that can only be a good thing.'

'That's true. How many girls have you trained, if you don't mind me asking?'

'From scratch? Just two, but I've helped many more along the way, and learnt for myself in the process.'

'How do you get to meet the right girls?'

'I've come to recognise the symptoms, as I did with you, but there are internet sites, and clubs, mainly in London but there's one in Peterborough.'

'Will you take me?'

'Once you are collared, yes. Meanwhile, there's something that needs attention.'

'What's that?'

Charles didn't bother to reply, but took her by the hand. They had reached a sluice, now closed so that the concrete channel was dry. Laura realised his intention immediately and allowed herself to be helped down out of sight. Nobody had been visible on the bank, leaving them safe for at least several minutes and probably a great deal longer. She made no protest as he peeled her dress up and off to leave her in nothing but her shoes, nor when he turned her to face the sluice gate.

'Take hold of the frame and stick out your bottom.'

Laura obeyed, setting her feet a little apart and arching her back to give him the best possible view from behind her. He gave a pleased nod, then planted a hard smack on her bottom.

'Ow! I thought you said I'd only get spanked when I deserved it?'

'No, you only get punished when you deserve it, but do you really think that calling me a dirty pig is acceptable?'

'You stuck your thumb up my bottom!'

'That's no excuse. Stay as you are.'

'Yes, Mr Latchley.'

Laura hung her head, her hands gripped tight to the iron

163

frame as her bottom was firmly and methodically smacked, making her already bruised flesh ache and sting. After just twenty slaps he stopped, ordering her to her knees, and fed his cock into her mouth. Laura sucked willingly, her eyes closed in bliss and her hand already between her thighs, revelling in the warmth of her bottom and doing her best to ignore the slight chill in the wind that signalled the approach of evening and the end of her time with her lover.

18

When she woke on the Monday morning, Laura's first thought was that she would be visiting Charles again the following weekend. Her second thought was that she would be seeing him again within a couple of hours, which produced a sharp thrill. She bounced out of bed and began her morning routine with an energy she hadn't felt for years. The shower seemed more refreshing, her coffee delivered a better kick, while her enthusiasm infected Smudge so strongly that he was behaving like a puppy.

She had been forbidden to wear knickers until further notice, an instruction that kept her obligation to obey Charles firmly in her mind as she dressed and as she walked to the station. He now came first, before work and before her home life, her feelings for him so strong that she realised she had never really understood what love meant before, while all the unpleasant aspects of her life she had previously struggled so hard to put from her mind now seemed trivial.

The train was full as usual, but she found herself smiling brightly at Hovis Boy and Mr Brown, and avoiding Darcy's eye just in case he got the wrong idea. When Charles got in she immediately embraced and kissed him, now keen to show that they were together and no longer obliged to pretend she didn't know him. He returned her affection, even patting her bottom and briefly moving her skirt over her bare skin to check that she was knickerless.

On reaching Cambridge she walked a little way with him

before a last kiss, then hurried to work. Even there she felt a new enthusiasm, applying herself to the presentation they were putting together for a Spanish firm with such efficiency that Mr Henderson complimented her on her work. At lunch she was able to give several of her friends a carefully edited version of her weekend, provoking both excitement and envy for her experiences. The inevitable result was that the entire office knew that she was in a new relationship by the end of the day, and she was able to snub Brian and Dave with a new assurance.

Tuesday was better still, as she'd managed to tidy her flat properly and was able to invite Charles back in the evening. Just to be with him felt wonderful; walking the dog, eating and talking together, then christening her cane with two middleweight strokes put across her bottom as she knelt on the bed. They made love twice that night, to leave her with a warm glow in the morning, but also a little tired. It had been after two o'clock before they'd got to sleep, while she had woken early to the feel of her hand being placed on his morning erection.

She was smiling sleepily as she sat down at her work station, and hoping that Mr Henderson wasn't going to demand anything that would require her full concentration. He didn't, instead telling her that he would be entertaining the head of purchasing from Barrington Barnes to lunch and leaving her in charge of the office.

The day passed as lazily as she had hoped, with only one curious incident. An email came through to confirm an order, which she was obliged to discuss with Mr Bannerjee. She put her chin up as she entered accounts, as usual, intent on conveying her utter contempt for Brian and Dave's remarks. This time they had placed a litter bin in the centre of the aisle, forcing her to step over it, but Brian paid no attention to her whatsoever, apparently intent on his computer screen, while

Dave let out a muted but distinctly dirty snigger. It was the same when she came back, only this time she allowed herself the luxury of calling them a pair of juvenile cretins as she stepped over the bin. Both of them sniggered.

Their behaviour was still preying on her mind as she walked to the station, and she was pleased to see Charles already there, with his briefcase on her favourite window seat in order to reserve it for her. He listened sympathetically as she explained what had happened, finishing with an appeal to his understanding of human nature.

'You always seem to be able to read my mind, so what do you think?'

Charles gave a thoughtful frown before replying, his voice low to avoid any risk of being overheard.

'I think they are a couple of dirty little urchins, and that you would do best to ignore them.'

'I've been ignoring them for years. It only makes them worse, particularly Brian. I've never been nasty to him. Even when he tried to chat me up at my first Christmas party I let him down gently. He seems to resent my existence.'

'There we are then. You rejected him and instead of accepting that the two of you are incompatible he grew resentful. Typical behaviour of the beta male.'

'Beta male? More like zeta male.'

'The last letter of the Greek alphabet is omega.'

'Omega male then, but my version sounds better.'

'More rhythmic, certainly. Tell me something, Laura. How would you feel about one or both of these men seeing you naked, or catching some intimate glimpse of your body perhaps?'

'I'd feel sick, and angry.'

'And yet you enjoyed the moment when a complete stranger caught you bare chested at the weekend?'

'That was different. They're creeps. No, men never seem to understand that. It's ... it's hard to explain. I like to feel attractive to men, but they've put themselves outside the box.'

'Because they are unattractive to you?'

'No, it's not like that. The guy who passed us the other night might have looked like Quasimodo, but it was still exciting. If he'd been Brian I'd have wanted to curl up in a ball.'

'I see. So is it that you don't see them as men, in the sense of your sexual opposite, that they've betrayed their role as men.'

'Yes, I suppose so. Something like that.'

'I think I understand, in which case I really do urge that you ignore them, for your own peace of mind.'

'I can't! You might be able to do that, because you're so in control. I want to know what's going on. You know something, don't you?'

Charles drew a sigh.

'No, but I suspect something. What was in the bin?'

'I don't know, rubbish. Why would I look in a litter bin?'

'Exactly. You wouldn't think of inspecting the contents of a litter bin, ever, which makes it the perfect hiding place.'

'What for?'

'A camera.'

It took Laura a fraction of a second for what he was saying to sink in before she spoke, aloud.

'But I've got no knickers on!'

Her face had begun to colour even as Darcy, the Grey Man, Mr Brown, Miss Scarlett, Hovis Boy and several others turned to look at her.

Charles had insisted that he was only guessing, but Laura was convinced that he was right. Not only did his theory fit the facts to perfection, but it was all too easy to imagine Brian and

Dave planting a camera to peer up girls' skirts. Her first thought, at least once she had got over the first agonising embarrassment of revealing that she had no knickers on to an entire carriage of commuters, was to report them for sexual harassment. Unfortunately she had no proof, as they were far too sneaky to leave any incriminating evidence around.

Yet the thought of them gloating over pictures of her naked bottom and sex was enough to make her grind her teeth in anger, and made worse by an unpleasant certainty that merely looking would not be enough. Once they were alone they would be pulling their dirty little cocks over her body, and no doubt imagining themselves taking out their lust on her. Something had to be done.

Charles had suggested that she attempt to rise above it, but had refused to make it an order, which she would have tried to obey. As it was she found herself scheming from the moment he got out at Ely. Somehow it had to be possible to catch them red handed, or to find the picture and take it to Mrs Jeffries, the head of personnel. If they tried the same trick again it would be easy, a simple matter of picking up the litter bin and showing the camera to the rest of the accounts department. Otherwise it would be more difficult.

The following day she put a pair of knickers in her bag and put them on when she arrived at EAS, just in case. It was easy to contrive an excuse to visit accounts, but while Brian gave her a look that sent the blood rushing to her face, the litter bin was where it belonged under his desk. Frustrated and embarrassed, she returned to her office, now haunted by the look in his eyes, not of mischief and lust as usual, but of a dirty, squalid longing, while Dave's snigger had seem disturbingly meaningful. Evidently they'd seen what they wanted, and would not be caught out so easily.

Laura returned to her scheming. Brian would be the ringleader, she was sure, and the one to keep the picture hidden, because both she and Charles had been sure it would not be destroyed. The camera would have to be quite advanced if it could be operated remotely and was almost certainly digital. That meant that the image would be stored electronically on at least one device, but probably not the network at EAS. She had also seen Brian using a laptop in the canteen, and there had to be a good chance that the image was stored on that. It was tempting to accuse him and demand to inspect the laptop, but if the image wasn't there she would just look ridiculous. First she had to make sure it was there.

She considered setting off the fire alarms and stealing the laptop before going out to the assembly point, but had to dismiss the scheme as impractical, not least because it was certain to get her sacked. When she spoke to Charles he agreed and once again urged her to rise above it, but by that evening she had thought out a better method of getting at his laptop with minimal risk to herself.

On the Friday morning she used the computer in the copying room to send out an anonymous email to Brian and others, claiming that one of the girls working as temps had been persuaded to streak, running across the yard at lunchtime in knickers and bra. A dozen things might have gone wrong, but none did. By lunchtime the accounts department was deserted, and as Laura had hoped, Brian's laptop was in his desk.

She turned it on, only to find herself confronted with a demand for a password. The hint was 'Leggy Laura doesn't wear', which left a sick feeling in her tummy despite her instant triumph. Her fingers were shaking so badly she could barely hit the keys as she typed in what she was sure would be the password – 'knickers'. It was rejected.

A single, nervous glance to the door and she tried again – 'underwear'. Again it was rejected. She swore, stabbing frantically at the keyboard as she tried to think what word Brian would use for women's underwear – 'knicks', 'undies', 'briefs', 'panties', ...

The screen changed, an explosion of colours clearing gradually to leave a picture of some powerful sports car with a silicone-assisted blonde in a bikini draped across the bonnet. She began to search his picture folders, only to discover that they contained several thousand pornographic images which would take hours to search through. Now close to panic, she called up a search, typing the single word 'Laura' into the box and biting her lip and the computer set to work.

It took just moments, an item coming up almost immediately, listed as a JPG with the name 'Leggy Laura upskirt'. She clicked on it, now sick to the stomach but also triumphant as the picture appeared, of a view clear up her office skirt, showing her stocking covered legs and bare flesh beyond, her thighs, the tuck of her bottom, and her sex. Every intimate pink fold had been captured in appalling detail, and to make it worse she was plainly wet, no doubt from memories of her weekend.

'The dirty little bastard! Right.'

She stood up, determined to take the laptop straight to Mrs Jeffries, only to hesitate. It was not the sort of picture she was keen to show around, let alone to the prim, fussy head of personnel. Worst still, Brian might simply deny that the picture was of her, as her plain grey-wool office skirt, stockings and suspender belt proved nothing, and nor did the small area of plain white ceiling or the fuzzy arc of the litter bin edge. The only way she could prove beyond doubt that the picture was of her would be to lift her skirt, take down her knickers and allow Mrs Jeffries to compare her vulva with the picture. It didn't bear thinking about, and while Brian would be booted out of the office before Laura was inspected he would know what was happening. Even if he and Dave got the sack the story would be around the office in minutes, an unbearable humiliation, and not the nice sort.

Laura cursed, hesitating as she weighed her need for justice and revenge against the awful cost, before deciding that Charles was right. She would delete the picture but do nothing, or better still, format the hard drive. Her mouth was set in a hard line as she called up the commands she needed, setting the laptop to destroy its own software, Brian's vast collection of smut, the appalling picture and any others he might have taken, along with copies.

The laptop was still running as she returned it to his drawer, but she knew it could only be so long before somebody came back, even if Brian himself remained in the canteen waiting to watch a streak that would never happen. He was sure to guess anyway, but would be no more able to do anything about it than she had been about him. That felt good, but not good enough, and as she walked back to her office she was conscious of a growing sense of disappointment. He had spied on her, intruding in the most obnoxious manner conceivable, and to all intents and purposes he was going to get away with it.

She tried to swallow her feelings, wishing she was as strong and self-assured as Charles, but it wouldn't work. The more she tried the more aggrieved she felt, and only the need to work kept her from storming back to accounts and accusing Brian to his face. It had been bad enough before, when she merely suspected, but far worse to actually see the picture of her most intimate parts displayed in a detail more appropriate to her gynaecologist than a lover and to know that Brian and Dave had been gloating over her, probably masturbating over her. At length Mr Henderson's calm, authoritative voice broke through her angry thoughts.

'Are you all right, Laura?'

'Just a slight headache, sir. I think I need some fresh air.'

'Have a few minutes, by all means, but would you mind taking these instructions over to Mr Gallagher in production first?'

'Certainly, Mr Henderson.'

Laura took the file he was holding out, grateful for the distraction but not too happy about having to go the full length of the walkway above the shop floor to reach Mr Gallagher's office. That meant running the gauntlet of the workers beneath, but as she reached the door leading onto the walkway she saw that it was worse than she'd expected. Brian himself was on the shop floor, talking to two men she didn't recognise. They were a fraction to one side, in a perfect position to see up her skirt. She hesitated, thinking of waiting until he'd gone, but the three of them were talking and might not notice her at all.

She hurried forward, walking as fast as she could, although the metallic click of her heels on the walkway seemed loud even above the throb and hum of machinery. One of the store-room doors was open, forcing her to stop out to the edge of the walkway just as she reached the point above Brian. She held her breath, hurrying on, only for his voice ring out from beneath her, thick with mockery.

'There's a view and half, eh lads, I can see right up to heaven.'

One of the workers laughed, the other wolf-whistled as Laura hurried past, her face now scarlet. She had to talk to Mr Gallagher for several minutes in order to explain exactly what the clients wanted, and was praying Brian had moved on as she left. He hadn't, but had been joined by Dave and another worker, all of them smirking openly. She looked out at the long perforated steel walkway to the safety of the door at the far end and began to walk, her thighs close together, taking tiny fast steps, but as she drew close the men began to chant.

'Leg show! Leg show! Leg show!'

Laura tried to walk faster still, her chin lifted, but her defiance only served to encourage them.

'Nice pins, love.'

'Come on, give us a bit of a show. It's only your legs.'

'I don't want to see leg. I want to see cunt.'

Laura stopped, her face burning, her anger pushing up past the point at which she could hold herself in. The storeroom door was still open, showing line upon line of five litre tanks of the metallic blue paint that was a trademark for the company switchgear, guaranteed proof against all weather for ten years. She was on automatic as she went in, selected a tank, levered the lid open with her door key and returned to the walkway, leaning over the edge.

'Hey, boys, here's something for you to remember me by.'

Brian looked up. Dave looked up. The three workmen looked up. Laura tipped the can, pouring out the full contents onto their heads.

19

The sight of Brian and Dave with their heads shaved and their skin still showing a subtle azure tint almost compensated for being called up in front of the disciplinary committee. Laura even managed to daydream for a little as they talked at her, imagining the men being sent out of the room and Mrs Jeffries and the other two women on the committee awarding her six strokes of the cane on the bare bottom for what she'd done. Indeed, Mrs Jeffries looked quite capable of doing it, but her sympathies lay entirely with Laura.

It wasn't even necessary to admit to the photograph incident, as she had more than a dozen witnesses to Brian's behaviour over a period of four years, which Mrs Jeffries considered more than enough provocation for Laura's act of vengeance. After nearly an hour Brian and the other men were given the option of withdrawing their complaint or facing a counter complaint of sexual harassment, terms both they and Laura accepted. Instead of the sack, which Laura had expected, she was given a formal warning.

She was still less than happy as she left the boardroom, where the hearing had taken place. It was all very well being the toast of the entire female staff of EAS, and not a few of the males, but Brian had a reputation for being vindictive and was not likely to accept what had happened as fair. They were bound to meet, which would be unpleasant even if he kept his comments to himself in the future, and she was extremely glad to leave when five o'clock came around. Charles was already on the train, and she found herself smiling despite her ill feelings, and pleased to be able to talk to somebody openly.

'I'm afraid I've been a very naughty girl.'

'You have a confession?'

'Yes. I poured five litres of paint over somebody's head, Brian, who I was telling you about the other day.'

'I was right then?'

'You were right. He'd hidden the camera, exactly the way you said, and he'd put the image on his laptop. I wiped the hard drive, but I didn't know if he had a copy and he'd seen anyway, which is what matters. Then he and some other men were teasing me, and there was the paint pot, and well . . .'

'You poured it over them?'

'Yes, from a walkway about ten feet over their heads. You should have seen it!'

Charles laughed, giving Laura a warm feeling. She laid her head on his shoulder, indifferent to the people around them. He began to stroke her hair, now silent, letting Laura relax and allow her cares to begin to fade. At Ely he stayed on the train and Laura knew that they would be spending the night together without the need for discussion or an invitation.

At King's Lynn he adapted himself to her evening routine, joining her as she walked Smudge down the river bank and back through the fields, then cooking a delicious pasta from ingredients picked up in her corner shop. By the time they had finished and were sharing the last of a bottle of red wine on her sofa, her feelings had mellowed sufficiently to allow her to enjoy the thought of accepting the consequences of her behaviour.

'I suppose I deserve to be punished for what I did to Brian?'

Charles looked surprised.

'Absolutely not. I consider your reaction fully justified and, besides, the situation was nothing to do with me.'

'Oh. I thought that you'd keep an eye on me in general, if you see what I mean?'

'I do, and if that's how you want it to be, then I'm happy to take on the responsibility.'

'Yes. I'd like that.'

'Very well. In a relationship like ours, it is important to have formal boundaries, which both of us agree on, in writing.'

'That sounds ... OK.'

'It is essential, especially if you wish to commit to me completely.'

'I do.'

'Do you?'

'Um ... OK, I'm not sure about this property thing. It sounds so one-sided, but it feels right.'

'You need a little time, I suspect, and perhaps to learn a little more.'

'Perhaps. You treat me so well though, giving me cuddles when I need it ...'

'Spanking you when you need it?'

'Yes, that too. Just to hear you say that gives me butterflies. If I were to be your property, would it be the same?'

'Naturally. If anything, more so. I would cherish you, as a man should cherish his partner. The ideal relationship, for me, and I suspect for you, is really not that dissimilar to the ideal of Christian marriage, in a historical sense that is. Nowadays we seem to have a very watered down version.'

'I thought you didn't believe in God?'

'I don't, which allows me to cherrypick the full range of established religions, selecting those things I approve of and discarding the mumbo-jumbo.'

'I wish I could be as certain as you.'

'You are young, but if you put your glass down I'll introduce you to something I expect you will enjoy.'

Laura purred, expecting to be taken into his arms, but instead found herself guided over his lap and into spanking position.

'I thought you weren't going to punish me!'

'I'm not. Spanking has other uses. In this case as therapy.'

Laura giggled.

'That just sounds like an excuse to get my knickers down!'

'Not at all, although naturally your knickers are coming down.'

'But what about a punishment being a punishment?'

'This is not a punishment, far from it, now be quiet, or it will be.'

Laura made a face, bracing herself for the pain of having her bottom smacked as he rolled up her skirt and adjusted her knickers to the top of her thighs. His hand settled on her bottom, lifted, and came down again with a gentle pat, just firm enough to make her skin tingle. The second was no different, but on her other cheek, the third lower, across the tuck of her bottom, and as he set up a rhythm her tension began to slip away.

'It's like being given a massage.'

'Perhaps, but far more fun for the masseur.'

She sighed, closing her eyes as he continued to smack her bottom. Just to be lying across his legs and exposed to him felt wonderful, open and free, while the now firm pats were slowly but surely bringing the blood to her cheeks and to her sex. Before long she'd begun to push her bottom up, letting her cheeks come apart and offering herself to his fingers. Charles merely adjusted her knickers a little, pulling them down far enough to let her sex show behind, and continued to spank.

'This is nice. You can do it a bit harder if you like.'

He changed his rhythm, using just the tips of his fingers to make her flesh sting. The same glorious, warm feeling she had experienced after her punishment spanking had begun to spread across her bottom, while she could feel his cock starting to press against her side, adding a sense of being wanted to her pleasure. She let her knees come apart, responding to her need, until her knickers were stretched taut between her thighs and her sex open to the air. Charles immediately slid a hand between her thighs, cupping her and squeezing gently as he continued to spank her with his other hand.

Laura moaned, pushing her bottom up to the pressure as he began to masturbate her. The smacks were harder now, making her cheeks bounce and the slaps echo around the room. She knew she'd be red behind, and how she would look, with her office skirt rolled up and her knickers pulled down, her hot bottom framed by her suspenders and stockings, the tight pink star between her cheeks on show to him, all of which was exactly as it should be as she came under his fingers in a long shuddering orgasm that left her feeling as relaxed as it did satisfied.

Laura awoke after a night of eager lovemaking to the feel of Charles getting out of her bed. She rolled over, bleary-eyed with sleep, as he tugged the bedclothes down, leaving her naked.

'Time to get up.'

Laura gave a weak moan. Charles threw the curtains open to let in bright spring sunlight, warm on Laura's bare skin even as she turned away to shield her eyes from the sudden glare. Charles opened the window and stretched in the fresh air.

'What a beautiful day. I don't think you'll be needing any clothes at all, Laura.'

She managed a sleepy response.

'I have to wear something, or I'll get arrested.'

'Shoes, yes, and I suppose you'd better have a coat so that we don't frighten the prudes. Otherwise, you're to go nude. Come on, lazy bones, out of bed.'

He had come back to the bed, and slapped her bottom before making for the bathroom. Laura pulled the covers back up, allowing her senses to come together as she listened to the hiss and splash of water. Smudge appeared, looking sorry for himself at having been shut out of the bedroom for the night and she tousled his head before finally throwing her legs over the side of the bed.

Work already seemed very distant, the incident with Brian and her formal warning no more than minor niggles, very much to the back of her mind in comparison with the excitement of the night before and the possibilities that lay ahead. Charles emerged from the bathroom and she took his place, enjoying her shower and making a thorough job of her morning routine before once more joining him in the bedroom. He was already dressed, and had put out a pair of lipstick red heels and the three-quarter length leather coat she had treated herself to on her last birthday, nothing else.

'You really meant it? You want me to go naked?'

'Under your coat, yes. Look on it as proving yourself, if you like, or simply as a little exhibitionism.'

'I can't take Smudge to Mrs Phipps like that! She'll guess, and what she knows, everybody knows.'

'Then I shall take Smudge to Mrs Phipps while you sort yourself out.'

'He might not go with you. I think he's a bit jealous.'

'Nonsense. Smudge likes me, don't you boy?'

He reached out to the dog, and to Laura's surprise Smudge simply nuzzled his hand. She gave in.

'I'll need to put my stuff in my red bag then, if you insist on me going about like a seaside tart.'

'I confess that the image rather appeals to me.'

Laura didn't reply, but made a face as he gave his wicked chuckle. He led Smudge from the room as she began to put her things together, and was back before she was fully ready, wearing nothing but her red heels and clutching her coat and bag.

'Like that will do nicely, if you prefer.'

'I wouldn't dare! Not around here, anyway. Perhaps somewhere lonely?'

'I might very well hold you to that.'

She gave a nervous smile before slipping her coat on. Even with the buttons done up she felt naked, and from the moment she stepped out of the door the sensation was stronger by far than it had been simply going without her underwear, but balanced by the security of having Charles by her side. Several of the people they passed looked at her, and she was sure they were thinking she was a call-girl walking with a client after spending the night together, an idea both arousing and pleasantly embarrassing.

It was worse at the station, because two of the staff recognised her, and in the train, where their fellow passengers were able to consider her at leisure. Her coat covered her to just above her knees and closed at her neck, yet the belt held it tight to her figure and she was sure that the way the leather clung to her breasts and hips and bottom made it obvious she was naked underneath, and that everybody had guessed. Worst of all, Hovis Boy was in the carriage, his eyes repeatedly flicking to her legs, attention Charles quickly noticed. He spoke quietly.

'He's very interested. I wonder, perhaps you should treat him to a flash?'

'Charles, no!'

'Why not? It would make his day, very possibly his entire year.'

'I can't, not him!'

'Why not him? For the same reason as Brian?'

'Yes ... no, not really. He's just not my type, too young, too spotty!'

'So if he was a handsome young man you'd be happy to flash him?'

'No! I mean ... it's just that ... I don't know, it's too embarrassing, in front of him.'

'But he hasn't given you any particular reason to dislike him?'

'No, but ...'

'Then we will strike a bargain. If there is nobody else in the carriage but him when we leave Littleport you are to flash as we pull in to Ely. If there is anybody else you escape, but if you decline, or fail, I will set you some other task.'

Laura had nodded before she could think better of it, the idea too exciting to be turned down, while the risk was clearly worth taking. Besides themselves and Hovis Boy there were five people in the carriage, and two of them looked like students and so would presumably be going all the way to Cambridge. Charles grinned.

'Good girl, although a very good girl would have obeyed without question.'

'I'm sorry, Mr Latchley.'

'That's better. So, let's see ...'

They were pulling into Watlington, where two of the passengers got out but another got in. At Downham Market both the supposed students got out, to Laura's dismay, but the other two stayed. Charles was plainly enjoying himself, his eyes twinkling as he watched her reaction, while she had begun to shake and her nipples had grown painfully stiff and sensitive beneath her coat. By the time the train began to slow for Littleport her heart was beating so strongly she was sure he could hear.

One of the two remaining passengers got up, but the other stayed firmly rooted to her seat as the train drew to a halt, only to rise and nip through the doors at the last moment. Nobody else got in, and Laura's mouth had come open in an O of horror as the train started once more. Charles rubbed his hands together.

'There we are then. I wonder if you have the courage to go through with it?'

Laura shook her head, then nodded, determined not to let him down or break her word and heavily aroused despite herself. Her fingers went to the top button of her coat, easing it open to leave a little of her cleavage showing, but her nerve failed her as she tried to tug her belt loose.

'I can't!'

Charles reached out, to tweak the second button of her coat open. She let him, unable to resist, trembling uncontrollably as he opened the third button, to leave her coat held closed over her naked body by her belt alone. Hovis Boy had noticed, but was trying not to look, his attention fixed firmly in front of him but his eyes constantly flicking towards Laura and Charles. Laura struggled to think of some way to justify what she had to do and hit on it almost immediately, the old trick of making it seem that he was the dirty one and not her.

When the train began to slow she was ready, her belt buckle loose, her fingers locked in the supple leather of her coat, Charles smiling as he watched. The platform of Ely station came in sight. Laura's heart was in her mouth as she spun on her heel, pulling her coat wide to show herself off, her breasts, her belly, the full length of her legs and the neat V of her sex between.

'Here you are, you little pervert. Is this what you want to see? Have a good look.'

Hovis Boy's jaw dropped, his eyes popping as he drank in

Laura's naked body, his bag of sandwiches dropping to the floor. She held her pose, until her nerve broke at the sight of a railway guard standing on the platform. Snatching her coat closed, she jumped from the train the instant the doors opened, to hurry down the platform as fast as her heels would permit, with Charles striding along beside her.

'Wonderful! Beautiful! I really didn't think you'd do it.'

'Nor did I!'

Despite her panic, nobody else seemed to have noticed, and they reached Charles' car without incident. Only when they were underway did she start to relax, and she was still holding her coat tightly closed until they had pulled off the main road. As she calmed down her arousal began to take over, immensely powerful. Charles realised, as always, and quickly turned onto a lane bordered by twin rows of poplars.

Laura gave a grateful sigh and let her coat fall open. Charles reached across to make a quick adjustment, baring her breasts properly as her thighs came wide and she slid a hand between.

20

To be with Charles, deep in the country, with nothing more to her name than her coat, her shoes and those few essentials she had put in her bag gave Laura the same mixed feelings of freedom and restraint she had already come to associate with the way he treated her. As he had explained, to be his meant to hold nothing back, and so she stayed naked in the house and garden, allowing him to see her and to access her body without qualification.

On the Saturday morning they went walking, along quiet footpaths and through woodland where Laura could keep just a single button of her coat done up, maintaining a constant, gentle arousal. Twice he took her in among the bushes and had her drop the coat from her shoulders to go nude, the first time simply because he wanted to admire her in the bright sunlight, the second time in an old hut at the edge of a copse, where she was put on her knees and fed his cock until he was erect in her mouth. Eager to make him come, Laura had begun to tug on his shaft and squeeze his balls when he pulled her gently back.

'Not yet. I have something else in mind for you.'

'What's that?'

'Let's just say I want you ready. Touch yourself, and show me.'

Laura rocked back on her heels, her thighs wide, excited simply to be showing herself so openly even before she'd begun to tease at her sex. Charles watched, nursing his erection but

185

making no effort to take advantage of her rising excitement, until at length he spoke again.

'That will do, for now.'

'I'm right on the edge.'

'Stop it, now!'

She obeyed, reluctantly, and they continued walking, she now on edge, while Charles seemed to return to his normal easy self instantly. Beyond the copse they reached a point at which the path divided, one route broad and clearly marked as a footpath, the other leading between high banks of vegetation. Charles chose the smaller route, leading them in among a dense growth of elder that made the air still and hot, while the path had vanished almost completely. It seemed very unlikely that anybody would see them.

'Shall I go naked?'

'Why not? This is all water company land, so we're safe enough.'

Laura quickly shrugged off her coat, provoking the quick thrill she was coming to enjoy so much. Charles took the garment, leaving her in nothing but her shoes as they moved on, Laura now sure that he would take advantage of her at any moment and looking forward to being stark naked outdoors while she was fucked or they made love, depending on his mood. He made no move, contenting himself with watching her until they came out from the elder copse to a long straight stretch of grass between two high banks. Charles paused, listening.

'It might be wise to cover up, unless you'd like to risk giving a few engineers a treat?'

'Not fully naked, maybe a flash if we're safe. Hang on, I just need to nip into the bushes.'

'Why?'

'To pee.'

'What did I say about hiding yourself?'

'Yes, but ... well, I suppose so, if you feel that it's important?'

'It's only important if you feel I shouldn't be allowed to see.'

'No, of course not, but ... I don't know, it's ...'

'Rude?'

'Well, yes, but more than that. I don't know, but I remember an article I read, about how a woman should never let a man see that sort of thing because it spoils her mystique.'

'That might be true, if you were in a relationship with Hovis Boy from the train. You are not. Now do it.'

Laura was blushing hot, but did as she was told, squatting down to one side of the path, her thighs well open to make sure nothing was hidden despite her misgivings. Charles watched, his face calm, with none of the shame or lust she might have expected, making it far easier to let go, and as she peed in front of him she realised that she had broken one more barrier in the way of the complete intimacy she craved. He waited until she had dabbed a tissue from her handbag to her sex before speaking again.

'Does that feel better?'

'Yes, and you don't mean because I don't need to go any more, do you?'

'No.'

'And you knew how I'd feel, didn't you?'

'Naturally.'

She pulled her coat back on and fastened the belt, leaving the buttons loose. As they walked on she took his hand, needing to feel she was being led by him, not only as lovers, and as his plaything, but as a pupil to her master. He walked a step ahead, taking the position naturally as they followed the path to where a bridge of metal gridwork crossed a dyke, from the top of which they could see back across the flat fields. The top of Charles' pump tower was visible in the distance among the trees.

Twenty minutes later they were once more indoors. Laura immediately shrugged off her coat and kicked her heels away, taking a moment to massage her feet before padding into the kitchen after Charles. He was at the work surface, with one of the cupboards open, just taking down a blue china dish in which sat an oblong pat of deep yellow butter with a rounded knife pushed into the top.

'Are we having lunch?'

'In a while. Once I've dealt with you.'

'Yes, please.'

'Kneel on a chair.'

Laura did as she was told, pulling a kitchen chair out from under the table and climbing on with her arms rested on the back and her spine pulled in to make her bottom as prominent and vulnerable as possible. Charles gave an appreciative nod.

'You have a natural instinct for sexual display, Laura.'

'Thank you.'

She felt ready, and was sure that if he'd intended to punish her she would have been taken upstairs to the necessary room, but he still seemed intent on his preparations for lunch, using the butter knife to cut a piece generous enough for the largest of baked potatoes. He glanced at her bottom, then stepped close.

'Hold still.'

Laura's mouth came open in an O of surprise as the butter was wiped off between her bottom cheeks, the still firm tip pushing into her anus.

'Charles!'

'Sh.'

'But ...'

'Sh, I said.'

'Oh God.'

She hung her head, trying her best to surrender to her fate in the way she wanted to, and felt she should. Already the piece of butter had begun to melt in her bottom hole, a sensation both rude and full of promise, but more than a little frightening. He took hold of her around her waist, keeping her firmly in place as he began to rub the butter in with gentle circular motions, pushing occasionally until his finger slid into her body without pain. Laura had begun to shake, fully aware of what was about to be done to her and both expectant and scared. When Charles spoke his voice was full of consideration, but also firm.

'Are you virgin behind?'

The blood rushed to Laura's face.

'No. Sorry.'

'There's no need to apologise. I prefer a little experience, and besides, only the weakest of men resent a woman's previous partners. You can even tell me about it, if you like?'

He had worked his finger deep, and was using his thumb to rub her sex as he got her ready, making Laura gasp and sigh as she struggled to answer him.

'It ... it was Tommy Fuller. We used to play cards for ... for forfeits. I always lost, and ... and ended up naked, having to do rude things for him, and suck him, until ... until one night he said he wanted to put it up my bum, and I ... I let him.'

'Just the once?'

'No.'

'I bet he used to cheat, and I bet you used to lose on purpose, didn't you?'

'Yes.'

Charles gave a soft chuckle.

'An enterprising young man, this Tommy Fuller, by the

sound of it, and a good judge of women. Did he bend you over, or prefer you to sit in his lap, or take you from the side?'

'He always bent me over. He … he liked to see it go in.'

He gave a full throated laugh.

'A man after my own heart! Now then, I need to be ready too.'

Laura's face was burning as she watched him pull out his cock and balls, but her arousal had come back as high as when she'd been made to play with herself in the woods. Her mouth came open as he offered her his cock, to take him in as far as he would go. She sucked eagerly, thinking of what was about to be done to her and the absolute surrender of bringing a man to erection in her mouth so that he could enjoy her bottom.

Charles took her by the hair, easing his cock in and out as he continued to prepare her. She could feel the warm butter trickling down her sex, and an open helpless feeling behind, familiar from the times Tommy had treated her the same way. He'd been even bigger than Charles, but that did nothing to reduce her apprehension as the now stiff cock was finally withdrawn from her mouth.

'Be gentle, please, Charles. Do it slowly, and stop if I say.'

'I know how to bugger a girl, Laura. Now just relax.'

She did her best, hanging her head in submission once more as he got behind her. His finger left her bottom, her cheeks were pulled open and she felt him push. Her mouth came wide as she began to fill, and she was already panting and wriggling her toes as he took a grip on her hips. Slowly, carefully, he eased his full length inside her, until she could feel his balls pressed to her empty sex.

'Is that good?'

'Yes.'

'Tell me, Laura.'

'Yes ... yes, it's good. It feels good to have your cock up my bottom, Mr Latchley. Thank you.'

'That's my girl. Now, I expect you'd like your treat?'

She wasn't sure what he meant, until she felt his arm snake in under her belly to find her sex and realised that she was to be masturbated while he was in up her bottom. He'd begun to push as he did it, adding to her overwhelming sensations of surrender and of pleasure. In just moments her muscles had begun to contract and he was pushing hard inside her as her orgasm rose up, to explode in her head, a screaming, panting climax so strong that her legs went beneath her. Charles snatched at her hip as he felt her body start to give way, supporting her as he thrust deep and hard, with Laura's body jerking helplessly on his cock until he too came, holding himself deep up her bottom as he took his satisfaction.

Laura lay face down on Charles' bed, naked and feeling content and completely in love. All her adult life she had craved a man who would make her feel not only wanted, but looked after, or, as Charles had put it, cherished. Tommy had never even come close, obsessed with sex and delighted by her body, enjoying her feminine reactions to his abundant, almost grotesque masculinity, but not protective at all, while he had neither expected her to be faithful, nor promised to be faithful himself. No other man had even come close, despite several who had been merely possessive.

Charles was downstairs, preparing lunch, which was something he insisted on doing himself, much to her relief. One of her concerns about his philosophy of owning her had been that as his property she would be expected not only to be his sexual plaything, but also his skivvy, cooking and cleaning while he took his ease and also beating her if he was unsatisfied with her work. He plainly had no such intention, although she was unsure if that was through a sense of fairness or because he was too controlling to let anybody else make choices that affected him. Certainly his attitude to cooking suggested the latter, with every item in his kitchen spotless and in its own place, right down to an alphabetised spice rack.

In fact, she reflected, his chosen role for her was not so much that of a girlfriend, or even a slave, but a pet. The idea was rather appealing. He would treat her as she treated Smudge, providing food, shelter, company, and looking after her health. The only difference would be that Smudge provided Laura protection, while with her and Charles it would be the other way around. She would be his, completely, and in a way she found increasingly arousing the more she considered it.

She jumped up from the bed, enthused and pleased with herself for coming up with the idea. Charles was cutting a square of blue cheese into precise cubes and looked around as she entered the kitchen.

'We're nearly ready. The wine is in the fridge, if you'd care to open it?'

'Of course, and I've come to a decision. I don't want to be your slave girl. I want to be your pet.'

'My pet? What sort of pet?'

'A pet pet, like Smudge, only of course, I'm a girl not a dog.'

Charles didn't answer, immediately, leaving her to extract the cold bottle of wine from the fridge before he spoke again, slowly and evenly.

'It's an interesting idea, but we would need to have rules.'

'Of course, and if I break them, a smack!'

'That goes without saying, but there would need to be house rules, about what you wear for instance …'

'I'd be nude, all the time.'

'I prefer you in stockings, and there would also be absolute rules, such as no peeing on the carpet.'

'Of course!'

'And it wouldn't be an excuse for laziness or misbehaviour.'

'Even a teeny bit?'

He paused to consider.

'I need to think about this, Laura, and so, I suspect, do you. If we're to be together we need to reach a mutual agreement, and put it in writing.'

'A sort of contract?'

'Exactly. In an ideal world it would be possible for you to simply declare yourself mine, to do with as I wish but knowing that I will cherish you.'

'That seems reasonable.'

'It should be, and that will form the basis of the contract. However, we live in the real world, so we need a little more detail. I'm beginning to see that while you are naturally feminine and appreciate how a man and a woman should interact, you are not, at heart, a slave.'

Laura felt a sudden emptiness.

'Is that a problem?'

He came towards her and kissed her.

'With any other woman, yes. With you, no. For you I will compromise, just so long as it is absolutely clear who is in charge.'

'Yes, Mr Latchley. Would you like me to suck your cock, Mr Latchley?'

'I hope that wasn't intended as sarcasm, Laura?'

'No, I promise.'

There had been amusement in his voice as he spoke, but she was left feeling a little uneasy, desperate to please and yet defiant in defence of her needs. He carried on as he began to mix the cubes of blue cheese into a bowl of salad.

'The thing is, Laura, that I had expected your deepest need to be to serve me, but while I can't fault your obedience or your need to please, it seems to me that your deepest need is to be protected. After all, you never ask how I wish you to dress, you haven't suggested that you strip for me, you didn't offer your bottom to me. I could train you to do these things, yes, but I prefer it to come naturally.'

'I prefer to be told to do it, and anyway, I probably would have offered if I'd known you liked that sort of thing.'

'Laura, it would take a saint not to bugger you, if given the opportunity.'

'I'm not sure about that. Not many men are that dirty.'

'Dirty? As in dirty pig?'

'Oops! Sorry.'

'I'm sure you will be, presently. For now, if you would pour the wine, we'll eat.'

The table was already laid, and Laura poured their glasses as he put some of the salad onto plates. As she had expected, it was delicious, and she ate a few mouthfuls before speaking again.

'I get spanked now, don't I?'

'Yes, after lunch.'

'I'm sorry if I'm not your ideal slave girl. You can punish me more severely if you want to, even cane me, or use one of those vicious looking leather straps, or whip me.'

'I will choose when you are punished, and how, but don't worry about not being my ideal. Attitude adjustment is an essential part of your training.'

'Oh.'

'Besides, there's really no such thing as an ideal. I adore the rich brown of your hair, but I would be equally happy if you were blonde, or a redhead, or had a green Mohican three feet tall. I'd also be perfectly happy if you were black, or shorter, or had a fuller chest, or taller with tiny breasts. The same is true for your personality. There are limits, both physical and in your character, but you fall well within those, as I trust I do for you?'

'Oh, yes, absolutely. And you're right about me wanting to feel protected, but it's more than that, because I like you to be wicked with me as well. I suppose you could say that you're halfway between my ideal hero and my ideal villain.'

Charles laughed.

'You have a very romantic nature, Laura, in the old-fashioned sense.'

'Yes, only for me the hero always arrives a little too late.'

'Or not at all, if he is also the villain. You said you liked the idea of being a captive even before you thought about spanking?'

'Yes. That was my favourite fantasy for years.'

'Good, because you're spending this afternoon in the cage.'

21

'This is not a punishment, more what the Americans call a time-out, an opportunity to calm down and reflect.'

As Charles spoke he closed the heavy padlock, leaving Laura trapped inside the tall metal birdcage. She was naked, but warm enough even in the shade with flecks of bright sunlight marking the concrete floor of her prison.

'How long will I be in here?'

'You won't know. The passage of time very quickly becomes hard to judge. When you wish to be released, call out, but I expect you to last at least an hour. Should you fail, you will receive one stroke of the strap for every minute you are short of your target. That will be after the spanking you have earned for referring to me as a dirty pig, again. Is that clear?'

'Yes.'

'Good.'

A casual wave and he was gone, leaving Laura to her thoughts. She knew she was supposed to contemplate her attitude to him, her role in their relationship and what it would mean to be completely in his control. That was all very well, but she was helpless, imprisoned, something she had fantasised about more times than she could remember, and better still, when she was released she was going to be spanked.

It was much easier to think of Evangeline Tarrington, trapped in the harem, kneeling on a bench with her gauzy pants pulled down and her wrists tied behind her back, one of a line of four bare-bottomed girls awaiting punishment.

Yet that had been very different, much more public and with the real restraint not her bound wrists but the scimitar-wielding harem guards. She had read other, more suitable scenes, but she was supposed to be thinking about Charles.

Laura sat down, the concrete base of the cage cool and hard against her flesh. Gripping the bars, she let her eyes flick to the padlock. It was heavy duty, too strong for her to break even had she had tools, while the cage itself was no less formidable. She was genuinely helpless, completely at Charles' mercy, and it did feel good, but still the sense of reliance he had told her to expect wouldn't come.

She tried hard, picturing herself as his slave girl, put in the cage to learn what it meant to be a man's property. He was older and wiser than her, she told herself, and understood her personality better than she did herself, but he had already admitted she was different. There was also a crucial element to her fantasies of captivity that he seemed to have overlooked: defiance.

A heroine who gave in and accepted her lot was no fun at all. Evangeline Tarrington had still been proud and defiant even tied up while her bare bottom was smacked in front of laughing girls and prurient guards. Laura wanted the same, to be caged not in order to reflect on what Charles felt should be her true nature, but in an attempt to break her spirit before she was taken out, spanked, strapped and fucked.

The punishment was one thing. It would hurt, and she deserved it, but to submit to discipline was part of her. So was reliance on a man as her protector, her hero, but he also had to be something more, the sort of man who found it amusing to make her go bare in public or to butter her bottom, a wicked man. Charles was that man, without question, and with that thought Laura reached an epiphany. For her to be happy, there would have to be certain things she was made to do, which made her the perfect foil for his natural cruelty, something that would be lost if she became completely subservient.

She almost called out, only to realise that she had probably been in the cage no more than ten minutes, which would mean fifty strokes of the strap. If it was anything like the cane, that would be unendurable, although if she was tied down over the whipping bench, gagged and blindfolded she would have little choice. The thought sent a sharp thrill through her, but caution prevailed and she went back to her thoughts.

Another scene she had often enjoyed in the darkness of her bedroom was a lot closer to her current predicament than anything from *Taken to Turkey*. In *The Marquis of Montauch* the brilliant but insane Human Chameleon had kept the heroine, Eloise de la Tour, in a sort of display case in his cellar, making her earn her meals by removing a piece of clothing each day.

Greatly to Laura's disappointment, Hugo be Montvilliers had rescued Eloise when she still had her camisole to cover her modesty, but it had been easy to extend the fantasy, imaging herself in the case, stripped naked, made to exhibit herself, to touch herself in front of her leering captor, to suck on his cock through the bars.

Laura shivered, imagining Charles coming back to tell her she would only be released once she'd satisfied him in her mouth. He'd push his cock through the bars, already erect, and she'd have no choice but to suck him, all the way as she knelt naked on the hard concrete floor. Better still, once he'd come he'd simply walk away, laughing, to leave her in a state of helpless consternation in her cage, cheated and exploited but unable to keep her fingers from between her thighs in response to what he'd done to her.

She stood up, clutching the bars as she wondered if he would comply with her fantasy or take her straight to the necessary room for her strapping. The answer was easy. This was Charles Latchley, the Devil. He wouldn't take any nonsense. She'd get strapped, one stroke for every minute under the hour, exactly as he'd promised, and with that thought came a new, more powerful thrill. Charles was not a man to be manipulated, and she could only ever hope to relate to him on his own terms.

Now feeling thoroughly confused as well as aroused, she began to pace the cage, turning at every second step in the narrow space between the bars. She wanted to call out, but didn't dare, to talk to him in an attempt to explain feelings she didn't understand herself, to take the punishment she feared so badly and end up trembling against his chest with her hot bottom thrust out behind and her fingers busy between her thighs.

She had to bite her lip to prevent herself from calling out in her frustration, sure that he'd hear and assume she wanted to be released. That would mean the strap, but he had been right about her sense of time. She was no longer sure how long she'd been in the cage, whether it was even as long as the ten minutes she'd guessed earlier, or twice that, three times even. It had not been an hour, of that she was certain.

Once again Laura sat down, determined to achieve the state of calm reliance Charles had told her she would go into. Closing her eyes, she began to chant quietly, a mantra she'd taught herself in order to help face exams. It wouldn't work, her head full of urgent thoughts, of her own condition, of her fantasies, of Charles and the strap, of his reaction to her request to be made his pet.

In a sense he'd done it already, because anybody who came across her in the cage would get a fine view. She was naked, her legs up, the lips of her sex on plain show, no more hidden than had she been some caged animal to which modesty and intimacy had no meaning. That felt good, and she imagined herself not at the back of the secluded garden where nobody but Charles could possibly see her, but in a public zoo, paraded nude in her cage for everybody to see, to laugh at her, to feed her bananas through the bars, the men to feed her their cocks through the bars.

Laura shivered, on the edge of giving in to her fantasy, but the idea was a little too ridiculous. It would be better if Charles treated her as the Human Chameleon had treated Eloise, keeping her in a display case, to be taken out for his amusement when he felt so inclined. She'd go in the cage in the necessary room, naked and helpless, all day while he worked, until he came home, when she'd be made to suck his cock through the bars in order to pay for her evening meal.

The fantasy was too good to miss. Her hand stole between her legs and she began to masturbate, already sighing with pleasure as she teased her sex and imagined how she'd feel. For eight hours or more there would be no escape, her cage securely locked and the key in his pocket. She'd be naked, her natural state, every detail of her body on show as she crawled on the floor of the low cage or lay on her back with her thighs carelessly open, imprisoned and yet completely secure.

Laura jumped at the sound of a cough from beside her, her hands instinctively snatching at her sex and breasts to cover herself an instant before Charles stepped from the undergrowth.

'The idea is to meditate, Laura, not masturbate.'

'Sorry.'

'Don't be. I should have known that to fulfil one of your favourite fantasies would have this result. You are incorrigible, and also rather distracting.'

He looked up as he spoke, and pointed. Laura followed the direction of his gaze, to find a small camera unit wedged into the V between two branches some twenty feet off the ground.

She felt the blood rush to her face as Charles began to grin.

'I was trying to compose our contract, never an easy task but especially difficult with you.'

'Sorry. I was thinking of you, about how it would feel to spend all day in the cage in the necessary room while you're at work, then have you come home and . . . and make me suck you through the bars to earn my dinner.'

'How every imaginative of you. Perhaps I'll do that, one day, who knows? For the time being . . .'

He trailed off, approaching the cage as he peeled down his fly. Laura gave an eager purr, getting onto her hands and knees as she pressed her face to the bars, allowing him to feed her his cock. Without the slightest trace of inhibition she began to play with herself once more, teasing her sex as he grew in her mouth. She played what was being done to her over and over in her mind: naked on her knees, locked into a steel cage and sucking cock through the bars for the man who had imprisoned her.

She had come before he was even fully erect, but continued to do her best and to enjoy herself, quickly bringing him to orgasm in her mouth. Spent, he unlocked the cage, allowing Laura to climb out. As she stretched her stiff limbs he was looking at his watch.

'Forty-two minutes, which make eighteen strokes of the strap.'

'But it's not fair!'

'I am always fair. You came out of the cage after forty-two minutes, which means eighteen strokes of the strap. Would you rather I went back on my word?'

'No, but . . . I thought you'd finished with me. You unlocked the cage!'

'A simple test, which you failed. Now stay still.'

Laura gave in, trying not to pout as her ankles were fixed into the straps on the whipping bench. She had already been spanked, turned over Charles' knee the moment they were indoors and slaps rained down on her bottom as she was lectured on her language. It had been sudden and hard, too much so to allow her to react sexually, but as he led her upstairs she could already feel the heat of her cheeks starting to get to her, allowing her anticipation to rise despite her fear of the strap, but not enough to still her protests.

'Yes, Mr Latchley, but I really did think I was done!'

'A punishment, once decided on, must never be revoked.'

'Yes, but ...'

'Sh.'

It was a gentle, soothing sound and Laura went quiet as he continued to fasten her into place. She was in the same thoroughly undignified position as before, with her bottom the highest part of her body, although from the design of the bench it was clear that she could have been fixed into place the other way around and left a good deal less exposed. There was a trace of panic in her voice as she tried to make a joke of her position.

'You always like me bum high, don't you?'

'Naturally. Besides which, exposure and shame are an important part of punishment. There are some people, purists, who say that a Master shouldn't enjoy punishing his girls, but that has always struck me as unnecessarily hidebound, or stiff if you prefer the term. Do you want a gag?'

'Um ... no, not this time. I haven't any knickers anyway.'

'No you don't. There are plenty of alternatives, but if you think you can cope without, so be it.'

'I'm not sure. How much does it hurt? As much as the cane? Because it ... I mean ...'

She stopped, realising that she'd begun to babble in a panic stricken attempt to delay her punishment. Charles chuckled.

'I bet you're the same at the dentist, talking about your last holiday or the weather instead of opening wide like a good girl.'

'Yes.'

'Talk all you like, if it helps, bearing in mind that I'm planning to go to work on your bottom and not your mouth. In fact, you can count your own strokes.'

He had gone to the rack of implements as he spoke, and reached out to touch first one and then a second among a line of supple leather straps. Some were longer, some shorter, some brown, some black, some with two or even three tails, one of which he chose, hefting it in his hand and bringing it down across his palm with a meaty smack that made Laura wince.

'A tawse, the traditional implement for corporal punishment in Scottish schools, and very effective, so I believe.'

'Oh God.'

Laura had already begun to wriggle in her straps as he approached, panic taking hold sooner than it had with the cane. Then, she had had no idea what a beating felt like, and only six strokes to take. Now she knew, and had been awarded eighteen. Yet she was determined to take her medicine, gripping the legs of the whipping stool despite her uncontrollable shaking and the huge bubble of panic welling up in her throat as Charles lifted the tawse over her bottom.

'I will keep this even and regular. I will not stop until you are done. Remember to count.'

'Yes, but, Charles, wait ...'

The tawse smacked down across her cheeks, making her jerk and gasp, then again, almost immediately, and a third time.

'Count.'

'Four! I mean three ... ow! Four! Five!'

'Good girl.'

The tawse was falling across her bottom at an exact rhythm, applied with hard precise smacks that gave her no opportunity to recover herself, nor for fear of the next, and only just allowing her to pant out the numbers between each crack of leather on flesh. Before she'd got to ten she lost control completely, writhing and kicking in her straps, wiggling her bottom and begging for mercy. It made no difference, the straps keeping her firmly in place as smack after smack was applied, and at last she found her voice once more.

'Twelve! Thirteen! Fourteen, you bastard, you pig, pig, pig! Ow, fifteen and sixteen!'

He carried on, applying the last two smacks, then stopped.

'That's three pigs and a bastard, Laura. What did I say about your language?'

'I'm sorry.'

'Four more strokes.'

'Oh God!'

She began to panic again, kicking hard against her bonds, and as the tawse cracked down one more time she was wishing earnestly that she'd hadn't called him names. Yet the pause had let the heat of her bottom start to get to her and he was spacing the strokes, deliberately allowing her arousal to rise. By the last two she had begun to push herself up to the strokes, drawing a light chuckle from Charles as she called them out.

'Twenty-one! Oh my poor bottom ... twenty-two!'

He put the tawse down. Relief flooded through Laura, and pride for having taken her punishment. She looked back, smiling crookedly at him from her upside down position.

'Thank you. Mr Latchley. Please may I have a cuddle now?'

'Naturally, just as soon as I've fucked you.'

'But you only came just now!'

'I know, but you affect me like nobody else, Laura. Maybe

it's your body, maybe the way you behave, but either way, you get fucked.'

He had unzipped himself as he spoke, and quickly fed his cock into Laura's mouth. She sucked, letting her feelings come as he grew in her mouth, from the heat in her bottom and the delicious shame of being made to suck the man who had beaten her erect so that he could use her. It was an outrageous thing to do and, for her, perfect.

As soon as he was ready he took her, straddled across the whipping bench to drive his cock down into her sex from behind. She could feel the muscles of his belly pressing on her aching bottom as she was fucked, her head full of thoughts of what had been done to her, strapped up, beaten and then casually used in a way she'd fantasised over a thousand times and which was at last her reality. Soon she was wriggling herself against him, close to orgasm as he pumped into her and left her on the edge once he'd come.

She was begging immediately, pleading for him to take mercy on her and bring her off. His response was to pick up the tawse once more, again applying it to her bottom with a firm, even rhythm, but lower, to send a powerful shock to her sex with every stroke. Laura stuck up her bottom, glorying in the pain and indignity of being strapped until she came under the blows.

Sunday was a lazy day, with Laura unselfconsciously naked about the house and Charles alternately cooking and working on their contract. The very thought of signing it gave Laura a sharp thrill, and she was determined to make a ritual of doing so, much as she had once imagined her wedding day, only with her naked on a collar and lead rather than in a white dress.

By lunchtime she had evolved an entire ceremony, as elaborate as it was impractical, including the use of a temple of sorts and a large audience to witness her acceptance of his will. On a more realistic note, she had been enjoying the sight and feel of the marks left by his strap across her bottom, and was hoping that some sort of punishment would be involved, so that when she put her name to the document she was in the state of perfect surrender that came no other way.

After their meal Charles went back to work, entrusting Laura with the washing up, after which she went out to lie on the lawn. Before long she half asleep in the warm sunshine, only to be brought back to her full senses by the sound of Charles rearranging the crockery and cutlery she had just put away but evidently not in exactly the right place. When he came outside a moment later she instinctively rolled face down, offering her bottom to whatever he had in mind for her, but he contented himself with a remark.

'I admit to liking my things just so, but having seen your efforts at putting crockery away I'm rather more inclined to accept your offer to be my pet.'

'Woof, woof.'

'Be careful, or you'll be spending next weekend wearing a pair of big floppy ears and a tail. Right, in this envelope is a draft of our contract. I don't want you to read it now. I want you to read it at home, sober, and you're not to start fantasising over it and playing with yourself. Is that clear?'

'Yes, Mr Latchley.'

'I somehow doubt that, but I do at least know that you're honest enough to admit it if you do get carried away. Seriously, it needs your careful attention, because once you've signed it becomes law.'

'Is it legally binding?'

'Our law, not the law of the land. Think of it as a business contract, valid only in so far as it's subject to the law, but with you as the goods involved.'

'Hmm ... that's quite sexy. There's bit in *Brigands of Barbary* where the heroine is sold for three camels and a goat ... ow! That was my thigh!'

'Girls with bruised bottoms get smacked thighs, and thighs sting more, as you will learn. Now will you please listen?'

'Yes, Mr Latchley. Sorry, Mr Latchley. Ow!'

'Sarcasm, Laura.'

'Sorry.'

'That sounded a little more genuine. No, it's not legally binding. It's a private agreement between you and me. As you're young, and not very experienced, we'll review it after a month, and again at suitable intervals but, in between, it governs your behaviour. Can you accept that?'

'Yes, as long as I've agreed to everything in it.'

'Naturally.'

He put the envelope down on the grass beside her. Laura put her chin on her hands, her bliss now slightly marred by the prospect of parting and work the next day, yet there was no hurry, and no denying the message the faint tingle of her slapped thighs was sending.

'I'm all yours, if you want me.'

...

22

In her flat that evening, after a boisterous reunion with Smudge, Laura began to read the contract, face down on her bed while he busied himself with a yellow plastic duck he had found at Mrs Phipps'.

As she had expected from Charles the contract was long and detailed, leaving very little to chance. The essence of it was that she would be his. That meant accepting discipline, obeying his orders and having no secrets from him whatsoever. It also gave him complete access to her body, but subject to a few common sense conditions. She was also to dress as he pleased, but on the understanding that if he wanted some exotic costume it was his responsibility to pay for it, while she had an alternative available at all times, to go completely nude.

By the time she'd reached his description of how she might be expected to dress she was itching to put a hand down to her sex, but the next section proved to be a very dry assurance that he would not exploit her financially by taking her wages or insisting on her signing over her assets. The idea had never occurred to Laura, but she could see that it made sense, being designed to provide an assurance that his desire to own her was genuine and not simply a way of exploiting her nature.

There was a great deal more, much of which she felt could have been taken as read, and none of which she wanted to change. Charles was naturally thorough, something she'd only ever been able to achieve with a great deal of conscious effort, but more importantly he had taken her needs into account as carefully as his own. He had even included guaranteed limits to her discipline for the sake of health, something she was sure she would never have been able to consider once she was in the strange, ecstatic headspace brought on by punishment.

When it came to sex, she was to be his and his alone, something she would have taken for granted in any case, as an inevitable part of being in love, while to her relief he also gave an assurance of faith, although there was one crucial exception, an exception that put butterflies in her stomach. He could punish other women, if the situation arose, just so long as the encounter was not openly sexual and, far more importantly, she could be punished by other women in any way he felt appropriate.

The very thought made her shake, first bringing her thoughts back to Hazel Manston-Jones, and then to the implications of the agreement. Even to imagine being spanked to the sound of another woman's disdainful laughter was almost too much, but to think of being put across the knee, on Charles' command, her bottom exposed and smacked by some smug bitch was the last straw. Best of all, it could be Hazel herself.

Laura gave in to the inevitable. Bouncing onto her knees, she pushed her bottom up and slowly eased her pyjama trousers down over her cheeks as she let her imagination run tree. Hazel would come to the cottage, it didn't matter why. She and Charles would get on well, too well, so that after an alcoholic lunch the two of them would be swapping happy reminiscences of how much fuss Laura made over a spanking. From there it would be a small thing for Charles to suggest that Hazel dish out the punishment Laura had earned that week.

She would protest, but it would be too late. The contract would have been signed and she'd have no choice. She'd be put across Hazel's legs on the big leather sofa in Charles' study, made to stick her bottom in the air, adopting the same exposed position she was in on her bed. Quickly she pulled her pyjamas back up, for the pleasure of easing them down again and imagining the agonising sense of shame that same exposure would bring with her body draped across Hazel's lap as her knickers were pulled down.

That alone was more than enough to get her there, and she began to run the scene over and over in her head as she rubbed at herself and tried to ignore the plaintive squeaking of Smudge's duck. Charles would be watching, amused by her reaction to Hazel, enjoying her shame as much as the sight of her bare bottom. He'd get his cock out, bringing himself erect in his hand as Hazel administered a firm, no nonsense spanking, making Laura squeal and writhe as her bottom turned red and her cheeks bounced to show off every intimate detail between. Worse still, she'd surrender her dignity completely, begging Charles to fuck her while Hazel held her in place, and with that thought Laura began to come, and to babble.

'Yes, please ... fuck me! Fuck my spanked bottom, Charles. Fuck me while she holds me. Fuck me!'

She was screaming as it happened, exactly as she had anticipated, her brain aflame with the image of how she would look as her sex filled; kneeling with her pyjamas pulled down and her bare bottom pushed high as she was mounted, the big cock pushed deep into her body, pumping frantically as she came in a long hard orgasm that seemed to last forever. Even when she was done she stayed as she was, her mouth curved into a little happy smile, content to be used and imagining how Charles would react if she confessed in the morning.

Over the next few days Laura fell into a pleasant, easy routine. When she admitted to her sin Charles told her he had already guessed, that for her honesty she would not be punished, and that she could have a dispensation as long as she continued to be truthful. She accepted happily, glad that it was out in the open. They discussed the contract over drinks in a pub near to Cambridge station, and Laura asked that the signing be made an event. Charles agreed immediately and they decided on the weekend after next as the ideal time.

On the Thursday morning she could not have been happier, leaving Charles at the station with a goodbye kiss and walking into EAS with her head full of erotic and romantic fantasies. Even the sight of Brian and Dave in the lobby didn't dent her mood, and she greeted Mr Henderson with a cheerful good morning, only to realise that there was a yellow file on the desk, the colour used for disciplinary procedures, while the expression on his face was far from agreeable.

'Is something the matter?'

'Yes. I regret to say that a complaint has been made against you, Laura, by Christopher Drake at Maxwell-Boyce, and a very serious one. He claims that you offered sex in return for a better price on our 36,000 volt units.'

'I did not!'

'He claims you did.'

'Well it's not true!'

'He claims otherwise, that you encouraged him to get drunk at the Horseshoes in Abbots Ripton and made it very clear that sex was available if he agreed to your terms.'

'No!'

'Think carefully, Laura.'

'It's not true.'

Mr Henderson gave a weary sigh.

'He expected you to deny it, and therefore sent this. I do not approve of his actions, needless to say, but I do think you have some explaining to do.'

As he spoke he took something from the yellow file and pushed it forward across the desk, one of the photos taken in Sheringham. It was the very rudest, showing her posing against the cliff. Her bottom was pushed out with most of her cheeks bulging from the sides of her tiny bikini bottoms, the swell of her sex barely concealed beneath a minute triangle of scarlet material, the top pulled open to show off her breasts, her nipples stiff, her lips pouted in an insolent kiss.

'The utter bastard!'

Mr Henderson gave her a moment for the full horror of her situation to sink in before he went on.

'Do you still deny that you had sex with him?'

'No, but ... OK, I had an affair with him, but I wasn't trying to bribe him. Anyway, that photo was taken on Sheringham beach, not at Abbots Ripton.'

'Answer me truthfully, Laura. Did you offer sex to Christopher Drake when you met him at the Horseshoes?'

Laura hung her head.

'Yes, we had sex, but it wasn't a bribe.'

'But you did have sex, with a client, on company time?'

'Yes.'

'Even leaving aside the issue of bribery, Laura, that would be grounds for dismissal, while I need scarcely remind you that you are already on a formal warning. I'm sorry, Laura, but I'm going to have to let you go. You can of course appeal, but Mrs Jeffries supports my decision. I doubt you would find much sympathy from a tribunal.'

'But ... please, wait a minute. He can't ... and anyway, what about him?'

'That's not our concern, and he indicates that if you are dismissed the matter need go no further.'

'He can't do that! That's completely unfair.'

'Fair doesn't come into it, Laura. Look, off the record, this is all to do with company politics. The Maxwell-Boyce account is worth a great deal of money, and Christopher Drake is something of a golden boy with them, not to mention being the nephew of their CEO. You've been an excellent PA, but I really have no choice, because if we keep you on we will be obliged to contest his accusation, which will mean losing the account and a costly court case, not to mention becoming the laughing stock of the entire industry. Therefore, as I'm sure you would understand if you weren't personally involved, you have to go. If you want to pursue the matter privately, of course, it is up to you, but I advise very strongly against it. I don't know why Drake has chosen to make this allegation, or why he has waited so long to do so, but ...'

'I do. It's his excuse so that he can keep his vicious bitch of a girlfriend!'

'I beg your pardon?'

'Hazel Manston-Jones. She caught us at it in Sheringham, and this way it makes him look as if I'm the one who tried it on, although if she believes him she's a stupid bitch.'

'Calm down, Laura.'

'But don't you see what's happened? He'd been trying to sweet talk her out of dumping him because he was seeing me, and she's stuck the knife in to make sure I get the sack.'

'Can you prove this?'

'No, of course not.'

Mr Henderson sat back in his chair, his hands spread in a helpless gesture.

'I've been sacked.'

Charles didn't answer, but immediately took her into his arms, indifferent to the commuters streaming past them towards the waiting train. Laura burst into tears, letting out all the emotions she had struggled to hold back during her interview with Mr Henderson and for the rest of the day as she tidied up her work, cleared her desk and as a final act engaged a temp from the very same agency who had put her forward for the job four years before.

Only when the train had started did Charles ease her gently down into a seat, directly opposite Darcy, whose presence was enough to embarrass her into digging into her bag for tissues. Charles waited until she had had a chance to tidy herself up before speaking.

'Do you have to go into work tomorrow?'

'No.'

'Then come home with me.'

'I can't. Smudge ...'

'Then I'll come home with you.'

'OK. Thank you.'

Laura went quiet, resting her head on Charles' shoulder and staring morosely out of the window at the passing countryside. With so many people around them, there was nothing to be said, but as the train picked up to full speed she was earnestly wishing that she had some way of magically transferring Christopher Drake to the rails in front of it. It was bad enough to have seduced her behind his girlfriend's back, but surely he should have had the decency to let things be, instead of getting her sacked in order to try and patch up the relationship he had been so willing to risk for a bit of variety in bed. The thoughts remained with her, but only when they were back in King's Lynn and walking by the river with Smudge bounding ahead did she admit to them, now more resentful than furious as she finished her explanation of what had happened that morning.

'I want to kill the bastard. Not literally, but you know what I mean.'

'Rise above it, that's my advice.'

'You said the same about Brian, but it was much more fun tipping paint over him. I'll cherish the memory forever too, but if I'd let him get away with it I'd always feel bad. I'm not as strong as you, Charles, and I'm no good at all at putting bad things behind me. For Christ's sake, I still resent Charlotte West for not inviting me to her fifth birthday party!'

'You are a very sensitive girl, but please, take my advice. Be proud and rise above it.'

'I can't, and I'll tell you what's worse. I told you Hazel Manston-Jones spanked me, didn't I, and how many times I've come over the memory? How do you think that feels, now she's cost me my job?'

'Is she necessarily to blame? It strikes me that the responsibility lies entirely with Mr Drake, who has obviously lied to her just as he lied to you.'

'Do you think so? I reckon she put him up to it, just to get back at me.'

'I admit that is possible, but I don't think it's very likely. I think it much more likely that he instigated the demand for your dismissal in order to impress her with the supposed truth of his story.'

'He still cheated on her though.'

'Yes, but as you were caught *in flagrante delicto* he can hardly claim that nothing happened, so that trying to blame you becomes his best option while he may well have painted himself into a corner, so to speak, and therefore found it necessary to make his claims formal. Lies, after all, have a nasty habit of needing fresh lies to support them.'

'That's true. Oh well, maybe she won't believe him anyway.'

'That's always possible, or she might believe him but reject him anyway.'

'Or take him back but use what happened to keep him in line. He would not like that.'

'In any event, their relationship is almost certainly doomed to failure.'

'Good.'

23

Charles left in the morning, on the same train Laura had taken day after day for so long, failing to catch it on only a handful of occasions and staying in bed only during rare bouts of illness. It felt strange to be lying there with the sun on her face and Smudge sitting in the corner with his lead in his mouth, looking hopeful, exactly as if it had been the weekend. She felt curiously numb, despite the occasional instinctive flicker of panic at the thought that it was a Friday and she was still in bed when she should have been at work.

At last she got up, but only to potter around the house doing minor and largely unnecessary jobs. Again and again she thought of Christopher Drake, cursing him and wondering what chance she had of getting another job after what had happened. The UK switchgear industry was far too small for her to avoid becoming the girl who'd offered sex to seal a contract, even if anybody did take her on, while in any other industry she would have problems without specialist knowledge or a track record, to say nothing of the difficulty of getting references.

Charles had suggested selling up and moving in with him, so casually that he had made it seem the obvious solution. She could see the appeal, but while sacrificing her sexual independence was as desirable as it was exciting, it was harder to let go of her financial independence. If she did, and signed her contract, she would be his completely, all day and every day, making her surrender to him an immediate reality.

She had said she needed time to think before she could give an answer, which he had accepted with the same level-headed calm he brought to everything. Now, with nothing to do but think, she found it impossible to separate her emotional needs from the cold practicalities of her situation. She had built up enough equity in her flat to leave her with money in the bank, but that didn't seem to matter, nor the clause in her contract allowing her to manage her own work affairs, because she knew that once she had signed, the last thing she would want was a job, let alone one in which any man other than Charles had authority over her.

In an effort to cheer herself up, she tried to think about the coming weekend, but she knew she wouldn't be able to recapture the sense of absolute freedom she had enjoyed so much, nor fully enjoy Charles until she had managed to clear her head of what Christopher Drake had done. She was also taking Smudge, Mrs Phipps having dropped a heavy hint that four weekends of dog sitting in a row would be stretching what could be expected of good neighbours. Despite Charles' affinity with animals, Laura wasn't at all sure he would be able to spank her in Smudge's presence without alarming consequences.

That put a smile on her face, but only briefly. She had soon begun to brood again, and picked up *Brigands of Barbary* in the hope of losing herself in the wilds of North Africa and the travails of the heroine, Olivia Silverthorn. Olivia had a bit more spirit than Evangeline Tarrington, and rather than simply feeling proud and resentful while waiting for the hero to turn up, actually did something about it for herself. On the other hand the hero, Daniel Lock, seemed a bit of a dead loss. Despite considerable provocation he had failed to put Olivia across his knee once in nearly a hundred pages. Nor had the Arab slave traders proved any better, more concerned with the quality of her skin and teeth than with tying her up or smacking her bottom. However, now that Olivia had been sold for three camels and a goat it seemed entirely possible that her new owner, Hasan Hasan, would know how the heroine of an adventure romance ought to be treated.

... beside his single remaining goat stood Hasan Hansan, his physical aspect alone enough to cause Olivia to place one dainty hand to the rosebud of her mouth. Six feet six he stood, crabbed and gaunt, his body wiry from the deprivations of the desert and scarred by the knives of old enemies long since fallen. A meagre loincloth shrouded his scrawny shanks, his sole garment save for sandals, crossed dagger belts and a cloak of rich peacock blue he must have stolen, probably from the body of some luckless merchant. His visage was more alarming still: a nose like the beak of a monstrous hawk, eyes like those of a slinking, predatory cat, a mouth like the slit of some horrid hell barred by teeth like broken tombstones. To make matters worse, his expression was a crapulent leer as he spoke.

'So, my pale petal of the chilly north,' he drawled dirtily, in, to Olivia's considerable surprise, remarkably good English, 'what has my purchase bought me? Come, I wish to see you – naked!'

Olivia Silverthorn screamed in horror and shame for the thought of having to disrobe for this repulsive specimen, and, without thinking, lashed out one dainty foot at the tip of a long, dancer's leg. Hasan Hasan, caught squarely in the wind, vanished over the precipice, along with his goat.

Laura pursed her lips with a touch of irritation. She had been hoping for more from Hasan Hasan and his goat, but after dropping over the edge of a precipice described as – '... a wall of naked rock higher than the topmost topaz of some ancient tower' – it didn't seem likely that they'd be up to much, while Olivia was now alone in the Atlas Mountains, not even at anybody's mercy, never mind in imminent danger of having her bottom compromised. Nevertheless, there was a certain satisfaction to the scene.

Olivia, Laura was sure, would not have meekly resigned herself to being pushed out of her job by some lying little bastard. Had Christopher Drake turned up in *Brigands of Barbary* he would have been some unprincipled rake and seducer, and with any luck have ended up at the bottom of the precipice with Hasan Hasan and the goat. It was just a shame that reality always had to get in the way, or she might have taken a leaf out of Olivia's book herself.

She went back to brooding on Christopher Drake, the book held limp in her hands. The more she thought about him, the less she felt able to enjoy the prospect of the weekend. To submit herself sexually to Charles she needed to feel good, confident and feminine, not crushed, and yet it was appalling to think of Christopher Drake spoiling her relationship with Charles as well as getting her the sack. Something had to be done, even if it was only to tell the bastard what she thought of him to his face.

Laura swung her legs off the sofa, determined to confront him. She knew the address of the Maxwell-Boyce plant off by heart, and if she drove fast she could catch him before lunch, or better still, in the works canteen where she could show him up in front of his colleagues. It had to be done, before common sense could get the better of her, and she had gone into automatic as she grabbed her bag and left the house.

She drove fast, with the radio turned up in an effort to keep her emotions high as she thought of all the things she could say to him. The list was long enough for a sizeable speech by the time she reached Peterborough and her nerve held as she parked the car and started towards the plant. Only as she approached reception did she begin to falter, realising that her plan of marching straight in and asking some random employee for his office was impractical. A smart, blonde-haired receptionist sat behind the desk, looking horribly efficient, while two large security guards flanked the doors. They had seen her, and it was too late to back down. Walking at her most businesslike clip, she approached the desk.

'Good morning. I am Miss Silverthorn. I wish to see Mr Drake, in purchasing.'

'Good morning, Miss Silverthorn. Mr Drake is out of the office at present. Did you have an appointment?'

Laura hesitated, all her stubborn determination gone on the instant.

'Um . . . no, that is . . .'

'Ah, here is his personal assistant. Perhaps she'll be able to help you?'

Laura turned sharply, to find Hazel Manston-Jones stepping out of a lift, just yards away, as tall and cool and elegant as ever. It was too late to avoid eye contact, while the receptionist was already speaking.

'Hazel. This is Miss Silverthorn. She was hoping to have a word with Mr Drake.'

Hazel had stopped, and to Laura's astonishment looked neither angry nor cold, but worried, while there was something close to panic in her voice as she gave a hasty response to the receptionist.

'Yes, I'll deal with this, thank you, Amanda. Laura, I think I . . . look, can we step outside?'

Laura nodded, cautious, but there was nothing in the other woman's manner to suggest hostility. Outside the main doors,

Hazel ran a hand across her brow, speaking quickly but in little more than a whisper.

'I owe you an apology, I know. I was angry and I shouldn't have done it, and I know Chris hadn't told you about us, but . . . anyway, I did it and I'd like to say sorry.'

'I don't understand.'

Hazel had been about to speak again, but stopped. Laura went on, her confidence rising in the face of Hazel's obvious alarm.

'Sorry for what, for spanking me or for costing me my job?'

'Costing you your job?'

'Yes, my job. What do you think happened when my boss got your bastard boyfriend's complaint?'

'He didn't send that, did he?'

'He did. I got sacked.'

'Oh hell. I am sorry, Laura. I told him not to, but . . . look, could we talk somewhere else? There are too many ears flapping around here.'

Laura sipped at her gin and tonic, listening as Hazel struggled to explain her situation. They were in the back bar of a small pub, once isolated, now swallowed by the industrial estate on which the Maxwell-Boyce plant was built. With some time yet to go before the lunch hour, they had the tiny room to themselves.

'. . . but it's not as simple as that. His uncle is our CEO, and Daddy's on the Board. They've been friends since school, they both think the sun shines out of his backside and that we make the perfect couple. We're supposed to be getting married in June, the Full Monty, in the cathedral with half-a-dozen bridesmaids and flower girls and bishops and . . . you get the picture. I wouldn't mind. I always wanted a big wedding, but not to Chris Drake.'

'Why are you still together then?'

'We're not. That's what I was trying to explain. After what happened in Sheringham I told him where he could stick himself, but he won't listen. He's unbelievably arrogant, and thinks he just has to wait until I calm down. I told Daddy, but he tried to talk me out of it, telling me that boys will be boys and then inviting Chris up for the weekend to have a quiet word. That's when Chris started saying you'd offered him sex in exchange for a good deal on the contract, just to save face, but Daddy's really old-fashioned about that sort of thing, and well, you know the rest. I did try to talk him out of it, Laura, and I am genuinely sorry for what happened.'

'Thank you. So, what are you going to do?'

'Have another drink. Let me get you one.'

Laura didn't object, and Hazel quickly returned to the table with two fresh gin and tonics but each twice the size of before.

'I have to drive.'

'I don't.'

Hazel took a swallow of her drink, then sat down.

'So that's the story. I can talk to him, if you like?'

'No. It's too late. There were problems at work anyway, and as it happens I'm with somebody else, somebody I met only a few days after ... you know. He's wonderful.'

'Good. That's something.'

She took another swallow, then laughed.

'I thought you were going to hit me when you came into the building. You looked fit for murder.'

'I felt fit for murder, but it wasn't you I was after. I was going to tell Chris what I thought of him.'

'I wish you had. He's at a conference in Lille.'

'Bad timing, like in Sheringham.'

Laura risked a cautious smile as she spoke. Hazel shrugged, embarrassed.

'I'm sorry.'

'Don't be.'

They fell into an awkward silence, eventually broken by Hazel.

'That wasn't the first time he's cheated on me.'

'No?'

'No. It was the first time I actually caught him at it, but I'm certain he's had at least one other affair. Most of the time it's been ... different.'

'How do you mean?'

Hazel didn't answer immediately, staring out of the window as if lost in thought before she replied.

'You seem quite tolerant?'

'I'd like to think so.'

Again Hazel paused, then went on in a rush.

'Chris. He's obsessed with getting another girl into bed with us.'

'Men like that, don't they?'

'He's always trying to get me to chat up other women, or to agree to put an ad on the net. The trouble is, I have to admit it's at least partially my fault.'

'Why? You're not responsible for his fantasies.'

'Well, no, but ... I was at an all girls' school, and I used to clown around a bit with my friends. Nothing serious, but it drives Chris wild and he used to like me to tell him. So I did, most of it made up just to get him going, and because I'd soon run out of real stories!'

Hazel's growing embarrassment was evident as she spoke, and she swallowed the rest of her gin and tonic before she went on.

'I just thought it was a bit of fun, but after a while he asked if I'd like to have one of my old friends to stay, with obvious implications. I tried to explain to him that just because we'd got a bit carried away together when we were eighteen and the only males we saw had hooves and antlers ...'

'Sorry?'

'Deer. I was at Klibreck School for Girls, in Sutherland. It has to be the bleakest place on earth, and believe me, on a winter's night you needed a cuddle. Chris didn't see it that way. To him it was all a big porn show, and he just wouldn't take it in that even if my friends might have enjoyed a reprise the last thing they'd have wanted was him watching, or sticking his cock in where it wasn't wanted. Another?'

'No, I'd better not.'

'I'm having one.'

Hazel went back to the bar, quickly returning with another double and taking up her story where she'd left off.

'Then he wanted to try swinging clubs. We went to a few, and ... and other sorts of clubs, but he couldn't bear the thought of me with another man.'

'He didn't seem to mind showing me off to other men. Sorry.'

'That's OK. Yes, he likes showing me off, but that's not the same. At the clubs there were women willing to play with me, but only if their partners were there, so if he wanted to touch he had to let another man touch me. That's what he couldn't handle, and I didn't want it that way either. Oh, no, he loves to show me off, as if I'm some sort of prize. He's put intimate pictures of me all over the net as well.'

'Ouch! He photographed me in that bikini, the one I was wearing ... half-wearing.'

Hazel smiled.

'You did look funny.'

Laura stuck her tongue out.

'What about his clothes?'

'Oh yes! He went berserk!'

'I wish I could have been there.'

'So do I. I got it on the phone, when he was trying to put you down to make me feel better. I told him I'd have done the same if I'd had the chance.'

'Good for you. So the swinging clubs didn't work out?'

'No. After that it was contacts, and I'd even agreed to try, just to please him. Then I caught him with you. One of the excuses he tried was that he was only after you in the hope that he could persuade you to join in with us.'

'The cheeky bastard! What are you going to do now?'

'I don't know. I'm under so much pressure to marry him, and I still love him even if that does make me a prize idiot. At the moment all I really want is to wipe that smug grin off his face.'

She went quiet and Laura didn't reply, only for a deliciously wicked inspiration to hit her.

'You should send him a picture of you with another girl and tell him he's never going to get it.'

Hazel grinned, but only for a moment.

'That would only encourage him. He reckons he can talk anyone around, and he doesn't believe in lesbian lesbians.'

'Lesbian lesbians?'

'As opposed to lesbians who only do it because they can't get a man and lesbians who do it to show off for men. I told you he was arrogant.'

'You're not joking!'

'No, I'm not. He'd just assume that she'd be game, unless it was you, of course!'

'Me!?'

'Why not? He'd hate it!'

'He would, wouldn't he?'

'Let's do it, come on. I've got my camera phone.'

'Yes, but ...'

'Come on, Laura. It'll be funny, and I'm not asking you to take your clothes off. We're in a pub, for goodness sake!'

'But what do you want to do?'

'I don't know, kiss and cuddle, I suppose. You've kissed another girl before, haven't you?'

'No. I haven't.'

'Oh. Well never mind, if you don't want to, but ...'

'Hang on ...'

Laura stopped, fighting to get the words out, but found courage in Hazel's complete candour about her own sexuality.

'Maybe I could lie over your knee, as if you were spanking me?'

Hazel laughed.

'You're terrible! OK, but quick, before the barman comes back or anyone else comes in.'

Laura was laughing as she got into position, but shaking too, with the memories of how many times she'd come over fantasies not a million miles away from what she was about to do, draping herself across Hazel's lap. They were on a long bench against one wall, allowing Hazel to hold her camera phone at arm's length while taking the photo as Laura stuck her bottom up as if waiting to be spanked.

'Here goes. Stick your tongue out at the camera.'

As Hazel spoke the palm of her hand settled across Laura's bottom, an electric touch. The camera flashed.

'Once again.'

Hazel's hand lifted and came down, applying a gentle smack to Laura's cheeks just as the camera went off.

'And again!'

'Oh God! Just do it, Hazel. Spank me!'

'Laura!'

Hazel was laughing, and the camera flashed again as she planted a second smack on Laura's bottom, much harder than the first. Laura stuck her hips up, lost to everything but the blissful shame of being spanked across another woman's knee, only to catch the sound of conversation from the passage. Hazel gave a squeak of alarm.

'Quick, get up! Get up!'

Laura scrambled to her feet, just in time to avoid being caught by an elderly couple with a small brown dog. Her face was burning red, and Hazel couldn't stop giggling, but the only reaction was a disapproving glance from the woman. Taking her drink, Laura swallowed what was left and sat down. Hazel leant close, speaking quietly but otherwise indifferent to no longer being alone.

'OK. It's not exactly exhibition stuff, but he'll get the general idea. What shall I say: "No boys allowed."? How about: "This was just the start, but never for you."?'

'Keep it simple, and obvious: "We'll never do this for you, and that means never."'

'You're right. I mustn't let him think I'm teasing. Which picture shall we use?'

Laura leant closer still as Hazel flicked through the options. The first showed her bottom up across Hazel's lap, both with their tongues stuck out. Hazel shook her head.

'Good, but too cheeky to go with the message.'

In the second Hazel's expression was stern and Laura looked shocked. Hazel clicked her tongue.

'That just looks as if you're getting it for being a naughty girl.'

The words made Laura's head swim and a guilty admission rose in her throat only to turn to a gasp at the sight of the third photo. Hazel was plainly enjoying herself, her mouth spread out in a wide cruel grin, while Laura was not only quite obviously pushing her bottom up to the smacks but looked as if she was about to come.

'That's the one!'

'No, Hazel! You can't let him see that!'

'Why not? He'll die of frustration. I'm sending it.'

'No, Hazel, please! Send the first one. He'll get the message.'

'No, it has to be this one. And it's for real. What was it you said? "Just do it, Hazel, spank me".'

'Hazel!'

Laura snatched for the phone, but Hazel held her off easily, still trying to punch her message in, only to relent as Laura started to beg.

'Oh, OK, I'll send the first one. It'll do the trick, but don't blame me when're you're the one who got turned on having her little botty smacked.'

Laura tried to find an answer, but no words would come. Her face was burning with blushes as she watched Hazel tap in the message and send it off, but her reaction had very little to do with Christopher Drake. She had been over Hazel Manston-Jones' knee, and Hazel knew she'd been turned on, and Hazel just thought it was funny. Her voice was a croak as she finally managed to speak.

'Could you send those to me too, please? And ... and maybe, if ... if sometime you'd like to do it again, properly?'

Hazel's eyebrows rose in surprise, then she smiled.

24

'I have a confession to make.'

Charles looked up from where he had been chopping a red pepper at his kitchen table, his expression as calm and controlled as ever.

'Yes?'

'I wasn't able to rise above it, the thing with Christopher Drake.'

'Yes?'

'No. I went to where he works to tell him what I thought of him.'

'Yes?'

'He wasn't there, but I did see Hazel Manston-Jones. She spanked me.'

'She spanked you?'

'I thought that might wake you up a bit. It was only in fun, to annoy Chris, but it felt ... right, and she says she'd be prepared to do it again.'

'Which is evidently something you want?'

'Yes, please, very much.'

'And would these spankings occur in my presence or not?'

'Um ... I didn't actually bring that up. She's fed up with Chris trying to push her into a threesome, you see, so it didn't seem a very good idea to suggest one with you. I would prefer it in front of you, of course, and it's not as if she has to take any clothes off, so maybe she'll come around to the idea? Would that be all right? I mean ... because you did say, in the contract ...'

'That you were allowed to receive discipline from other women, yes. I know it's something you need, but I had rather expected to be present, otherwise the situation does rather question my authority, and my position.'

'Sorry.'

'Not at all. Only a fool refuses to allow himself to be questioned, and an insecure fool at that. A genuinely dominant man remains flexible, prepared to learn and to adapt himself to circumstances. I have worked out my ground rules over a great many years, and while I believe them to be good I would never be so arrogant as to claim that they are absolute. Nevertheless, I'm not at all sure about this. Did you tell her about me?'

'Oh yes. Not everything, of course, mainly that I need to feel protected ... and that I like to be disciplined.'

'How did she react?'

'She understood, I think.'

His response was a thoughtful frown. Laura carried on.

'She certainly didn't disapprove, and she admitted she'd get a kick out of doing me. She's bisexual.'

'I see. Well, I shall have to think about this carefully, and frankly if I am not to be present I don't think it would be appropriate. Do you have the pictures you took?'

'Yes.'

Laura quickly extracted her mobile phone from her bag, calling up the three pictures and showing them to Charles. One corner of his mouth flicked up into his familiar grin as he saw, only for his expression to change to curiosity.

'I see. Put Smudge out, Laura.'

'What is it?'

'Do as you are told, Laura.'

'Yes, Mr Latchley.'

Puzzled, Laura hustled Smudge into the garden and returned

to stand in front of him. Charles gave a complacent nod, pushed his chair back, and with one smooth motion hauled her across his knee. She squeaked as she was turned bottom up, and again as her clothes were adjusted behind, with her dress turned high and her knickers taken down to her knees. The spanking began, with his arm holding her firmly in place as several dozen hard smacks were delivered to her rear cheeks. At last he let go and she got up, treading on her toes and rubbing at her hot bottom. Charles waited until she had recovered herself, then took her hand to lead her from the kitchen and upstairs. Laura felt her stomach start to churn.

'The necessary room?'

'Yes.'

'Oh God. What am I going to get? And what for? Why did you spank me?'

'I felt you needed it, and as for what you're going to get. You'll see.'

He let go of her hand to unlock the door and led her inside. At the sight of the whipping bench her body immediately started to tremble and she cast a frightened glance at the lines of implements, any one of which he might be about to put across her bottom. Instead to went to the cage, unlocking it and swinging open the door.

'Inside.'

Laura got down on her knees and crawled into the cage. Charles immediately shut and locked the door, leaving her trapped.

'How long will I be in here?'

'Perhaps a few minutes, perhaps a little longer.'

He made to leave the room, but Laura called out after him.

'Charles, hang on! What happens if I call for you?'

'You'll find yourself with a sore bottom and not just a hot one. Wait until I come back.'

'Yes, but ... what if I want to pee?'

'The floor of the cage is PVC. I dare say you'll find it easy enough to clean up when I get back.'

'Charles!'

He had gone, the door closed behind him and a moment later she heard the padlock click into place.

Laura had lost all track of time when she heard the doorbell ring. She knew she'd been in the cage a long time, because the sun had swung around to the other side of the house, leaving the room full of warm yellow light. He'd obviously eaten the lunch he'd been preparing when she arrived, but she'd had to go without, adding a growing hunger to her woes. Her tummy was also beginning to feel a little uncomfortable, but the worst thing was having no idea why she had been put in the cage and how he was going to react to her liaison with Hazel. The spanking meant very little, being just the sort of brisk punishment he liked to dish out for minor offences, or simply to keep her in trim. Something else was going on, but she had no idea what.

She had been curled up, half-asleep on the padded floor of the cage, but the ring of the doorbell had brought her back to her full senses. Kneeling up, she listened, but the thick walls and solid doors of the cottage made it impossible to pick up whatever was said between Charles and the caller, presumably one of his local friends. She was fairly sure she'd heard a car, and began to wonder if the man would stay long, leaving Charles unable to come for her, maybe until she'd wet her knickers, which was what was going to happen if he didn't take pity on her before too long.

There were no more noises, and after a while she slumped back into her curled up position, hugging her knees. Her bottom had been delightfully warm when he'd first locked her up, and she'd brought herself off under her fingers almost immediately, in a kneeling position with her knickers pulled down at the back and her skirt turned up, fully aware of the watching camera. Charles either hadn't been watching or had simply ignored her, much to her chagrin, and after a while she had tidied herself up and settled down to wait.

Now, as she rolled onto her back, she thought about playing with herself again, simply for something to do, but no sooner had she let her thighs come open and begun to stroke the front of her knickers than she heard footsteps on the landing. Turning quickly over, she got onto all fours, waiting as the key was turned in the padlock. The door swung open to reveal Charles, grinning wickedly as he looked down at her.

'Good girl, Laura. It's nice to be welcomed.'

Only then did Laura realise that she had reacted precisely as Smudge did to her own return at the end of the day. She found herself blushing and smiling as Charles unlocked the cage, and as she crawled out he tousled her hair.

'Maybe I'll take you up on the idea of keeping you as a pet, darling. For the moment, I have something else in mind, so into the bedroom with you and tidy yourself up. Don't rush, because I want you at your best.'

'Yes, sir.'

A pat on her bottom sent Laura on her way, to where she had laid out her weekend suitcase by Charles' bed. He had gone back downstairs, still grinning, making her wonder what he was going to do as she brushed out her hair and adjusted her make-up. Certain it would involve her exposure, and fairly sure they would be going outside, she made a brief trip to the bathroom and changed into fresh knickers, all the while with her imaginings growing more vivid. After a moment of hesitation she took her bra off, deliberately opening up yet more possibilities for embarrassment and exposure, then went downstairs.

Charles was in his study, seated at his desk but with the chair half turned so that he could face the open door. Laura entered, feeling a little unsure of herself as she went to stand in front of him, but he merely looked her up and down before giving an approving nod.

'Pretty, and also smart, as a young woman should be. Don't you agree, Hazel?'

Laura spun around, her mouth coming open in shock as she realised that they were not alone in the room. Beside the door, seated on a high-backed chair upholstered in green leather, was Hazel Manston-Jones, as immaculate as ever, if not more so, with her hair up in a tight bun, her body looking impossibly slender and elegant in a bright red skirt suit, one long leg thrown across the other and her feet encased in smart black heels.

'What are ... how did you get here, Hazel?'

'By car, you silly girl. Charles invited me over.'

'But you've never met!'

'As a matter of fact we have, although I was a little taken aback at first, I admit, but he's very charming, and persuasive. He called me on your mobile.'

'So ...'

Laura trailed off, glancing from one to the other, a wild, terrifying hope rising in her head. Charles smiled as if reading her thoughts, then spoke.

'Yes, I felt that in the circumstances it was reasonable to give Hazel a call, although I'd really only intended to pave the way for a surprise at some time in the future. However, as it happens she has the strength of character to know her own mind and not need coaxing, so she drove over. We've been having a little chat since she arrived, and I'm pleased to say that we've managed to find some common ground.'

'You have?'

'Yes. I thought we might when I recognised her in your photo. She wasn't entirely frank with you about the sort of clubs she and her ex-boyfriend had been visiting either. Some were swingers clubs, others rather different, which makes her the ideal person for this. I've made one or two small alterations, by the way.'

He had picked up a document from his desk, her contract.

'Hazel has kindly agreed to witness our signatures, and to lend an occasional hand with your discipline. Hazel is going to spank you, Laura, once a week, circumstances permitting, in front of me, and on your bare bottom.'

Laura's legs seemed to have been turning slowly to jelly as he spoke, but she managed to take the contract from him, holding it between trembling fingers but barely seeing the words. There were now three spaces at the bottom, the first for Charles, the second for her and the third for Hazel, as witness. Charles spoke again.

'Otherwise it is much the same, but if you'd like to read it through?'

'No, I . . .'

'Read it, Laura.'

She tried, hurrying over the words, but they were as before and she stopped before she'd reached the bottom of the page. Charles was offering her a pen, which she took. Going to the desk, she signed, as neatly as she could. He took the contract in turn, marking the line above his name with an elegant flourish. As he passed the simple piece of paper back, Laura felt as if something had changed within her and as she passed it to Hazel she found herself wanting to curtsey. She watched as Hazel signed, then returned the paper to the desk, feeling excited and expectant, also scared as Charles went on.

'You said you wanted to make this occasion special, and so it shall be.'

He had opened the draw of his desk as he spoke. Within was a collar, flat and about an inch wide, made of five rows of polished steel links. There was a small padlock at the front, which he opened, then stood up as he spoke once more.

'Collars come in many varieties, velvet for some, a steel torque for others. For you, I made a trip to the pet shop. Lift your chin.'

Laura obeyed, holding her head up to allow him to encircle her neck with the metal band. It felt cool and heavy, but her feelings went far beyond the simple reality of having a collar around her neck. She was now owned, his to do with as he pleased. For one long, blissful moment she could think of nothing else, until Hazel clapped, breaking the spell.

'That was beautiful. Now that she's collared, can I spank her?'

Charles made a suave gesture.

'Certainly, my dear. Laura, go over the Lady's knee.'

'Yes, sir.'

Charles could not have been more casual, smiling happily as he turned his chair to get the best possible view. Laura's feelings were anything but calm, fear and embarrassment bringing her close to panic despite the power of her arousal. Hazel adjusted her legs to make a lap for Laura, patting her skirt as she spoke.

'I'm going to enjoy this. Come on, Laura, over you go.'

Laura had gone into automatic as she moved forwards, scarcely able to accept what she was doing as she laid herself into spanking position across the other woman's legs. Hazel wasted no time, immediately taking a firm grip and laying her hand across Laura's bottom, at which Charles spoke again.

'Bare, naturally.'

Hazel had begun to squeeze Laura's bottom through her skirt as she replied.

'Yes, of course, but I like to expose them gradually.'

Charles gave a light chuckle and the blood rushed to Laura's face, not only for the embarrassment of having her bottom fondled by another woman, but at the realisation that she was not the first. Yet she could not bring herself to resist, or to complain, even as Hazel's touch grew more intimate still, cupping the cheeks of Laura's bottom as if about to push a finger between. Then the caresses stopped and her dress was lifted.

Laura closed her eyes, her whole existence focused on her exposure, picturing herself as her dress was raised, first to reveal the upper parts of her seamed stockings, then the bulges of soft white flesh above, her suspender straps, and last the swell of her bottom, now covered only by the tight black lace of her knickers. With the dress turned up on Laura's back, Hazel spoke again.

'Pretty panties, and a lovely round little bum. Stockings and suspenders too, I see. You've trained her well, Charles.'

'She was always a stockings girl, stay-ups generally, but usually seamed. It was one of the first things I noticed about her.'

'When I met her first I thought she was a complete innocent.'

'Oh no. A little naïve, maybe, but not innocent.'

'So you were saying! Aren't you a bad girl, Laura?'

Laura made to reply, increasingly alarmed by their conversation, but Hazel had begun to caress her bottom again and now delivered a sudden, sharp smack as she spoke again.

'Very bad, so very, very bad! You really deserve this, don't you?'

'I don't know! I ...'

Hazel had begun to spank, applying herself firmly to the seat of Laura's knickers with smack after smack, and all the while admonishing her.

'An absolute disgrace, in fact. One of the naughtiest girls I've ever come across, and believe me, I've come across some who needed their bottoms smacked night and day, but you, Laura, you need it done on the hour.'

Laura could no longer answer, her legs kicking as she lost control to the stinging pain of the slaps, her mouth agape and her hips wriggling in a futile effort to dodge Hazel's hand. Charles was watching in open delight, his face not merely wicked but rendered demonic by the scarlet light of the afternoon sun, and as Hazel paused Laura found herself babbling an appeal.

'I haven't been that bad, have I Charles?'

He chuckled.

'I rather think Hazel is referring to your little piece of self-indulgence earlier in the week.'

It took Laura a moment to realise what he meant.

'You didn't tell her!?'

It was Hazel who replied, laughing as she once more set about Laura's bottom.

'Oh yes he did, but don't worry. I don't mind. I think you're a slut, and a dirty bitch, but I don't mind, just as long as I get to take it out on your bouncy little bottom.'

'Oh God!'

Laura's face was burning, and felt as hot as her bottom, her embarrassment made worse by Hazel's open laughter and continued taunting.

'Oh yes, you know you deserve it, don't you, Laura? On the hour every hour, skirt up and panties down – speaking of which.'

The spanking stopped. Laura froze as the waistband of her knickers was taken in Hazel's hand, lifted, then pulled back, peeling the lacy black garment slowly down to let the air to her burning rear cheeks, and to show her off to her tormentors, first the tight pink knot of her anus, the full spread of her bottom, then the pouted lips of her sex. Now bare, Laura began to sob, overcome by her emotions. As her knickers were adjusted to halfway down her thighs she had hung her head, completely surrendered to her fate. Hazel spoke again.

'That's better, isn't it, Laura, all bare, just the way you should be.'

Hazel's grip tightened and the spanking started again, harder than before, to send Laura into a kicking, wriggling frenzy and to set her squealing, at which Charles spoke up.

'If you want to gag her, make her take her knickers in her mouth.'

'I like to hear her, thanks, but I might do that anyway, in a while.'

'As you please, but one refinement you might enjoy is to lift her dress. There's something wonderfully unnecessary about bare breasts during a spanking. Her bottom has to be bare, naturally, but to bare her breasts is pure indulgence.'

'And very undignified. Come on, Laura, lift up a little. We want to see your titties.'

Laura complied, unable to do otherwise, raising her body a little as her dress was tucked up around her neck, exposing her breasts to Charles' view, and to Hazel's touch, one slender hand cupping a dangling ball just long enough to feel the shape and weight.

'She's quite big, isn't she?'

Charles didn't answer, watching intently as Hazel went back to spanking Laura. The slaps were no longer as hard, and delivered lower, pushing to Laura's sex and reminding her forcefully of Hazel's liking for other women. She knew she was wet anyway, the scent of her arousal strong in the air, and it was no use trying to pretend that the spanking was purely for discipline, or purely for Charles. Already she wanted to masturbate in front of both of them, adding confusion and fresh shame to her woes as the spanking continued.

'Give in to your feelings, Laura.'

It was Charles, his voice a little hoarse, even he no longer able to be detached. With that Laura gave in, pushing her bottom up to the smacks as she burst into tears, now completely abandoned to her fate. She knew they'd organised it and that punishing her was making Hazel excited, but it didn't matter. Charles owned her, and what he wanted was good. Hazel gave a little purr at Laura's acquiescence, almost a growl, and spoke as she stopped.

'Let's finish you off.'

Laura knew what she meant, but made no attempt to resist, either as her knickers were hauled off and pushed tightly into her mouth, or as Hazel began to touch her once again, this time without holding back. Her mouth had come wide around her mouthful of satin and lace as her breasts were squeezed and slapped, her nipples pulled to erection and clawed nails raked across her skin, all the while with her bottom pushed high as slap after slap rained down on her cheeks. She tried to put a hand back, no longer able to resist her need, but it was slapped away.

'That's my job, I think, Laura.'

Hazel's hand found Laura's sex, reaching under her belly to masturbate her as she was spanked and pinched, her bottom hole tickled and her vagina penetrated, bringing her feelings up to ecstasy in no time and quickly tipping her over the edge into a writhing, gasping orgasm that finished only when Hazel suddenly let go. Laura tumbled to the floor, legs wide as she sprawled at their feet. Charles was looking down at her and she quickly spat out her knickers, offering her open mouth. He merely shook his head and pointed to Hazel.

Laura turned, to find Hazel tugging up her skirt. She was

bare underneath, and shaved, her neat pink sex wet with arousal. Laura swallowed. Hazel extended a finger, beckoning. Laura cast a glance to Charles. He rose, took her firmly by the scruff of the neck and walked her forwards. Hazel purred as she let her legs come fully wide, fully exposing her sex and the tiny pink wrinkle of her anus as well. Charles spoke, his tone allowing for no resistance.

'Lick her, Laura.'

'But Charles . . .'

'If you seek a master, Laura, that is what you expect to find. Do as you are told.'

With that, her head was pushed firmly between Hazel's thighs.

Visit the Black Lace website at
www.black-lace-books.com

FIND OUT THE LATEST INFORMATION AND TAKE ADVANTAGE OF OUR
FANTASTIC FREE BOOK OFFER! ALSO VISIT THE SITE FOR . . .

- All Black Lace titles currently available
  and how to order online
- Great new offers
- Writers' guidelines
- Author interviews
- An erotica newsletter
- Features
- Cool links

BLACK LACE — THE LEADING IMPRINT OF
WOMEN'S SEXY FICTION

TAKING YOUR EROTIC READING PLEASURE
TO NEW HORIZONS

LOOK OUT FOR THE ALL-NEW BLACK LACE BOOKS – AVAILABLE NOW!

All books priced £7.99 in the UK. Please note publication dates apply to the UK only. For other territories, please contact your retailer.

THE GIFT OF SHAME
Sarah Hope-Walker
ISBN 978 0 352 34202 7

Sad, sultry Helen flies between London, Paris and the Caribbean chasing whatever physical pleasures she can get to tear her mind from a deep, deep loss. Her glamorous life-style and charged sensual escapades belie a widow's grief. When she meets handsome, rich Jeffrey she is shocked and yet intrigued by his masterful, domineering behaviour. Soon, Helen is forced to confront the forbidden desires hiding within herself – and forced to undergo a startling metamorphosis from a meek and modest lady into a bristling, voracious wanton.

To be published in January 2009

DARK ENCHANTMENT
Janine Ashbless
ISBN 978 0 352 34513 4

In the follow-up to her peerless first collection, Cruel Enchantment, Janine Ashbless brings you more breathtaking tales of lust and magic, dark fantasy and even darker desire. An unearthly stranger who pursues a newlywed on her Mediterranean holiday, an opera production where emotions run out of control, and a ghost who wants one thing only from the descendant of her murderer are just three of the seductive and stylishly written stories that will tease, tempt and transport you to fantastic realms where dreams – and nightmares – can come true.

To be published in February 2009

SEDUCTION
Various
ISBN 9780352345103

From the enthralling gaze to the masterful kiss, the arts of the seducer are legendary and this anthology will draw you into a sinfully sensual world where the urge to seduce or be seduced is irresistible. Written by some of today's most talented and imaginative authors of female erotica, each story explores the timeless fantasy of giving in to temptation. Elegant, feminine and alluring, this collection will leave you longing to surrender over and over again.

ALSO LOOK OUT FOR

THE NEW BLACK LACE BOOK OF WOMEN'S SEXUAL FANTASIES
Edited and compiled by Mitzi Szereto
ISBN 978 0 352 34172 3

The second anthology of detailed sexual fantasies contributed by women from all over the world. The book is a result of a year's research by an expert on erotic writing and gives a fascinating insight into the rich diversity of the female sexual imagination.

Black Lace Booklist

Information is correct at time of printing. To avoid disappointment, check availability before ordering. Go to www.black-lace-books.com.
All books are priced £7.99 unless another price is given.

BLACK LACE BOOKS WITH A CONTEMPORARY SETTING

- ☐ THE ANGELS' SHARE Maya Hess — ISBN 978 0 352 34043 6
- ☐ ASKING FOR TROUBLE Kristina Lloyd — ISBN 978 0 352 33362 9
- ☐ BLACK LIPSTICK KISSES Monica Belle — ISBN 978 0 352 33885 3 £6.99
- ☐ THE BLUE GUIDE Carrie Williams — ISBN 978 0 352 34132 7
- ☐ THE BOSS Monica Belle — ISBN 978 0 352 34088 7
- ☐ BOUND IN BLUE Monica Belle — ISBN 978 0 352 34012 2
- ☐ CAMPAIGN HEAT Gabrielle Marcola — ISBN 978 0 352 33941 6
- ☐ CAT SCRATCH FEVER Sophie Mouette — ISBN 978 0 352 34021 4
- ☐ CIRCUS EXCITE Nikki Magennis — ISBN 978 0 352 34033 7
- ☐ CLUB CRÈME Primula Bond — ISBN 978 0 352 33907 2 £6.99
- ☐ CONFESSIONAL Judith Roycroft — ISBN 978 0 352 33421 3
- ☐ CONTINUUM Portia Da Costa — ISBN 978 0 352 33120 5
- ☐ DANGEROUS CONSEQUENCES Pamela Rochford — ISBN 978 0 352 33185 4
- ☐ DARK DESIGNS Madelynne Ellis — ISBN 978 0 352 34075 7
- ☐ THE DEVIL INSIDE Portia Da Costa — ISBN 978 0 352 32993 6
- ☐ EQUAL OPPORTUNITIES Mathilde Madden — ISBN 978 0 352 34070 2
- ☐ FIRE AND ICE Laura Hamilton — ISBN 978 0 352 33486 2
- ☐ GONE WILD Maria Eppie — ISBN 978 0 352 33670 5
- ☐ HOTBED Portia Da Costa — ISBN 978 0 352 33614 9
- ☐ IN PURSUIT OF ANNA Natasha Rostova — ISBN 978 0 352 34060 3
- ☐ IN THE FLESH Emma Holly — ISBN 978 0 352 34117 4
- ☐ LEARNING TO LOVE IT Alison Tyler — ISBN 978 0 352 33535 7
- ☐ MAD ABOUT THE BOY Mathilde Madden — ISBN 978 0 352 34001 6
- ☐ MAKE YOU A MAN Anna Clare — ISBN 978 0 352 34006 1
- ☐ MAN HUNT Cathleen Ross — ISBN 978 0 352 33583 8
- ☐ THE MASTER OF SHILDEN Lucinda Carrington — ISBN 978 0 352 33140 3
- ☐ MIXED DOUBLES Zoe le Verdier — ISBN 978 0 352 33312 4 £6.99
- ☐ MIXED SIGNALS Anna Clare — ISBN 978 0 352 33889 1 £6.99
- ☐ MS BEHAVIOUR Mini Lee — ISBN 978 0 352 33962 1

- ❏ PACKING HEAT Karina Moore   ISBN 978 0 352 33356 8   £6.99
- ❏ PAGAN HEAT Monica Belle   ISBN 978 0 352 33974 4
- ❏ PEEP SHOW Mathilde Madden   ISBN 978 0 352 33924 9
- ❏ THE POWER GAME Carrera Devonshire   ISBN 978 0 352 33990 4
- ❏ THE PRIVATE UNDOING OF A PUBLIC SERVANT   ISBN 978 0 352 34066 5
  Leonie Martel
- ❏ RUDE AWAKENING Pamela Kyle   ISBN 978 0 352 33036 9
- ❏ SAUCE FOR THE GOOSE Mary Rose Maxwell   ISBN 978 0 352 33492 3
- ❏ SPLIT Kristina Lloyd   ISBN 978 0 352 34154 9
- ❏ STELLA DOES HOLLYWOOD Stella Black   ISBN 978 0 352 33588 3
- ❏ THE STRANGER Portia Da Costa   ISBN 978 0 352 33211 0
- ❏ SUITE SEVENTEEN Portia Da Costa   ISBN 978 0 352 34109 9
- ❏ TONGUE IN CHEEK Tabitha Flyte   ISBN 978 0 352 33484 8
- ❏ THE TOP OF HER GAME Emma Holly   ISBN 978 0 352 34116 7
- ❏ UNNATURAL SELECTION Alaine Hood   ISBN 978 0 352 33963 8
- ❏ VELVET GLOVE Emma Holly   ISBN 978 0 352 34115 0
- ❏ VILLAGE OF SECRETS Mercedes Kelly   ISBN 978 0 352 33344 5
- ❏ WILD BY NATURE Monica Belle   ISBN 978 0 352 33915 7   £6.99
- ❏ WILD CARD Madeline Moore   ISBN 978 0 352 34038 2
- ❏ WING OF MADNESS Mae Nixon   ISBN 978 0 352 34099 3

BLACK LACE BOOKS WITH AN HISTORICAL SETTING

- ❏ THE BARBARIAN GEISHA Charlotte Royal   ISBN 978 0 352 33267 7
- ❏ BARBARIAN PRIZE Deanna Ashford   ISBN 978 0 352 34017 7
- ❏ THE CAPTIVATION Natasha Rostova   ISBN 978 0 352 33234 9
- ❏ DARKER THAN LOVE Kristina Lloyd   ISBN 978 0 352 33279 0
- ❏ WILD KINGDOM Deanna Ashford   ISBN 978 0 352 33549 4
- ❏ DIVINE TORMENT Janine Ashbless   ISBN 978 0 352 33719 1
- ❏ FRENCH MANNERS Olivia Christie   ISBN 978 0 352 33214 1
- ❏ LORD WRAXALL'S FANCY Anna Lieff Saxby   ISBN 978 0 352 33080 2
- ❏ NICOLE'S REVENGE Lisette Allen   ISBN 978 0 352 29984 4
- ❏ THE SENSES BEJEWELLED Cleo Cordell   ISBN 978 0 352 29904 2   £6.99
- ❏ THE SOCIETY OF SIN Sian Lacey Taylder   ISBN 978 0 352 34080 1
- ❏ TEMPLAR PRIZE Deanna Ashford   ISBN 978 0 352 34137 2
- ❏ UNDRESSING THE DEVIL Angel Strand   ISBN 978 0 352 33938 6